FIRE SEASON

IN THIS SERIES BY DAVID WEBER

For a complete listing of Baen titles by David Weber,
please go to www.baen.com.

FIRE SEASON

DAVID WEBER & JANE LINDSKOLD

FIRE SEASON

Copyright © 2012 by Words of Weber, Inc. & Obsidian Tiger, Inc.

A Baen Books Original

Baen Publishing Enterprises
P.O. Box 1403
Riverdale, NY 10471
www.baen.com

ISBN: 978-1-4516-3840-0

Cover art by Daniel Dos Santos

First printing, October 2012

Distributed by Simon & Schuster
1230 Avenue of the Americas
New York, NY 10020

Library of Congress Cataloging-in-Publication Data

Weber, David, 1952–
    Fire season / David Weber & Jane Lindskold ; [cover art by Daniel Dos Santos].
        p. cm.
    "A Baen Books Original."
    Summary: Fourteen-year-old Stephanie Harrington and her fellow Provisional Forest Rangers on the planet Sphinx must prevent disaster from befalling a treecat clan caught in a blaze while preserving the secret that the treecats of Sphinx are highly intelligent and deserving of rights that some would deny them.
    ISBN 978-1-4516-3840-0 (hardback)
    [1. Human-animal communication—Fiction. 2. Human-animal relationships—Fiction. 3. Space colonies—Fiction. 4. Science fiction.]
    I. Lindskold, Jane M. II. Dos Santos, Daniel. III. Title.
    PZ7.W38747Fir 2012
    [Fic]—dc23
                                                            2012023913

10 9 8 7 6 5 4 3 2 1

Pages by Joy Freeman (www.pagesbyjoy.com)
Printed in the United States of America

FIRE SEASON

CLIMBS QUICKLY'S TWO-LEG WAS UP TO SOMETHING she shouldn't be doing...again.

The emotions surging through her mind-glow made *that* perfectly clear. And it was just as clear that she knew her elders would have disapproved strongly. But Death Fang's Bane had a true gift for bending rules, and she was having a grand time.

Her friend, Shadowed Sunlight, or possibly "Karl" (if indeed the single sound most usually applied to this two-legs was a name, not some other designation), was less delighted. Climbs Quickly couldn't read Shadowed Sunlight's mind-glow as easily as he could that of Death Fang's Bane, but the basics were present. Shadowed Sunlight's mind-glow overflowed with determination, watchfulness, alertness, and apprehension.

Climbs Quickly leaned forward in his seat, watching intently as the "air car" (or "car"—a sound so very like "Karl" that the similarity had confused him for quite a

1

time) sped along a complex path through the maze of tree trunks among which they traveled.

Climbs Quickly couldn't quite figure out what precisely was the source of Death Fang's Bane's excitement. True, the air car in which they were traveling was moving very quickly—and sometimes rather erratically—but that didn't seem to be excuse enough for the surges of excitement and dread coming to him through their shared link.

The folding flying thing in which they had more routinely traveled before this new fascination had gripped his two-leg was far more erratic. Yet, unless the weather was particularly bad, Death Fang's Bane didn't react this strongly to piloting her folding flying thing.

The treecat thought a bit wistfully about the folding flying thing. He preferred it to the air car in which they were now traveling. The feeling of the wind on his fur was delightful and the winds carried such interesting scents. Also, the glider *felt* faster somehow. He'd figured out that the air car actually covered distances more quickly, but with the winds closed away, the sensation of speed simply wasn't the same.

A touch forlornly, Climbs Quickly pressed his remaining true-hand against Death Fang's Bane's shoulder, then used his left hand-foot to indicate the air car's closed side. From past experience, he knew the transparent panels here could open—although he hadn't quite figured out how to manage the opening himself.

To emphasize his request, Climbs Quickly made a small sound of pleading protest. In the time that he'd lived with Death Fang's Bane and her family, he'd learned how much emphasis humans placed on mouth noises. The People relied on mind-speech, using sound and gesture to provide emphasis. These alien two-legs, by contrast, seemed to have no equivalent to mind-speech, relying instead on complex mouth noises augmented by a bewildering variety of gestures—gestures that didn't seem to mean the same thing from occasion to occasion and could be eliminated completely.

He pitied them, for their mind-glows were brilliant and warm. It seemed sad that even two good friends like Death Fang's Bane and Shadowed Sunlight could not share them.

"Bleek!" Climbs Quickly repeated. Then, when Death Fang's Bane didn't acknowledge him, he extended his claws and struck them against the clear panel, making a noise like hail hitting rock. "Bleek! Bleek!"

When he felt Death Fang's Bane gust out her breath, then chuckle, Climbs Quickly tapped the transparent panel again, just in case she'd missed the point.

"Bleek!"

✧　　✧　　✧

"Bleek!" Tap! Tap! "Bleek! Bleek!"

Stephanie Harrington gingerly began to remove one hand from the air car's stick. Immediately, the car swerved alarmingly.

"Hands on the controls!" snapped Karl Zivonik. "Stephanie! I'm taking enough of a risk letting you fly without a permit. You want to wreck us and get my license pulled?"

"Sorry," Stephanie replied with uncharacteristic meekness. She knew perfectly well the risk Karl was taking. If they were found out, losing his license would be the least of the penalties. "Lionheart wants a window open. Since I'm flying low and pretty slow, I think it's okay."

She couldn't see Karl rolling his eyes, but she guessed at the expression even as he emitted a gusty sigh and turned to address the treecat directly.

"Back window," he said to Lionheart, pointing for emphasis. "Stephanie has enough distractions without you leaning over her shoulder and the wind blowing her hair in her face."

One of the things Stephanie liked about Karl Zivonik was that he was among the small handful of humans who addressed Lionheart as if the treecat was intelligent enough to understand him. Most humans either didn't bother to talk to the treecat, or, if they did, they adopted the syrupy tones they used to address very small children—or pets. More annoying were the handful who seemed to think that if they spoke very slowly and used very simple phrases the treecat would understand.

Stephanie supposed this last bothered her so much because it was actually probably the best approach, but those who used it didn't employ a consistent and scientific approach.

Karl pushed a button. As the back left side window slid down, the air car swerved slightly. Stephanie corrected, but overdid it—in part because Lionheart had just removed his weight from her shoulder—and she was off-balance.

"Steph!" Karl turned the single syllable into reprimand and protest in one.

"Sorry," Stephanie repeated.

She scanned the control panel: direction indicator, elevation, engine temperature, fluid levels. There was so much to keep track of. Worse, unlike with the hang glider, where an accident meant some busted struts and fabric (and if she wasn't careful, some busted Stephanie, as she remembered all too vividly), here she might damage expensive equipment.

Worse, Karl didn't own this air car. At sixteen T-years, he had dreams of owning one, had even admitted that he was saving towards a used model, but this air car was "his" only because he needed to get to his job as a provisional ranger with the Sphinxian Forestry Service. His parents considered use of the car fairly compensated by the time they saved shuttling Karl back and forth from Thunder River, which was about a thousand kilometers away—an investment of a couple hours each way, even at the speeds an air car traveled.

Since Karl and Stephanie were the only probationary rangers in the Sphinxian Forestry Service, they were regularly assigned to work as a team, allowing only one ranger's time to be taken up with supervising them. Since Stephanie couldn't pilot, this meant that usually they worked in the vicinity of Twin Forks, the town nearest to the Harrington freehold and where Richard Harrington had his veterinary clinic. There was plenty of room in the Harringtons' sprawling stone house, since Stephanie's parents definitely planned on additional children. That was one of the reasons they'd emigrated from their heavily populated homeworld of Meyerdahl, and Stephanie was looking forward (guardedly) to the novel experience of siblings. In the meantime, Karl often stayed with the Harrington family, taking advantage of all that currently unoccupied space, although sometimes he stayed with friends in Twin Forks.

They were coming into an area where the forest giants were more widely spaced, so Stephanie hazarded talking in addition to piloting.

"I think I'm getting better," she said, "but I'll admit, I never thought handling an actual air car on 'manual' would be so hard. I mean, I was getting perfect scores on the simulator, even in the 'auto-pilot-off' setting."

"Wonder-girl," Karl retorted with a grin. "You always get perfect scores on everything. If you hadn't, I would never have let you try this. Reality is different than a simulator. What I don't understand is why you can't wait until you have a learner's permit like everyone else. Your fifteenth birthday isn't that far off."

Stephanie was glad that concentrating on piloting gave her an excuse to pause before answering. She knew she tended to "push." Only lately had she tried to figure out why. It wasn't as if her parents didn't love her or expected her to win their approval. If anything, Richard and Margery Harrington were almost too approving, too fair, too balanced.

They'd let Stephanie know, gently and in small increments, that she had advantages most people did not. For one, although they'd tried to hide this from her lest she get either lazy or smug, Stephanie knew her IQ scored nearly off the charts. Karl's statement that she always got perfect scores on everything was only a slight exaggeration.

For another, Stephanie was a "genie," her genetic mutations making her stronger and tougher than average. She paid for these advantages with a higher than usual metabolism, but given that Mom and Dad always made certain there was ample interesting stuff to eat—they shared her metabolism, after all—she never suffered for this. What she did suffer from was the flashes of hot temper that came with the package. She simply didn't get along easily with most people—especially people her own age. They seemed dumb, fascinated with things she wasn't in the least interested in.

Karl Zivonik—who was over a T-year and a half older than her—was the closest Stephanie had to a friend her own age, the first she had made since her family emigrated to Sphinx from Meyerdahl a bit over four T-years ago. Even Karl was more like a big brother than a friend, watching over her, scolding her, teasing her, practicing target shooting with her, and, well, letting her fly his car, even though it was against the rules.

However, despite the amount of time they spent together, Stephanie still felt there was a lot she didn't know about Karl. At times he'd fall into a brooding silence or snap at something she didn't think was all that bad. From Karl's aunt, Irina Kisaevna, Stephanie had learned that much of Karl's family and many of his friends had died during the

Plague. Stephanie guessed that probably had something to do with his moods, but she sensed there was more. Occasionally, someone named "Sumiko" would get mentioned—usually by one of Karl's host of younger siblings—and there would be this uncomfortable quiet.

Anyhow, despite the amount of time she'd been spending with Karl, Stephanie's best friend was Lionheart.

I mean, look at him, now, she thought affectionately, glancing into the rearview mirror to do so, *hanging out the window like some cross between a gray-and-cream floppy toy and a six-legged weasel. No one would ever guess how smart he is....*

At long last, Stephanie answered Karl's question, "I don't want just a learner's permit. You know as well as I do that you can qualify for a provisional license at fifteen."

"At need," Karl said. "You can get a provisional license 'at need.'"

"My family does live pretty far from Twin Forks," Stephanie was beginning, when an overwhelming sensation of alarm surged into her from Lionheart. The strong wave of emotion was far stronger than the normally faint, elusive sensations she received, yet its very strength made it hard to define: apprehension, anxiety, yet somewhat removed.

"Bleek!" Lionheart spilled the meter and a half of his furry length over into the front seat, landing in Karl's lap, rather than Stephanie's, as would have been his more usual choice. "Bleek!"

Showing Lionheart understands more about operating machinery than most would grant a treecat, Stephanie thought, but the thought was fleeting. Lionheart was pointing off to the southwest. Every line of his body was tight with urgency.

Stephanie immediately shifted course. Karl didn't protest.

"What's bothering Lionheart?" he said, stroking the

thick gray fur along the treecat's spine in a effort to soothe him.

"I don't know," Stephanie admitted, "but whatever it is is over that way. Let's go find out!"

✧   ✧   ✧

Pleased when the clear side panel was opened, Climbs Quickly immediately poked his head out the opening. Again, he was reminded that the air car moved more quickly than did the folding flying thing. His fur flattened against his face and his inner eyelids dropped into place. Even so, this was an infinitely better experience.

During the seasons he had lived with Death Fang's Bane and her parents, he had come to the conclusion that two-legs and the People did not use their senses in the same fashion. Two-legs were so sight-oriented that, as in this wonderful fast-traveling vehicle, they would actually eliminate signals from scent or sound. Taste—except when eating—did not enter into their experience of the world. The importance of touch was harder for him to judge.

By contrast, the People relied on the triad of sight, scent, and hearing about equivalently. As hunters—especially when moving through the treetops—they were very aware of the usefulness of touch, including signals carried by vibration. He had *no* idea how two-legs managed without whiskers! Taste was also important, especially in how it could add dimension to the sense of smell. And in the pleasure it brought to food...

At this speed, Climbs Quickly found himself relying primarily on scent for his assessment. He caught a variety of tantalizing odors: bark-chewer mingled with the sap of the golden-leaf it had been sampling; the tangy scent of purple thorn; the musky perfume of tongue-leaf in summer flower. At one point his fur bristled when an upward eddy brought him the rank odor of death fang, liberally associated with the blood of some unlucky ground runner.

Climbs Quickly wondered how the two-legs could think they knew anything of a world most of them merely saw as they passed over faster than a winter wind, glimpsing what lay below only as a blur of green and brown. Perhaps the two-legs had senses he couldn't guess at, just as most of them had no idea how the People used mind-speech.

In any case, today, Death Fang's Bane and Shadowed Sunlight were traveling below the canopy—and not at too great a speed. Climbs Quickly, for one, was going to make the most of it.

Drawing in a luxuriously deep breath of the warm late-summer air, Climbs Quickly caught a new scent, one that shocked and appalled him as even that of the death fang had not... The scent of smoke and, behind it, the hot, brain-snapping odor of freshly burning fire.

Arboreal as they were, the People were all too aware of the danger brought by forest fire. It offered a danger to them greater than any death fang or snow hunter. Those could be escaped by flight into the upper branches or even—with cooperation—fought and killed, although rarely without injury, as his own scars attested. However, even the greatest cooperation could not fight a forest fire. The best the united strength of an entire clan could hope to achieve was to forestall the fire's spread while the weak and young got away.

Climbs Quickly shivered inside his skin and breathed in the scent again. It was hard to pinpoint where it was coming from with so many conflicting winds, but he was a trained scout.

The course on which Death Fang's Bane was taking the vehicle was erratic, but it did not seem to be going in the direction of the smoke and fire. For a moment, Climbs Quickly almost gave in to the impulse to ignore what he had smelled. After all, he was far away and this was nowhere near the range of his own Bright Water Clan.

However, his own natural curiosity had not been dulled by his seasons with the two-legs. Moreover, the songs of the memory singers—of whom his own sister was one—provided a connection to clans that would never meet, even if that connection was attenuated by distance.

Usually, Climbs Quickly's first impulse would have been to get Death Fang's Bane's attention, but he knew that not only was she responsible for the vehicle's movement, she was not handling this chore with her usual ease. Therefore, although his alarm was growing as the scent of smoke became more intense, he leapt over the seat and into Shadowed Sunlight's lap.

"Bleek!" he said, pointing in the direction in which the smell of smoke was strongest. "Bleek! Bleek!"

His faith in these two-legs had not been misplaced. Almost immediately, he felt the vehicle change direction. Nor was the impulse entirely that of Death Fang's Bane. Shadowed Sunlight's mind-glow was less easy for Climbs Quickly to read, but he could feel in it acceptance that he had some reason for his urgency—even if the reason was as of yet a mystery.

❖   ❖   ❖

"What's in that direction?" Stephanie asked, trying to increase the speed while not losing control of the air car. "Let me know if Lionheart seems to think we're going the wrong way."

"He's still pointing southwest," Karl said. "Let me call up the area map. We're within a Forestry Service district, but I'm pretty sure it's close to private holdings near here."

Stephanie knew Karl wasn't being in the least slow, but she felt an intense sense of impatience—or urgency. Not for the first time, she wondered if her feelings were

always entirely her own. For example, she could always locate Lionheart, no matter how far away he was. She knew he could do the same with her. However, she felt certain Lionheart knew what she felt sometimes even better than she herself did. However, how much did the link work the other way? Might the urgency she felt now not be her own impatience, but Lionheart's?

"Oh, Steph," Karl said with a chuckle. "You're going to love this. The private lands we're heading toward belong to the Franchitti family."

Stephanie made a rude noise. The Franchittis were not among her favorite people on Sphinx. In fact, it wasn't stretching the point too much to say that they were among her least favorite. Certainly Trudy Franchitti, who was roughly a year older than Stephanie, was on Stephanie's "Most To Be Avoided" list.

"Well," Stephanie said. "Maybe we don't need to go that far. I wonder what has Lionheart so riled. If it was something on the ground, we should have flown over it already. I mean, we're not moving all that fast."

"I've been thinking the same thing," Karl said. "Which means it's something he could smell from a long way off. Take the car up, Steph. Maybe we can see what he can smell."

Unspoken between them was that they both had guessed what this threat might be. The season was very late summer—on Sphinx the seasons lasted for approximately fifteen T-months. This summer had started out normally enough, but as it had progressed, conditions had grown increasingly dry. Drought status had been declared. Fire warnings were posted everywhere.

Very carefully, Stephanie brought the air car up above the canopy. The gigantic crown oaks and near-pines that dominated this area were so widely spaced that it was possible to steer between them. Since steering without the

autopilot and radar assistance was something Stephanie had wanted to practice, they had stayed at trunk level. This choice had the added advantage of keeping Stephanie's more erratic maneuvers away from casual observation.

"Steph!" Karl was pointing southwest, his gesture unconsciously mimicking that of the treecat who rested in his lap. "Smoke!"

Looking in the direction indicated, Stephanie saw the faintest wispy grayish-white traces threading through the thick arboreal canopy.

Karl was already on his uni-link, comming the SFS fire alert number. "This is Karl Zivonik. We're at . . ." He rattled off coordinates. "We've spotted smoke. It's pretty faint and might be coming from private land, but we thought we'd better report it."

The voice of Ranger Ainsley Jedrusinski came back over the com. "We've got it, Karl, and one of the weather-watch birds is just clearing the horizon. Give me a sec."

There was a brief delay while she queried the weather satellite for a downlook. Then her voice came back. "*Definitely* a hot spot over accepted limits, especially given wind direction. We're going to send in a crew. Good work. Out!"

Stephanie had set the air car to hover and now she glanced over at Karl. "So, do we go to help?"

Karl considered. "Well, Ainsley didn't say we shouldn't, and it *is* our fire, sort of. But if we go, I pilot."

"No problem," Stephanie said, setting the auto-pilot to hover and sliding so they could change places. "No problem at all."

✧   ✧   ✧

Actually, though she wouldn't have admitted it aloud, Stephanie was glad to give up having to pay attention to the surprisingly demanding role of pilot—at least a pilot

without autopilot. Freed up from those responsibilities, she brought up her uni-link and downloaded information on the location of the fire.

"Winds are rising," she told Karl. "Unless there's a miracle, the fire's going to spread—and fast. I wonder what started this one?"

Karl shrugged. "We can rule out lightning. The usual summer T-storms are really late. This might be a ground fire that's finally broken out to the surface, so we're seeing the smoke. The area is so dry almost anything might start a fire."

Stephanie nodded. She also knew what Karl wasn't saying: on Meyerdahl, eighty to ninety percent of forest fires had a direct or indirect human cause. The percentage wasn't as high on Sphinx, since the population was so much smaller, but that didn't matter. When the forests were this dry, even a stray spark could find ample natural tinder.

Whatever their cause, forest fires were never comfortable events. Intellectually, Stephanie knew wildfire was actually a necessary part of a forest ecology, a means of clearing away deadwood, underbrush, and accumulated duff that contributed to disease. Moreover, many plants actually *needed* fire in order for their seeds to germinate. Browsing and grazing animals benefitted, too, since new growth was higher in nutrient value. Thus, a bit more indirectly, the predators benefitted as well.

Despite knowing all of this, Stephanie still found it hard to think of forest fires as *good*. The skeletons of burned-out trees, the carcasses of animals that failed to outrace the spreading flames, the fallen bodies of birds choked by smoke, even though they were never close to the fire, all seemed evidence of evils to be fought.

Yet what was true on any planet with forests was even more so on Sphinx. Eighty percent of Sphinx's land surface was forested. Some of the plants—like the picketwood, on which the treecats were so dependent—might look like forests. However, picketwood groves were actually one vast plant. The parent tree sent down runners from the branches of a nodal trunk. These in turn became their own trunks and sent out more runners. Damage to one area of picketwood could have a definite—although usually short-term—effect on related groves, even if those groves were kilometers away.

The policy of the Sphinx Forestry Service was to manage rather than simply put out natural fires. This did not make SFS popular with many of the human settlers, who felt that they and their property should be protected no matter what—even if that property was located where it should not be. When the fire was of human origin and SFS started handing out reprimands and fines...Well, then the SFS found itself even less popular.

Karl had switched the com so they could listen to the Forestry Service chatter as the unit was assembled and sent out. Although the SFS had what many of the planet's residents considered an overly large staff, they were actually stretched pretty thin. Ranger Jedrusinski's call had alerted any and all on- or off-duty rangers in the immediate area of the fire. Some would delay long enough to fetch specially equipped firefighting vehicles.

However, at this time of year, all rangers—and that included Stephanie and Karl, who were only probationary rangers—routinely carried with them a kit that included a Pulaski, a shovel, a bladder bag, a portable fire shelter, and a fire-suit. Many of these tools would have been perfectly familiar to firefighters some thirteen hundred years before. Others, like the modified vibroblade cutting edge of the Pulaski (a combination hoe and fire axe that had been in use for centuries even before humans reached for the stars) or the fire-retardant chemicals that the bladder bag automatically mixed with water, would have surprised and delighted them.

When he'd taken over piloting, Karl had closed the back window they'd opened for Lionheart. The treecat had remained in the front seat, perched on Stephanie's lap. Once they'd set course in the direction of the fire, Lionheart stopped pointing. Some of the tension had left the lines of his long, lean body, but through their shared link Stephanie could feel that the treecat was clearly conflicted about heading into—rather than away from—a fire.

She stroked Lionheart, even going so far as to roll him over onto his back so she could ruffle the cream-colored fur on his tummy and tickle under his chin. Usually, this relaxed him, but soon enough, Lionheart put his one remaining true-hand and his two hand-feet on her forearm and gently shoved her away.

Stephanie offered him a perch along the back of her seat. He flowed up, sinuously graceful, and settled where he could rest his true-hand on the top of her head while looking out the window.

Despite their name, treecats were not all that feline. For one, no Terran cat had ever possessed six limbs or a fully prehensile tail. Their build was longer and—beneath their fluffy coats—leaner. They were also larger, averaging sixty to seventy centimeters through the body, with their tails doubling their length. And, of course, no Terran cat had three-fingered hands with fully opposable thumbs.

However, quite like Terran cats, male treecats, like Lionheart, were tabby-gray above, cream below. Their gray tails were ornamented with a varying number of darker bands. There were other similarities as well: slitted pupils to the eyes (these almost always green), retractable claws (although these were far sharper than those possessed by any Terran cat), pointed ears, and long whiskers. Moreover, when tense, treecats bristled out their fur much as a Terran cat did. As Karl piloted them closer to the fire, Stephanie could feel from the tickling along her neck that Lionheart was distinctly puffed.

Stephanie wondered what treecat clans did when faced with a forest fire. They didn't have fire retardant chemicals. They were tool users, but the tools she had seen were limited to ropes, nets, stone knives, and small stone axes. These last were fine for hacking off the branches treecats used to build sleeping platforms, but could not fell a burning tree so the flames consuming it would not spread through the canopy.

She supposed the only thing treecats could do was run in the hope they could get their kittens and old ones out fast enough they didn't need to watch—and what she suspected was worse, *feel* them burning to death—as the flames licked out greedy tongues, devouring all with a mindless hunger.

Shuddering at the thought, Stephanie pulled up a template and overlaid it on the map of their location. Immediately, she felt relieved. The map the Forestry Service had put together indicating the locations of known treecat clans did not show a clan in this area. The map was far from complete, but this close to human-inhabited lands, she felt pretty confident that it would be accurate.

Stephanie knew she shouldn't have favorites among the creatures that lived on Sphinx. As Frank Lethbridge and Ainsley Jedrusinski kept reminding her, every creature— even hexapumas—had their part to play in the complex planetary ecology. Stephanie couldn't help it. She didn't like hexapumas. She liked treecats a lot—more, in fact, than she did most humans.

To distract herself, Stephanie thought about a particular litter of hexapumas, the kits of a mother she and Lionheart had killed just under three T-years ago. When she had become a probationary ranger she had learned, to her surprise, that SFS rangers had rescued and hand-raised the kits. Like the cubs of many Terran "higher" predators, hexapuma kits required parental care for their first several years.

As a probationary ranger, Stephanie had been required to take her turn cleaning the pens and bringing the little monsters food. Lately, she and Karl had been included in discussion as to the best areas in which to release them. Care had been taken to make certain the hexapuma kits did not bond with their human caretakers, but a certain greater familiarity could not be avoided—even if merely that these hexapumas would be accustomed to human odor and might even associate it with food.

A surge of anger filled Stephanie as she recalled how she'd struggled not to point everyone's attention at Lionheart's horrible scars, his missing right true-hand. Quick heal and considerable medical attention had made certain her own scars did not show, but they were there nonetheless. She wanted to scream, "Hexapumas are dangerous monsters!" but knowing hers would be the minority opinion—suspecting she was probably even wrong—she'd kept her opinions to herself.

When Lionheart suddenly stiffened, Stephanie thought that—as so often—he was reacting to her internal turmoil. However, instead of reaching and patting her gently on one cheek as he usually did to soothe her, he now began to bounce in place, pointing both ahead and down. Stephanie could almost feel his frustration that he couldn't make his point more clearly.

"What is it, Lionheart? What's wrong?"

✧　　✧　　✧

Climbs Quickly hadn't exactly relaxed when Shadowed Sunlight and Death Fang's Bane had demonstrated that they understood his warning about the fire. From past experience, he knew that two-legs took fire at least as seriously as did the People. Moreover, being what they were, the two-legs would likely deal with the fire in some fashion, rather than merely running from it. He had witnessed such actions in the past and seen Shadowed Sunlight and Death Fang's Bane being trained to fight fire. While he was still uncertain why some fires were put out promptly while others were permitted to burn in a contained area, he had come to trust that any danger this fire offered would not be ignored.

Now, settled comfortably across the back of Death Fang's Bane's seat, Climbs Quickly decided that it couldn't hurt to spread the warning a bit further. He was no memory singer to send his mind voice out between clans, but he knew his mind voice—especially since he had bonded with Death Fang's Bane—was stronger than that of most males. Moreover, his sister Sings Truly was considered one of the most remarkable memory singers of this generation. Even at this distance, he might be able to reach her. She could spread the word to other memory singers and so alert the clans. At the very least, he might reach some scout or hunter who would relay the warning.

Climbs Quickly sent out a call, then opened his mind to "listen" for a reply. One came almost immediately, but it was not his sister's voice he heard. This was an unfamiliar voice, male and much closer.

<Help!> it cried. <My brother and I are trapped by the fire. Help!>

There was a desperation to the cry, as if the one who gave it had been calling for some time and had lost hope that any would hear. The mind-speech included information not included in the simple message. The two treecats were high in a green-needle, within a grove of such trees.

This was not good for several reasons. Unlike the net-wood groves in which clans tended to make their central nesting places, green-needle trees did not have interconnected branches. Instead, branches tapered off, ending in needles that would not bear an infant bark-chewer, much less a full-grown Person. To make matters worse, green-needle trees burned fast and hot. These brothers must have been hard-pressed to take refuge there.

The fire had not yet reached their refuge.

<Can you get down? To another tree?> Climbs Quickly asked.

<No,> the speaker—he called himself Left-Striped—replied. *<The ground is very hot. We tried. My brother—he insisted he could run fast enough—badly burned the pads of his hand-feet and true-feet. We made our way up into a green-needle and hoped the winds would carry the fire elsewhere, but...>*

Climbs Quickly knew then what this call really was. It was not so much a call for help—for what help could come in such a situation? It was Left-Striped's last attempt to make certain that the clan to which these brothers belonged would learn of their deaths and so not be left to empty mourning.

So the situation must have been in the days before the coming of the two-legs, the tragedy accepted as something to be sung of in sorrow, but now...

Climbs Quickly's "conversation" with the stranded treecat had taken only breaths. Now he rose onto his true-feet and began pointing. He tried to show that he was indicating a specific portion of the fire-affected area by angling his gestures precisely along the lines where he could "feel" the other treecat's mind-glow.

Death Fang's Bane made mouth noises at him. One of these was the one she used as his name; the rest was only noise. Yet Climbs Quickly sensed concern in her mind glow, a desire to comfort, to reassure.

She made more mouth noises. Climbs Quickly felt

fairly certain that she understood he was not merely repeating his warning about the fire, but a frustration that matched his own indicated that his new message was not reaching her.

"Bleek!" he said desperately, wishing the sound carried different meanings the way mouth noises seemed to do. "Bleek!"

❖   ❖   ❖

"Easy, Lionheart. Easy," Stephanie said soothingly.

The treecat flowed down from her seat back onto her lap. Then he stood and turned, his flexible spine meaning that his feet could remain oriented forward even as he turned to face her. He placed his remaining true-hand on her face and looked deeply into her brown eyes with his green.

"Bleek," he said with a sort of pathetic intensity. Then, gently but firmly, he grasped two locks of her short, curly brown hair and began tugging them.

Stephanie heeded the prompt—not to do so would have been to have her hair pulled, since the treecat was very strong. She found she was looking down.

"Karl," she said, her voice coming just a little choked from the tight angle of her throat, "I think he's telling us that whatever has his attention is lower."

"Well," Karl replied. "That's a given, since we're flying above the tree canopy."

Despite the sardonic tone of his reply, Karl began guiding the air car lower. Stephanie felt precisely when Lionheart let go of her hair.

"Okay, Karl! I think we're at the right elevation. Can we level off here?"

"Pretty well," Karl replied. "There's a lot of mature near-pine here and they tend to leave space between as they develop. If it was picketwood, no way. What direction does he want me to go?"

The treecat had adopted his "pointer dog" stance again. "Still the same," she said. "I'll let you know if he changes direction."

"So we're still heading into the fire," Karl said. "Check the Forestry Service reports."

Stephanie pulled the maps up on her uni-link screen.

"The heart of the fire is further west," she said, "definitely on what my grid shows as Franchitti lands. However, the winds are pushing a tongue out this way—right toward these near-pines."

"Bad. Very bad." Karl said, "Near-pines burn super hot and fast."

Stephanie nodded. At firefighting orientation, she had learned that the high profile of the oldest trees was meant to attract lightning. Basically, when a stand reached the point in its life-cycle where new growth was impossible, the oldest trees became lightning rods—inviting fire that would open up the area, fertilize it with ash, and accelerate the germination of seeds by burning away the resinous covering.

Now all that theory was becoming real. She and Karl had helped with a few firefighting operations this season, but always as support: bringing in supplies, coordinating communications, answering questions from concerned residents. This was the first time they'd flown directly into a fire—and all the warnings they'd been given about how dangerous and unpredictable fire could be were becoming very real.

"Lionheart's changing his point now," Stephanie reported a few minutes later. "He's indicating more south."

She took a compass reading along the line of the treecat's hand and gave it to Karl. He then refined their course. This was repeated several times.

"I think," Stephanie said, "we can guess where Lionheart wants us to go. I'm marking your nav map. See where the fire's sent out a tongue? The place isn't really 'on fire' yet, but it's close."

"Why do you think he wants us to go there?" Karl asked, adjusting the course and accelerating the air car's pace.

Stephanie pressed her lips together. "I think someone— some treecat—must be right where that tongue of the fire is. I think we're its only chance not to get burned to death."

<WE ARE COMING,> CLIMBS QUICKLY SENT TO LEFT-
Striped as soon as he was certain that Death Fang's Bane
and Shadowed Sunlight were indeed heading in the right
direction. <*Can your brother move?*>

The reply was muddled. Through it Climbs Quickly
felt an awareness of smoke and heat. All People knew
that smoke was as dangerous as fire. Despite this, the
only place the brothers had been able to take refuge
from flames that were eating along the ground was in
a tree—and smoke rose. Climbs Quickly sensed that the
brothers had already climbed as high as the flexible length
of the green-needle would bear them.

<*Coming?*> came Left-Striped's faint reply. <*How?
Flames lick up the trunk beneath us. This green-needle is
tallest of its kin, but only a hand or so of body-lengths
are between us and the fire.*>

This did not come at once, but in little spurts, the usual
almost-instant communication of mind-speech broken as

Left-Striped struggled to concentrate on more than holding fast to the tree and gathering in his next breath. There, too, a flood of worry for the brother contaminated his thoughts. Climbs Quickly caught a fragment of sensation containing weight against Left-Striped's shoulders and upper body. He knew then that his new friend had positioned himself beneath his brother, making of his own body a platform to hold the other as the grip of his burned limbs weakened.

The brother then could not move. Indeed, he was barely conscious, and when he lost consciousness, likely he would plummet into the hungry flames beneath.

Climbs Quickly looked up over his shoulder at Death Fang's Bane.

"Bleek!" he said to draw her attention from the little device she held in one hand. "Bleek!"

When Death Fang's Bane was looking, Climbs Quickly made as if he was running. It was awkward to do so without actually moving, but Death Fang's Bane was swift to comprehend. She made urgent mouth noises to Shadowed Sunlight. Immediately, Climbs Quickly felt the vibrations as the air car picked up speed. Shadowed Sunlight was flying much less carefully now, permitting the feathery tips of the green-needle and even small branches to brush against the outside of the air car.

Death Fang's Bane was making urgent noises, then she was pointing, pointing...

Climbs Quickly looked with his eyes—rather than following the guidance of Left Striped's mind-glow—and saw a horror. The two treecats clung high in the branches of the tallest green-needle in this grove, their weight enough to bend the tip of the tree to one side. Flames licked up the trunk, consuming smaller limbs at once, spilling out along the larger limbs for a more leisurely meal.

Wind was rising, both that which was driving the fire

in this direction and that generated by the fire itself, for by feeding on the old green-needles that thickly carpeted this area, the fire was growing hotter by the moment. The flames took sustenance from the wind as well, dancing in delight.

A new sound entered the complex of images as some part of the air car began laboring to cool the interior of the vehicle. An odor of smoke came where there had been none before. Aware from experience how neatly the air car usually sealed away any indication of the world without, Climbs Quickly felt panic rising.

He had possessed such faith in these two-legs that he had brought them here without thought for their safety, but what if in bringing them here he had doomed them all?

✧　　✧　　✧

"I see him," Stephanie shouted. "No! Them. There are two of them. Two treecats up in that bent-over near-pine!"

Spilling into the backseat, she grabbed her kit and slipped on the fire-suit that rested on top. This was an emergency model, made of fire-resistant fabric, basically a coverall with built-in boots and a hood.

An adult might have found donning this difficult in the confines of the air car, but Stephanie was a flexible fourteen—almost fifteen—year-old girl. Lastly, she netted her curly brown hair under the matching hood, slinging the breathing mask to cover her face. An earplug included in the hood put her in immediate contact with the air car. Goggles with an optional heads-up display covered her eyes.

Karl had been maneuvering the air car over toward the burning near-pine. He might not have managed, except that near-pine was among those breeds of trees that shed lower limbs as they grew, so the under-story was comparatively clear. Karl had a steady hand on the controls, but even with the guidance systems enabled, the updrafts of hot air were giving them a bumpy ride.

"Steph," Karl said, the measured tones of his voice showing just how tense he was. "What are you planning?"

"Someone's going to have to stuff the 'cats in the car," she said tersely. "I'm sure Lionheart has been trying to tell them we're here to rescue them, but I don't think he's getting through. How close can you get me?"

"To that large limb about two meters below the 'cats," Karl said. "I think."

"I have my counter-grav unit," she said. "So whatever happens, I'm not going to fall."

She didn't need to tell Karl that while the counter-grav unit would assist her in rising and falling, it wouldn't let her "fly." Moving through the burning tree—for rising sparks were now igniting the needles of the upper branches—would be up to her.

When Karl had the air car into position, Stephanie opened the back side door. Smoke immediately gusted in, making both Karl and Lionheart cough and sneeze. Stephanie wished she'd thought to hand Karl at least the breathing mask from his kit, but she couldn't delay now.

Lionheart did not attempt to follow her out onto the burning near-pine. As Stephanie stepped onto the limb, she could feel it bobbing. Part of this would be from her movements, but she thought more was due to the conflicting air currents of wind and thermal updraft.

Her goggles automatically adjusted for the available light, but even so, the conflicting brilliance of the flames warred with the darkening of the smoke. Even odder was the way her coveralls shielded her from the worst of the environmental changes. Stephanie *knew* she was walking through a rising fire, but she didn't feel it—which didn't mean she wouldn't burn if exposed to enough heat for long enough.

Long ago, Stephanie had learned that she kept her head

in situations that would turn most of her peers—even most adults—into gibbering idiots. As when she had fought the hexapuma in an effort to save Lionheart's life, she now felt herself concentrating on the situation, fears pushed aside in the urgency of a need to act.

She'd gibber later.

Moving purposefully toward the trunk, Stephanie assessed the situation more closely. From a distance, she had seen two treecats huddled together. What she hadn't been able to see through the smoke was that the lower one was holding the other in place, his limbs bracing the upper treecat while his strong, prehensile tail anchored him to the near-pine limb. The upper cat was limp but breathing.

Stephanie's original plan had been to grab the lower one, then see if she could get him moving towards the car. Now she adapted.

She touched the lower 'cat. Bleary green eyes opened and looked at her with surprising lack of panic. Stephanie guessed that Lionheart must have reached this 'cat at least. When she touched him, she could feel him trembling from the strain of maintaining his awkward hold on the other treecat. He hissed when he felt her touch, and she guessed why.

"Don't worry. I'm not going to pull you out from under your buddy," she said, hoping the tone of her voice would soothe him and trusting Lionheart to do the rest. "Did he get a bad dose of smoke? Let's see if I can move him."

The hissing stopped as soon as Stephanie reached up for the other 'cat. This one's ears flickered when she touched him, but his eyes did not open. Moving as quickly as she could without risking her precarious balance on the tree limb, she struggled to free his claws from their death grip in the tree bark. She managed more easily than she had thought possible, given that treecats had

six limbs with retractable claws that could rip through even tanned leather and artificially reinforced fabrics—as Stephanie had learned to the detriment of her wardrobe in her early days with Lionheart, before he learned just how fragile her clothing was.

This 'cat was only holding on with his true-hands. The other two sets were badly burned, the grip of their claws easily released.

Stephanie winced as she worked the claws free, trying hard not to hurt the 'cat but very aware that a fate far worse than burned paws was awaiting him if she didn't get him into the car as quickly as possible.

Karl had set a closed link between her fire-suit and the air car. Through this he had provided a steady update as to immediate conditions, his voice almost as impersonal as a computerized weather report.

Now a note of emotion entered his voice. "Steph, the flames are within a meter of your feet. The limb you're standing on is starting to smoulder. It's going to go up soon."

"I've almost gotten this 'cat loose," Stephanie replied. "I think the other one can move on his own. You're not going to believe it, but he was holding the other one up."

"I saw," Karl said. "Hurry."

So Stephanie did, pretending to herself that the tears that leapt hot to her eyes were from some trace of smoke that had gotten in past her mask, not because she knew she was causing the treecat considerable pain. Once he snapped as if to bite her, but stopped in mid-motion. She was relieved.

At last, well aware that flames were now licking around her feet, Stephanie got the upper treecat loose. He dropped into her arms, not as heavy as his bulky fur might suggest, but still a considerable weight that threw off her balance. For a terrifying moment, she teetered, then recovered.

"Steph!"

"I'm coming!"

To her relief, as soon as his burden was lifted, the lower treecat had uncurled himself from the awkward position he had adopted to hold the other in place. He was running now, scampering with odd, leaping jumps meant to minimize his contact with the burning tree limb. Despite this awkward gait, he flowed rapidly toward the open door of the air car. There he hesitated momentarily. The opening was bobbing alarmingly as the air car was tossed by the updrafts.

Lionheart poked out his upper body, true-hand and hand-feet extended, beckoning urgently, reaching as if to grab the other. Perhaps seeing how Lionheart's missing limb made this a very precarious position, the other treecat jumped into the air car. Stephanie and her burden were only a few steps behind. Feeling the limb under her feet creaking alarmingly, Stephanie half-leapt, half-lurched through the open door.

"Get your feet in!" Karl yelled. "I'm pulling us out."

Stephanie hauled her legs in after her and felt the open panel sliding shut. Almost immediately, the jouncing of the air car settled somewhat.

"I'm taking us back to your freehold," Karl said. She noticed he was wearing his breathing mask and goggles. "I called and your dad is home. I told him we have a patient for him. Did the other 'cat get burned?"

"I don't think so," she said, "or at least not badly."

Stephanie twisted carefully in the now cramped confines of the backseat, the injured 'cat in her lap. Lionheart was sitting next to the other treecat, thrumming gently.

She grinned at him. "Good job, Lionheart."

He bleeked and gave her a "thumbs up" gesture with his one true-hand. Then he motioned for her to put the injured treecat on the seat between him and the other cat. Now they both sat pressed against the injured one, making soothing sounds something like a Terran cat's purr.

At the time of her own injury, Lionheart's clan had done something similar for her, somehow making her mind able to ignore the pain of a very badly broken arm, nearly broken leg, and several cracked ribs, so Stephanie did not interfere. Instead, she climbed into the front seat to give the 'cats more room.

Karl, she noted, now had both respirator and goggles hanging loose on straps around his neck. She took off her own, but left the fire-suit on.

"Were you able to get those out while keeping the car steady?" she asked. "I'm impressed."

Karl chuckled. "Actually, Lionheart got them for me. I was coughing my head off and that wasn't doing any good for my piloting. Next thing I know, he's shoving the respirator at me, bleek-bleeking like mad. I got it on and he brought me the goggles."

"Good for him!"

"We got to add that to our list for Dr. Hobbard," Karl said. "The one to show that treecats are human smart, no matter what some people say."

"Human smart," Stephanie laughed. "You and I both know they're smarter than some people we know."

Lionheart bleeked, reaching forward to pat Stephanie with approval.

"Lionheart agrees with us," Stephanie said. Then the background chatter from the SFS team cut into her thoughts. "Oh! Have you reported in to SFS?"

She still felt a thrill when she referred to the Sphinxian Forestry Service by its initials—that was one of the "in" things she and Karl had picked up during their training as probationary rangers. She also got a kick out of addressing Frank and Ainsley by their titles, rather than first names, when they were on duty. Doing so acknowledged that they were all part of a group that went from the newly created Probationary Rangers up to Assistant

Rangers, Rangers, Senior Rangers, with Chief Ranger Shelton overlooking them all from the very top.

"I did," Karl said. A sly grin stretched one corner of his mouth. "I told them that we'd been coming in from the north, but had encountered a tongue of fire that made going that way a bad idea. They told me not to circle around, that the fire was under control and that aircraft were coming in to dump water and fire retardant to halt the spread of the fire in that area, so we'd better clear out."

"So you did..." Stephanie giggled.

"And was praised for my prudence," Karl said, a lopsided grin turning up one corner of his mouth. "Of course, they're going to find out eventually, but why add to their stress?"

❖   ❖   ❖

<Are you badly burned?> Climbs Quickly asked Left-Striped.

<My hand-feet and true-feet are tender,> the other admitted, *<and I have some blisters where sparks or flying embers burned through my fur. Nothing at all serious. I am more worried about my brother. He is very sluggish.>*

<We are going to one who can help him,> Climbs Quickly said reassuringly. His mind voice filled with images of Healer, the father of Death Fang's Bane. *<This one specializes in helping those who have been wounded—and not only those of his own type. I have seen him help his daughter or mate, but usually he gives his skills to other bloods. He is the one who saved my life after a death fang tore me into little more than bloodied scraps of fur.>*

<I have heard that song,> Left-Striped said, a note of excitement coloring his mind voice. *<When I realized that your voice was coming from the two-leg's flying thing, I wondered if the one who had offered hope when there was none might be you.>*

Climbs Quickly felt pleased at this generous recognition, but he did not bask in it.

<Then you realize that the two-leg who came out onto the burning green-needle is the one our people call Death Fang's Bane?>

<Yes. She is as brave as the songs tell.>

<We are going to her home. She is a youngling by their count. Her father is a healer. Her mother does interesting things with plants. It was in the clear-walled plant place attached to their house that I first tasted cluster stalk.>

<And were seen in the process,> added Left-Striped, his mind voice mingling admiration for boldness with traces of disapproval. *<The elders of our clan—my brother and I are of the Damp Ground Clan—are still arguing as to the wisdom of Bright Water's choice. As for me, having been saved when I had no belief such rescue was possible, I am interested in learning more about the two-legs.>*

<They are as different from each other as the People are,> Climbs Quickly cautioned. *<One cannot meet Death Fang's Bane or Darkness Foe—both of whom have shown themselves friends and protectors of the People—and say "Now I know what two-legs are." There are those such as Speaks Falsely or the one who caused the burning destruction of Bright Heart Clan who also walk on two legs.>*

Much of this conversation was augmented with a flow of images. There was no chance that Left-Striped would mistake which specific two-leg Climbs Quickly referred to. The names were accompanied by mental images: sharp in the case of Darkness Foe and Speaks Falsely, both of whom Climbs Quickly had met personally, less sharp in the case of those he had only heard about from another treecat. The People could lie—however, when they did, it was usually by leaving out some important piece of information, as Sings Truly had done when encouraging the Bright Water Clan to come to the rescue of Climbs Quickly and a "youngling."

<I think,> said Left-Striped, *<based upon what you have shown me, that there must be greater variation between these two-legged people than there is among our own people. They have no memory singers to bind them together with shared histories. From what we witnessed when Speaks Falsely preyed upon the People, they find it all too easy to deliberately hide what they are doing from each other.>*

Considering what he had seen Death Fang's Bane do, such as her venture in the pilot's seat of the air car earlier that day, Climbs Quickly could only agree.

Left-Striped went on. *<This lack of shared stories would make for dangerously varied ways of behaving. How can the People know which of the two-legs can be trusted and which should be avoided?>*

A good question, Climbs Quickly thought to himself. *But one for which I do not yet have an answer.*

❖   ❖   ❖

Stephanie was worried that her dad would ask all sorts of awkward questions regarding how she and Karl had come up with two more treecats, but whatever Karl had said over his uni-link had apparently left Richard Harrington with the impression that they had been working the fringes of a fire with the SFS and that the treecats had been handed over to them.

"Have I ever messed up the air car," Karl said, ruefully surveying the array of scratches and smoke stains, while the vet examined his two newest patients where they huddled in the backseat.

Richard Harrington pulled out a spray applicator and gave each treecat a light sedative. "This will let us move them without stressing them further."

"Help yourself to the supplies I keep in the hangar," he went on. "You won't be able to get the smell of smoke out of the upholstery, but this should go a long way toward your keeping your use-privileges. I've found a buffing compound that does wonders with scratches."

"Thanks, Dr. Richard. I was wondering what my folks would say. Do you need help moving the 'cats?"

"No, I can handle them. Once I get them out, you can take the 'car directly over to the hangar."

Of average height, but strong enough to carry his heaviest gear without assistance even under the pull of in Sphinx's 1.35 *g*, Dad easily lifted the two stranger treecats. Stephanie bent to give Lionheart a ride.

Without turning, Dad said, "Let him walk, Steph. It won't hurt him to work off some of what I've seen him devouring at the table. In any case, how many times do I have to tell you that you may be strong, but your skeleton is still pliable. Hauling that treecat around could give you curvature of the spine."

"But, Dad, I used to carry him all the time."

"That was before Scott gave you your last physical, young lady. Consider the facts. You are a hundred and thirty-five centimeters tall. Lionheart is sixty-five centimeters through the body. His tail adds another sixty-five centimeters, so he's one hundred and thirty centimeters long—only five centimeters shorter than you are."

Stephanie knew that was true. When Lionheart stretched out next to her in bed, he was just about as long as her. Still, she wasn't going to give up without trying at least a little more. Motioning for Lionheart to come along, she followed her dad toward his in-house clinic.

"He's not as heavy as I am, though."

"No, he's not, but when you consider that a poorly balanced backpack or even a large purse can contribute to scoliosis, you surely can see my point. Scott MacDallan may carry Fisher half-perched on one shoulder, but Scott's a grown man. When you're an adult, you can make your own choices, but for now, you—and your skeletal structure and soft tissues—are my responsibility, got it?"

"Got it," Stephanie sighed.

I can handle being short, Stephanie thought, *as long as one of these days I get around to having a figure. Mom's built okay. She keeps telling me she was a late developer, but what if I got the Harrington genes for figure and the Quintrell genes for height?*

The thoughts, a constant source of minor worry as her fifteenth birthday drew closer, ran like background music through her mind as Stephanie hurried after her father.

In the clinic, Stephanie assisted her father as he cleaned up the two treecats and treated their surface injuries. One good thing about having a resident treecat was that Richard Harrington had a solid idea of what medications would work and which would not.

The smoke inhalation was more of a problem, since Dad didn't like the idea of forcing a breathing mask over the treecats' heads.

"They're tense enough without scaring them with that, but from the wheezing in their chests, they took some damage. I'd hate for them to get pneumonia."

Lionheart had been standing by, making reassuring croons and bleeks when the stranger treecats—especially the one that had been more severely injured—bristled at being handled. Even though the burn medication was applied with a light spray, the treecat clearly hadn't liked it and had hissed back at the applicator.

Maybe he thinks the applicator was threatening him, Stephanie thought, and wished, not for the first time, that she could ask Lionheart a question more complex than "Want some celery?" (the answer to that was *always* enthusiastic agreement) or "Want to come with me?" (This also almost always met with agreement, although with varying degrees of enthusiasm.)

Now, remembering how Karl had reported that Lionheart had brought him his respirator when the air car had filled with smoke, she had a sudden idea.

"Dad, Lionheart was in the smoke, too, though not for as long. Do you think he could use a dose from the inhaler? Maybe if he used it, he could somehow let the others know it won't hurt them."

Richard Harrington had long gotten past the days when he underestimated Lionheart. He looked thoughtful, then nodded. "You show him what we want."

Stephanie did so, miming using the inhaler on herself, then holding the inhaler to Lionheart's mouth. He sniffed it carefully, then sighed gustily and opened his mouth. This revealed a remarkable array of very sharp teeth, but Stephanie trusted him not to bite her. The procedure completed, she held up the inhaler, then pointed it at the other two treecats.

"They need this, too," she said. "Can you explain?"

Lionheart bleeked and directed his attention at the other 'cats. Whatever he said also involved a great deal of wheezing and deep breathing, but in the end, the two treecats submitted to one deep breath each.

"Very good!" Dad said after they had finished with the breathing treatments. He leaned forward and took a closer look at the two treecats' coats, focusing particularly on their tabby-gray sections. "This is interesting. I think we have a pair of mirror twins here."

"Mirror twins?" Stephanie asked. The term sounded familiar, but she couldn't quite place it.

"Fraternal twins," Dad clarified, "but ones that have markings that match each other like reflections in a mirror. In humans, this would mean that one twin would be right-handed while the other was left-handed. Things like that. Look how the stripes and other markings on these two work. Our injured friend's larger stripes all go right. The other one's are a perfect match, but oriented to the left."

Now that the two treecats were cleaned up and brushed, Stephanie could see what her father meant. To a nonspecialist, all male treecats looked pretty much alike. Their upper coats were striped in shades of gray, while their stomachs were a contrasting cream. Female treecats (not that most humans got a glimpse of these, since they were less adventurous than the males) were dappled brown and white, rather like a Terran fawn. However, when you spent enough time with treecats, you learned there was a fair amount of variety within individual tabby patterns.

"Well," Richard Harrington continued, "that will make naming them for my records easier: Right-Striped and Left-Striped. I wonder how usual mirror twins are among treecats. You said you've seen litters of kittens, but do treecats often have identical twins?"

"I haven't," Stephanie said, rolling her eyes, "been able to ask them. Is the one who got worst burnt—Right-Striped—going to be okay?"

"I think so. In an ideal universe, I'd keep him in bed for a day while the skin healed, but in this case I think the best we can do is take him and his brother out to the gazebo. You still have a hammock rigged for Lionheart there?"

"A couple. He likes taking advantage of sun or shade, depending on the weather."

"Good. We'll put them out there and invite them to stay by bribing them with fresh food and water. Let's add some celery for good measure—that always seems to work with Lionheart."

From past experience, Stephanie knew that most treecats reacted to celery like a Terran cat did to catnip. This was really weird, since, although technically omnivores, the 'cats seemed to lean to the carnivorous side. It also meant that their teeth weren't really well equipped for eating the stuff and they tended to make a horrible mess.

"I've commed your mother," Dad went on as he scooped up first Left-Striped, then Right-Striped, "and she knows we have guests. She's bringing her car in on the side furthest from the gazebo so she doesn't startle them. Ask Karl if he wants to stay for dinner."

Karl did and was easily convinced to stay overnight as well, since he and Stephanie both had been asked by the SFS if they'd help with fire clean-up, and the Harrington freehold was a great deal closer than his own family home.

That evening, Karl showed Stephanie some images he'd taken of her going into the fire. By necessity, the pictures were wobbly and choppy, since he'd had to leave his uni-link balanced on the dashboard while he concentrated on keeping the vehicle steady. Even so, it was impressive. Stephanie hadn't realized just how close the flames had been or how badly burnt she would have been without her fire-suit. A couple of times, even knowing that everything had worked out in the end, she found herself distinctly scared.

Still, she knew that if circumstances demanded, she'd do it again.

❖   ❖   ❖

Sphinx! Anders Whittaker felt delight shiver through him as the shuttle touched down, followed some moments later by a not unexpected heaviness as the planet's higher gravity took effect. He switched on his belt-mounted counter-grav unit, already adjusted to compensate, and felt his weight return to normal.

It shouldn't be so easy, Anders thought, *to adapt to an alien planet.*

Of course, it really hadn't been easy. The counter-grav

unit could compensate for weight, but lightening a person didn't do anything to help the lungs deal with the denser atmosphere's concentrations of gases. For that he'd needed nano-tech treatments. Then there had been all the immunizations, not just against the plague, which had wiped out so many of the original settlers, but against anything else his parents could think of.

I bet I could swim in raw sewage and come out without the least trace of infection.

He grinned at the image, thinking how horrified his mother would be. She'd been worried about him accompanying his father to Sphinx on this research expedition. However, she hadn't been able to deny that it made more sense for Anders to spend the time in his father's company. She'd just been named to a post as a cabinet minister of the newly elected president of Urako. She'd been busy before, as Counselor Whittaker, senior representative for one of the highest population zones on the planet. As Cabinet Minister Whittaker, she was going to be nearly unreachable for the next six T-months.

In light of his wife's appointment, the timing for Dr. Whittaker's trip to Sphinx hadn't exactly been the best. However, although Bradford A. Whittaker could be called many things, "professionally uninvolved" would never be one. A rising light in the field of xenoanthropology, he'd long griped that his career had been held back by the lack of a new intelligent alien species to study.

When the earliest reports of the Sphinxian treecats had come to his attention, Dr. Whittaker had seen the opening for which he had longed. He had all but memorized every word of every press release, every report. He'd begun immediate correspondence with Dr. Sanura Hobbard, Chairwoman of the Anthropology Department, Landing University, on Manticore, the official head of official Crown inquiry into treecat intelligence. He'd fumed that his own responsibilities as a faculty member of Urako University on the planet Urako in the Kenichi System didn't let him take ship right away—this despite the fact that the Sphinxian Forestry Service wasn't allowing anyone much access to the treecats.

Anders had been infected by his father's fascination. Like Dr. Whittaker, he agreed that treecats just had to be intelligent, maybe not *humanly* intelligent, but no one was certain where they would fit on the sentience scale. Human exploration had turned up too few other intelligent species—and in at least one case, the species had been wiped out before it could become inconvenient. Long before there had ever been a chance to go to Sphinx, Anders had become an advocate for treecats' rights.

Then had come the fiasco with "Doctor" Tennessee Bolgeo, ostensibly of Liberty University in the distant Chattanooga System. Not many people knew what had happened, but enough had leaked out—especially within xenoanthropological circles—to create a scandal. In response, the Star Kingdom had decided that the best damage control would involve two steps.

First, they changed their policy of permitting relatively free access to the treecats. Second, they decided to bring in an officially sanctioned off-planet xenoanthropological team. Needless to say, Dr. Whittaker had immediately applied for this newly created Crown consultancy.

It was a long shot. There were many other xenoanthropologists with more seniority—and with a better chance at landing additional grants that would assure detailed investigations. However, Anders was certain that no other applicant had more passion than his dad.

So had begun several T-months of pure agony.

Between Dr. Whittaker waiting to hear if he had been selected for the Sphinx project and Counselor Whittaker waiting to hear if soon she would be Cabinet Minister

Whittaker, the tension in their household had been thick enough to cut into bricks.

Very much the son of a politician *and* the son of an anthropologist, Anders had weathered the situation with skill. From the politician side, he'd learned to say the right things and not commit himself to any course too soon. From the anthropologist side, he'd learned to step back and observe, weighing the data with as little added emotion as possible.

So it was that Anders was more prepared than either of his parents when—miracle of miracles—both of them had found themselves with fascinating new professional opportunities and the topic of "What do we do with Anders?" had arisen.

Anders knew his mother would want him to stay on Urako. He loved his mom, but he also knew how much time he'd spend alone—and that much of the time he'd spend with his mother would be within the context of official functions. Compared to the lure of treecats and a chance to live on a barely settled alien world within the fascinating Star Kingdom of Manticore, well, even regular dinners with the president of Urako and all the perqs that came with high public office held no attraction.

Bradford Whittaker wasn't exactly a warm and fuzzy parent—there was too much of the anthropologist in him for that. But he did believe in exposing his son to every possible experience, and he'd already taken Anders with him on trips to anthropological sites both on planet and in a few nearby systems. Given all of this, it wasn't hard to convince the new cabinet minister that her son would be better off accompanying his father. What had surprised Anders was how enthusiastic Dr. Whittaker had been about taking Anders with him.

"Anders is interested in treecats," he'd said. "I'm certain he'll be a real asset to the team."

Anders had glowed like a sun going nova. It wasn't often his father approved of him within the context of the anthropology that was his first love. Even Mom had been won over.

"But you'll write me every week," she'd fussed as she'd helped Anders to pack. "And I'll write, too. Send lots of pictures and make certain you don't fall behind on your studies. University may seem impossibly far off to you, but you're nearly sixteen and entrance exams will be on you before you realize it."

There was a lot more of this. Anders let it flow over him. He knew it was just his mom making sure he knew he was important to her. He'd let her pack him extra socks and underwear without protest. On some atavistic maternal level Mom seemed convinced that a relatively newly settled planet like Sphinx would lack such basic items.

Unspoken was her concern that Dr. Whittaker would forget such things as clean underwear and regular meals once he was within reach of his new test subjects. He'd always been a bit obsessive. Now, with his entire professional reputation resting on this trip (as he repeatedly stated), Dr. Whittaker had taken to addressing his son as if he was simply an unusually young graduate assistant.

In many ways, this suited Anders just fine. It beat being "the kid." Since the field season was going to be a long one, several members of the crew had brought family members. However, Anders was the only one who wasn't another adult.

Doctor Calida Emberly (xenobiology and xenobotany) had brought her elderly mother, a painter, who was on partial retainer to the expedition as a scientific illustrator. Both Kesia Guyen (linguistics) and Virgil Iwamoto (lithics and field methods) had brought their spouses. In Iwamoto's case, his was a very recent marriage, brought about in part by the impending departure of the expedition. Only Dr. Langston Nez, a newly minted Ph.D. in cultural anthropology who had been Dr. Whittaker's senior assistant for many years, had traveled alone.

Anders had overheard Peony Rose Iwamoto gossiping to Dacey Emberly, saying that Dr. Nez's long-standing relationship had broken up in large part because Nez preferred to continue working with Dr. Whittaker rather than seeking some prestigious position of his own. Apparently, Nez's partner had said some really nasty things about Dr. Whittaker being grasping, ambitious, and self-absorbed.

Anders only wished he disagreed. He loved his dad but, if it hadn't been for their shared fascination with treecats, these days he wasn't sure they'd have much in common.

Sphinx! Anders savored the thought as the passengers shuffled from the shuttle into the spaceport. *I'm really here! I wonder how long until I get to see a treecat in person? I wonder if it will be a "wild" or one of one of those who have adopted a human?*

Unarticulated, even to himself, was the question, "Will I get to meet Stephanie Harrington and Lionheart?"

Anders' fascination with Stephanie was almost as acute as his interest in treecats. It wasn't because she was a girl nearly his own age—he was about eight T-months older—although his mother had teased him about that when she saw he had a special file for articles on Stephanie. It was because Stephanie Harrington had been the first person to make contact with treecats. Until Stephanie had figured out a way to trap an image, no one had even known treecats existed.

Then she'd nearly been killed saving a treecat from a hexapuma—or the treecat had been nearly killed saving her—that part of the story was always a bit unclear. Basically, as Anders had told his mother, Stephanie Harrington could have been a century-old double-butted near-baboon and if she'd done what she'd done, he'd still have been interested in meeting her.

And Lionheart.

Therefore, Anders was shocked and horrified when, after welcoming them to Sphinx, Dr. Hobbard told them that Stephanie had nearly been killed that day while going into the heart of a raging forest fire to rescue a pair a stranded treecats.

STEPHANIE AND KARL WOULD HAVE PROBABLY COME in for a lot more grief over the risks they'd taken rescuing the two treecats if it hadn't been for three things.

First, the imagery Karl had so thoughtfully taken had demonstrated how very careful they had been. Stephanie had been in full gear, not rushing in with no thought other than for saving the 'cats.

Second, again the images provided a neutral witness that without their intervention, Left-Striped and Right-Striped would have died in the blaze. Although doubtless many treecats died in fires set in the course of nature, once it had been confirmed that this fire had been caused by human negligence, it was very hard to persuasively argue that humans shouldn't do something to save those endangered by it.

Third, the arrival of the team of out-of-system anthropologists on the very day of the fire had provided both Stephanie's parents and the SFS with a way of reminding

Stephanie that with great knowledge not only came great responsibility, but a liberal dose of boredom as well.

"Dr. Hobbard," Marjorie Harrington said that evening over dinner, "commed me earlier to say that the off-world anthropology team was arriving today. She wondered if we could arrange for you to come and speak to them. I told her you were out on SFS business, but that we'd com her back to arrange a time."

Stephanie had been about to protest that she couldn't spare the time, that it would be days before Right-Striped could go without care, but a certain narrowing about both her mother's and father's eyes, as well as the slight grin twitching the corners of Karl's usually serious mouth, told her that this was one battle lost before it was joined.

"Do they need time to settle in," she asked, "or would tomorrow be good?"

Richard Harrington's expression shifted to approving. Marjorie nodded.

"I asked. Apparently, Dr. Whittaker was disappointed that there weren't treecats waiting to greet him and his team at the spaceport in Yawata." She laughed at Stephanie's involuntary bleat of protest. "I don't mean that literally, Stephanie. It's just that Dr. Whittaker is very enthusiastic. Dr. Hobbard says the anthropologists can meet with you any time—the sooner the better. However, she did her best to give you time to prepare by telling them you'd been out doing fire rescue today."

"That's nice of her," Stephanie said.

Quickly, she weighed her options. If she said the fire had worn her out, she might buy some time to get to know Right-Striped and Left-Striped before they took off for wherever they lived. However, next time she wanted to help at a fire, that "tiredness" would certainly be remembered.

Anyhow, she wasn't tired. She'd rather spend time with the treecats, but she was pretty excited about the anthropologists, too. These were *real* xenoanthropologists, not fakes like that horrible null, Tennessee Bolgeo.

"Tomorrow, then," she answered, the words coming so swiftly on the heels of the others that only someone who knew her well—like her parents and Karl—would think them anything but impulsive. "As early as you want."

Richard nodded. "Good. We'll com Dr. Hobbard after dinner. Marjorie, did she say where this meeting was to be held?"

"Dr. Hobbard suggested the SFS ranger station near Twin Forks," came the reply. "There's just one problem. I have an appointment to be at the Tharch freehold to demonstrate some of the cooler-weather vegetable hybrids we've been developing. Sad as it is to admit, this glorious long summer is almost over, but since autumn also runs fifteen months, with the right cultivars we can take advantage of it..."

She paused and grinned. "Sorry. My enthusiasm running away with me. Short form. I'm booked all day tomorrow."

Richard Harrington looked concerned. "I am, too. I have a small gap early, but I was going to use it to work with my newest patients. I suppose they'll be all right, but if..."

Karl didn't quite interrupt, but a shift in his body language stopped Richard in mid-phrase.

"I could fly Stephanie in," Karl offered. "I could even get her back here. It's no trouble. I've been considering anthropology rather than forestry—or maybe in addition to forestry—when I start college, so I'd really like to meet these people."

Richard Harrington visibly relaxed. "That would be great, Karl, if it's okay with your folks. You've been away all day already, out in a forest fire, and now staying away overnight. If you were my kid, I'd want to see you with my own eyes."

That sadness Stephanie had noted was such a real part of Karl fleetingly passed over his face.

"Don't worry, Dr. Richard," he said, using the nickname he'd developed as a compromise between naturally good manners and the difficulty of having two Dr. Harringtons in the same household. "I'll com. They'll be glad enough to have a chance to chat. I'll go home tomorrow."

Have a chance to chat, Stephanie thought, wishing that, like Lionheart, she could reach out and offer comfort that was more than just words. *Unlike with all those people who died in the Plague. People who are gone forever and that those who are left will never have a chance to talk to again.*

✦   ✦   ✦

Anders was relieved when Dr. Hobbard told them that Stephanie Harrington was unharmed. More excitingly, she had agreed to meet with them the next morning.

"I must warn you," Dr. Hobbard said that evening when she met them for dinner, "to handle Stephanie Harrington with no less care and courtesy than you would any adult. She may be a girl of fourteen, but where treecats are concerned, she's old as the hills."

Anders could tell his father didn't believe that anyone—especially a girl of fourteen—could hold back any information he was determined to get. It wasn't until later, when he and his dad were back in their suite, that Anders realized to what extent Dr. Whittaker was prepared to go to get what he wanted.

"Anders," Dr. Whittaker said, "the time has come for you to show yourself a part of our field team."

He rubbed his hands together, and Anders was reminded of a coach he had once had, a man who had liked to proclaim himself his players' "buddy" and "pal"—that is, right up until he was screaming at you for "letting down the side."

The similarity went beyond attitude. Like that coach, Dr. Whittaker was a big man, both tall and broad. In earlier years, fieldwork had kept him trim, but lately most of his work had been in libraries and laboratories. This might be mentally arduous, but did not put the same demands on his body, making him fleshy if not quite fat. Over the last few years, Dr. Whittaker's brown hair had been retreating from his forehead at an alarming rate, Whittaker family genetics defying a wide array of "cures," both scientific and otherwise. The fact that genetic engineering had all but eliminated male pattern baldness only added to Dad's frustration since, in his case, tinkering with the associated genes created a solution that was far worse than mere hair loss.

Anders distinctly hoped he'd been spared this particular gene. He had even checked with his doctor during a routine physical a few years ago and had been disproportionately relieved to learn that his scans showed no evidence of the baldness gene. More likely, he'd wind up with a thick head of hair like his maternal grandfather.

Surreptitiously comparing himself with his father, Anders thought that overall he hadn't done too badly. He was showing promise of his father's height and solid build, but his deep blue eyes and sandy-blond hair came from his mother. His features were also shaping into a masculine version of hers, a throwback to Scandinavian ancestors who had favored clean lines, rather than the blunter, more polyethnic mix that dominated in his father.

"Part of the field team?" Anders echoed.

"That's right, my boy. You've shown yourself interested in the treecats, but have you considered that anthropology is more than studying interesting cultures? Sometimes you must also work with those who dominate the area."

Anders had a sneaking suspicion where this was heading, but he'd long ago learned that it was politic to hear the other person out before jumping to conclusions. He also had a creepy feeling that he now knew why Dr. Whittaker had been so enthusiastic about taking him to Sphinx.

"Oh?"

"That's right. In this case, of course, the ones who dominate the area are not the treecats themselves, although they are the indigenous intelligent species and therefore should have some rights themselves to decide who does and does not have access to them."

Anders noted with some admiration how Dr. Whittaker could use this complex conclusion—one that, as far as he knew, was not shared by the majority of the residents of Sphinx—to his own advantage. It made *Dr. Whittaker* sound like the true treecat advocate, not the Forestry Service, who had set themselves up as the treecats' protectors.

I guess I'm not the only one who has learned something from living with a politician all these years. Now if Dad could only learn to be as nice—as genuinely caring—as Mom, he'd be ahead of the game.

Anders nodded. "Like the treecat who made friends with Stephanie Harrington—Lionheart. He chose to make contact with the humans."

"Actually, that's not precisely correct," Dr. Whittaker said. "'Lionheart,' as Ms. Harrington has so quaintly named this treecat, actually was making contact with the greenhouse. All his actions show that he intended to stay away from humans. He showed remarkable ingenuity in avoiding the alarms. Only Ms. Harrington's admittedly brilliant deduction regarding the wavelengths in which treecats perceived light enabled her to catch a recorded image."

"But," Anders protested, "they've stayed friends since."

"Again, Anders, I fear you are jumping to the same romantic conclusions that so many have reached. Lionheart— I do wish we knew what manner of naming conventions treecats use for themselves—actually fled from that initial contact. It was not until Ms. Harrington pursued him, using tracking methods about which she has been very vague, and was injured, that Lionheart came to the rescue. Her actions were irresponsible, putting both herself and the treecat in considerable danger."

"She saved his life!" Anders said angrily.

"Only after endangering it in the first place. Really, Anders, I thought you were more capable of scientific detachment. Perhaps your mother is correct and you have developed a—romantic attachment, shall we call it?—to the idea of the heroic Stephanie Harrington."

Anders glowered and bit back a couple dozen things he would have liked to say. Instead, dreading more discussion on this subject, he steered the conversation back to his father's original statement.

"So, Dad, you said there was something I could do to help out the team?"

Dr. Whittaker brightened. "That's right. As I was saying, often well-meaning non-indigenous cultures assume a paternalistic attitude regarding what they consider vulnerable primitive cultures."

"That is," Anders couldn't resist saying, "the high-tech newcomers decide to protect those who might suffer otherwise."

"You are romanticizing again," Dr. Whittaker replied, waggling one finger at Anders. "Paternalism is not simply protectiveness. As the word—which has its roots in an old word for 'father'—implies, those who become paternalistic set themselves up in the role of parents, assuming they know better for no other reason than they have more technology and that technology enables them to dominate."

"So the Sphinx Forestry Service is paternalistic," Anders summarized.

"Yes," Dr. Whittaker agreed enthusiastically, "and not merely toward the treecats, but also toward Ms. Harrington herself. You heard Dr. Hobbard's warning."

"That didn't sound protective," Anders said. "I mean, except maybe of us. Dr. Hobbard was warning us that Ms. Harrington might button up if we pushed her too hard."

"I can see you are determined not to see things my way," Dr. Whittaker said. Since this was pretty much the truth, Anders said nothing, but waited for him to continue. "I do not plan to 'push' Ms. Harrington. Clearly, this would be a bad tactic. However, it has occurred to me that you are about her own age. She might loosen up around you. Moreover, you are a handsome young man and she is a young lady—a clever young lady, no doubt, but no less a female for all that."

"You want me to sweet-talk her so she'll tell us more about the treecats?" Anders didn't know whether to be indignant or to laugh.

"Befriend her," Dr. Whittaker said. "Flirt, if that is what you wish. Make her comfortable with us. Let her see us as humans who care as much about the treecats and their well-being as she herself does. Remember. Her initial contact with anthropologists was that fake Tennessee Bolgeo. She may retain some reflex aversion to our profession."

"So you want me to flirt with her," Anders said, amazed.

"Befriend her," Dr. Whittaker pressed. "Or, if you are unwilling, then I believe there is a young man who is also an SFS 'probationary ranger'—a post created, apparently, to enable the SFS to better control Ms. Harrington. Don't look at me so disapprovingly. I'm not asking you to seduce the girl. I'm not asking you to do anything more dishonest than what your mother does when she kisses strange babies and hugs little old ladies she's never met. All I'm asking you to do is be nice."

Anders didn't know what to say to that. Anyhow, refusing to talk to Stephanie or this other fellow—Karl something-beginning-with-"Z"—would be really stupid, since, in addition to seeing a treecat himself, there wasn't anything Anders wanted more. And if he could make his dad happy, earn points as a "team player," then what was he doing wrong?

"Okay, Dad," Anders said, putting on his most winning smile, uncomfortably aware of how much it resembled the one on thousands of his mom's campaign posters, "I see your point. I'll do what I can to befriend Stephanie Harrington."

✧   ✧   ✧

Climbs Quickly managed to convince Left-Striped and Right-Striped that they would be perfectly safe in the gazebo, but it took some doing. Not only was the gazebo far closer to the ground than a more usual sleeping platform, but it was uncomfortably close to the two-legs' own dwelling.

In the end, Climbs Quickly thought that Right-Striped's injuries had as much to do with convincing them to stay as any reassurance he offered. When Right-Striped had been forced to climb the green-needle, the pads of his hand-feet and true-feet had not only been burned, but also had been badly abraded. What skin remained had been blistered and swollen, leaking blood and slime, and in great danger of becoming infected.

Healer's treatments had minimized the pain and all but eliminated the swelling. However, the false skin he had misted over the injuries would not hold up under the demands of travel.

Then, too, the food Death Fang's Bane brought them was a selection based on Climbs Quickly's own favorites. The grand finale of the meal was a fresh piece of cluster-stalk for each of them. This fine and exotic treat brought rhapsodies of delight from the two guests, even bringing Right-Striped out of the silence that had shadowed him long after much of his pain had been alleviated.

Over cluster-stalk, Left-Striped told how they had happened to be so near an area inhabited by two-legs.

<The Damp Ground Clan recently relocated to a fresh central nesting place within our territory. Although this hot, dry weather has not drained the lands beneath our former nesting trees, many of the feeder streams that bring us fish and water crawlers have diminished their flow or dried entirely. Hunting was growing more difficult, since too few ground-runners come into the wetlands to make up the difference.>

The images that accompanied Left-Striped's words gave Climbs Quickly a fair idea of the area into which the Damp Ground Clan had made their new home. As with all treecat nesting areas, it was well-supplied with the net-wood trees that made travel without touching the ground so easy. He noted that the Damp Ground Clan's new nesting place also had exceptionally good overhead coverage, supplied in part by association with golden-leaf.

<Yes.> Right-Striped said in response to Climbs Quickly's unarticulated thought. *<One of the reasons the elders of our clan chose this area was that the golden-leaf provides further shelter from the two-legs and their flying things. Our territory is near enough to lands the two-legs have claimed as their own that there has been some disturbance.>*

Left-Striped added, *<Our new nesting place is not very near where the two-legs live, but some of the best hunting does take us close. My brother and I were scouting the region, checking to see if we could find what routes the two-legs use and gathering some idea of how frequently so our hunters could make appropriate plans.>*

Although the People had resolved to be cautious in their interactions with the two-legs, they were also learning that where the two-legs settled, interesting opportunities were to be found. Climbs Quickly himself had taken cluster stalk from their transparent plant places—an act justifiable for a scout, although it would be considered theft if a Person took such from another Person.

However, even if the People would not steal directly from where the two-legs grew their food, it could not be ignored that often the two-legs created secondary food opportunities. Small ground-runners often came to browse at the edges of their planted fields. The two-legs' practice of leaving out food for the animals they kept also drew scavengers. Some of the plants they grew also migrated outside the areas the two-legs had marked for their own. These were often quite tasty and very robust.

So, although doubtless the elders of the Damp Ground Clan would have argued otherwise, Right-Striped and Left-Striped had been sent to scout the forests near to where the two-legs had staked a claim precisely because the two-legs were there.

Climbs Quickly did not blame them, although he was growing a bit weary of how the People could fill their mouths with cluster stalk while their minds denied the value of those who had brought it.

He bleeked amusement as he tasted Left-Striped's— Right-Striped had drifted off into a doze—awareness of the irony.

❖   ❖   ❖

The next morning, Death Fang's Bane's actions made clear that she and Shadowed Sunlight were heading off again. Climbs Quickly debated staying behind to continue visiting with Left-Striped and Right-Striped. He thought his presence might reassure them that it was safe to remain in the gazebo. However, beneath the excitement in Death Fang's Bane's mind-glow was a sense of uneasiness. He could not read her thoughts, but he knew the taste of this particular emotion and knew it had much to do with her relationship with the People.

Time and again, Climbs Quickly had sat with his two-leg, reassuring her as she answered question after question. From her gestures and a few words—as well as the taste of her mind-glow—he knew when the People were the subject. There was a special note that entered into her mind-glow during some of these discussions. It reminded Climbs Quickly somewhat of the feeling of stalking or scouting—as if she was being very, very careful, as a hunter took care not to break a twig lest the prey hear and flee. Or as if she was scouting some dangerous creature, like a death fang or snow hunter, and knew that a slip might mean disaster.

For these reasons, although he would have enjoyed relaxing with these members of another clan—especially after the exertions of the previous day—he decided to join Death Fang's Bane and Shadowed Sunlight when they departed that morning.

This time, Climbs Quickly noted with amusement, there was no question as to who was operating the air car. Despite their traveling above the trees and at a high speed, Shadowed Sunlight slid down one of the transparent panels for Climbs Quickly without being asked, but Climbs Quickly did not enjoy the ride as much as he usually did. His thoughts were too full of the implications of change.

✧   ✧   ✧

When Karl brought down the air car at the familiar SFS regional headquarters complex, Stephanie noticed that several vehicles were already parked in the visitors' area.

"Dr. Whittaker and his team must already be here," she said, gathering Lionheart into her arms and hugging him. Surely Dad wouldn't mind if she carried him just a short distance.

"Ready?" Karl asked.

"You bet," Stephanie replied.

Inside, they were immediately directed to a conference room off to one side of the building. The room was large—it doubled as a lecture hall—but today seemed quite crowded. It smelled strongly of coffee—the beverage favored by the hard-working SFS staff—but there were under-notes that promised other options. When Lionheart bleeked in delight and strained in the direction of the refreshment table set up to one side of the room, Stephanie suspected the presence of celery.

"Little pig," she whispered. "You had some just last night!"

But she knew she'd give in. She suspected that Lionheart liked meetings as little as she did. She appreciated his company—and the support he gave her could go far beyond the comfort offered by a warm, furry body to hold.

She set Lionheart on the long table that bisected the room. Frank Lethbridge, one of the two rangers who had been assigned to train her and Karl, was the first to intercept her, but others quickly followed.

In addition to several representatives of the SFS, including Chief Ranger Gary Shelton himself, Dr. Sanura Hobbard was attending. Stephanie knew Dr. Hobbard all too well. At first she'd found the professor somewhat annoying, but now she had come to respect her devotion to careful and responsible study of other cultures. Eventually, they'd even come to a sort of compromise as to what Dr. Hobbard would and would not publish about the treecats.

As Stephanie politely greeted those she knew, sharing with Karl a mixture of ribbing and congratulations for their heroics during the fire the day before, she was very aware of the large group that clustered at one end of the room, clearly waiting to be introduced.

The group was dominated by an extremely tall, broad man. Somehow he gave Stephanie the impression of being made all of curves: the dome of his balding head, the arc of a budding gut, a round smoothness to his heavy, muscular limbs. This proved to be Dr. Bradford Whittaker himself.

When they were introduced, Dr. Whittaker shook Stephanie's hand. He gained a point in her estimation by neither patting nor poking Lionheart, but instead offering the treecat a little bow by way of greeting.

"This," Dr. Whittaker said, "is my chief assistant, Dr. Langston Nez."

Dr. Nez proved to be shorter than average, built along planes instead of curves. His most noticeable features were untidy brown hair that stood up in spikes, as if he ran his hands through it frequently, and bushy eyebrows from under which green eyes—darker than Lionheart's but no less alert—watched like animals from a forest.

Dr. Whittaker went on. "This is our linguistics specialist, Kesia Guyen."

No "doctor" in front of this one's name, Stephanie noticed. A graduate student, then, but certainly one who was done with classes and now working on her dissertation.

Kesia Guyen had lovely rich chocolate-brown skin and wore her hair in swirling curls that framed a face that seemed to find seriousness difficult. She had a rounded figure with breasts that could do double-duty as platforms, and full hips. Her clothing showed a penchant for bright colors, sashes, and jewelry, but Stephanie didn't think that this was a Trudy-like effort to emphasize her physical assets, more as if Kesia found life colorful and didn't mind showing it.

"Delighted!" Kesia said when Stephanie said she was happy to meet her, "Enchanted! So very, very happy to meet you both."

She might have said more, but Dr. Whittaker continued.

"This is Dr. Calida Emberly." He indicated a woman quite a bit older than the others, older even than himself, for she was easily in her mid-fifties. "She is our xenobiologist. Her first concentration was in zoology, but she also holds degrees in xenobotany."

Dr. Emberly extended a long-boned hand. "I've read several of your mother's papers. I hope to get to chat with Dr. Harrington while we're here."

Stephanie liked Dr. Emberly instantly. "I'm sure she'd be happy to meet you. She's always glad to hear other people's thoughts."

Dr. Emberly possessed a hawklike profile that made her seem very stern, but when she smiled, the hawk took wing. She wasn't nearly as tall as Dr. Whittaker, but her slender, lithe build made her seem taller. Her hair was either silvered or platinum blond—Stephanie couldn't be sure which—and she wore it long, in a thick braid intertwined with a contrasting violet silk cord. Stephanie admired this touch of vanity on a woman who otherwise might be dismissed as plain. It gave her character.

I wonder if Dr. Whittaker waited to introduce her because, in a lot of ways, she probably outranks him, Stephanie thought. *He seems like that sort.*

"Finally," Dr. Whittaker said, "we have Virgil Iwamoto. He's our lithics specialist. He's also an expert on the latest in field methods."

Iwamoto was the youngest of the group, probably in his mid-twenties. His face showed a distinct Asian influence that expressed itself in brown, almond-shaped eyes and small, neat features framed by silky black hair. He wore a short, tidy beard and seemed anxious.

"Pleased to meet you," he said in a soft, pleasant voice.

"Let me see," Dr. Whittaker said with a curious smile. "There's one other person I'd like you to meet."

He looked around, finding the one he sought at the end of the refreshments table, where he had apparently just filled a cup with coffee.

"I'd like you and Karl to meet an unofficial but important member of our team," Dr. Whittaker said, the words rolling out as if he was making a speech. "Over there, hiding behind Dr. Emberly, is my son, Anders Whittaker."

Anders turned and almost sheepishly toasted Stephanie and Karl with his coffee mug.

"Hi," he said. "I've read a lot about you both. Glad to meet you."

Stephanie knew she said something in reply. She could feel the words buzzing in her throat, but somehow she wanted to say something more than "Glad to meet you, too."

Anders Whittaker was, simply put, the most compelling young man Stephanie had ever met. It wasn't just his dark blue eyes, large enough to lose yourself in, or the thick wheat-colored hair that he wore gathered in a neat ponytail at the base of his neck. It was the shape of his mouth, the way it quirked in a sideways smile that invited you to join in on some unspoken joke. It was the rose-and-ivory glow of his unexpectedly fair skin—his father was several shades darker. Anders was already tall, taking after his father in that, but where Dr. Whittaker seemed to be made of curves, Anders was lean and supple.

Stephanie was saved from gaping stupidly by Chief Ranger Shelton saying, "If we could all grab drinks, then take seats, I'd like to get this gathering underway. Sadly, I have a meeting regarding yesterday's fire that's going to pull me away, but I'd like to get things started."

While all the predictable things were said—Dr. Whittaker holding forth on how very happy he was to be there and how proud he was to have been selected for this important, groundbreaking study, Dr. Hobbard and Chief Ranger Shelton responding in kind—Stephanie fought to keep her attention on what was being said. She wanted to move to where she could get a better look at Anders, see if he was maybe smiling one of those quirky smiles as the adults said all the things they already knew, but wanted to get on the record.

After Chief Ranger Shelton left, the mood immediately became less formal. Chairs were pushed back. Several people rose to refill their drinks.

Karl was one of these. "More cocoa, Steph?"

"Uh, sure." She blushed. That had really sounded polished, hadn't it?

"Bleek!" Lionheart said. The SFS staff had provided him with a stool so that he could sit next to Stephanie and still comfortably see over the table. When Stephanie had gotten her cocoa, she'd brought him some cubes of cheese, but she had no doubt what he was asking for now.

"Not really a good idea," she said.

"Is he asking for celery?" said Dr. Emberly, the woman who had been introduced as the xenobiologist.

Stephanie smiled ruefully. "He is. He's known it was here since we walked into the room—heck, he probably knew as soon as we got into the building. From what we can tell, treecats have a wonderfully sharp sense of smell."

"Is it all right if I give him some?" asked Virgil Iwamoto.

Stephanie considered. "Well, Lionheart had some celery just last night, so he shouldn't have too much. Treecats are more carnivores than omnivores and..."

She wished she hadn't started in on this, but having done so, she pushed on, inelegant though the subject might be. She hoped Anders didn't think she was being crass or crude.

"... Well, it makes them constipated if they eat too much of it. Lionheart had some real problems when he first came to live with us, but Dad figured out the problem. Now I give Lionheart doses of what's basically cod-liver oil a couple times a week. Since he likes fish, it isn't too much trouble."

"Interesting," said Dr. Emberly. "Extra fiber usually gives terrestrial animals gas. Eating it helps eliminate blockage. I wonder what the difference is in the metabolisms?"

She looked as if she would very much like to be given a treecat to dissect, but since Stephanie had heard her father say similar things, she recognized scientific fervor when she heard it.

Watching Lionheart make his messy way through the helping of celery sticks Iwamoto slid over to him broke the ice amazingly. Questions rained down from all sides. Karl—whose uncle by marriage, Scott MacDallan, had also been adopted by a treecat—helped answer them.

"What else does Lionheart eat?"

"Just about what the wild treecats do. We try to make certain he gets a healthy, balanced diet, but he does eat with the rest of us, so he's developed rather esoteric tastes."

Karl added, "Fisher and Lionheart do have different preferences. Fisher really loves fish. Lionheart seems to prefer poultry or red meat."

"Will the treecats eat celery to the exclusion of everything else?" This was from Dr. Nez, the cultural anthropologist.

"You mean, do they get addicted?" Stephanie asked back, hearing her voice sharpening.

She'd been asked this before, and knew that there were some humans who thought that the "pet" treecats stayed with humans more for access to this delicacy than out of affection—like a drug addict hanging around a pusher.

She went on before Dr. Nez could clarify his question. "No. They don't get addicted—at least the treecats I've known don't seem to be. They just like it a whole lot. It's like my mom and chocolate. She can go without it, but offer her a slice of apple pie or a slice of chocolate torte and she'll take the chocolate every time."

Ranger Lethbridge chuckled. "I'll second that. I'd

say there are some members of the SFS who are more
addicted to coffee than any treecat is to celery, but that
doesn't mean I'd leave a bunch of celery unsupervised
when Fisher and Scott come to call—not if I expect to
find it left untouched."

There were more questions about diet, which segued
pretty naturally into matters of food gathering and hunting.
Stephanie and Karl could handle most of these questions
without violating their sense of what was right. For the
questions they didn't choose to answer—Stephanie never
gave away quite how often she and Lionheart went to visit
Lionheart's extended family—one of the SFS rangers could
offer at least a partial answer.

After the fiasco with Tennessee Bolgeo, there had been
two treecats in need of care and rehabilitation before they
could be returned to their clan. Stephanie and Karl had
helped with that, but it hadn't been too long before the
treecats had returned to Lionheart's clan. There had been
another case when a human had done considerable harm
to treecats. In that case, an entire clan had come close to
being wiped out. The SFS had helped however they could,
relocating the 'cats and even giving them food and tools.

After they relocated the treecats, the SFS didn't quite
snoop, but they did take some long-range films. However,
since the treecats lived in the shelter of the picketwood,
satellite downlook was out for all but chance spottings.
The microbugs that had been attached to ears or skin
were meticulously groomed out of existence. Attempts to
plant observation mini-cameras in known treecat colonies had ended with a series of mysterious accidents to
expensive equipment.

Or not so mysterious, Stephanie thought, *once you realize that Lionheart and a couple of the others figured out
what those cameras were and passed the information along.*

Eventually, the voice Stephanie had been longing to

hear again without consciously realizing it spoke. His voice was clear, but there was a sense of hesitancy as well.

"Lionheart was really badly hurt," Anders said. "He lost one true-hand entirely. Even with his fur grown back, you can see the other scars. Could he go back to being a wild 'cat if he wanted?"

Stephanie always hated this question because it implied that—like one of those birds who had a badly broken wing and so couldn't be set free again—that Lionheart was a captive because of injuries he had taken protecting her.

She felt Karl stiffen slightly where he sat next to her, his foot moving to press against hers in a reminder to keep her temper. This time, though, maybe because Anders had asked so gently, the question didn't sting as it usually did.

"I think Lionheart could," Stephanie said. "He'd have to be careful. He doesn't climb quite as fast or run as well as I've seen other treecats do, but he has adapted. The middle set of limbs are basically—as far as we can tell, anyhow—used for expanding options. Treecats can run like centaurs, but still have their hands free. Or they can manipulate things with two sets of hands while standing on their back legs. Or they can run all-out on all six limbs. Basically, Lionheart's lost a few options, but he's not as crippled as a human would be even if that human had lost only a couple of fingers."

Karl, apparently not trusting this unexpected calm and wanting to give Stephanie a chance to collect herself, added, "Also, treecats are social. We haven't had a lot of opportunities to observe their community interactions, but we have plenty of evidence that they help each other."

He went on to tell about how Left-Striped had held Right-Striped in the burning near-pine. "Left-Striped did that," Karl continued, "even though any chance of rescue was pretty slim. I'd say Lionheart would have plenty of support from his clan if he chose to go back."

To a one, the anthropologists were eager for more details about this most recent treecat contact. This rescue, as well as the evidence of mirror twins among the treecats, was new material.

"It's lucky you two came along," Dr. Whittaker said, "or was it entirely luck?"

"Lionheart probably smelled the smoke," Stephanie said. "He likes to hang out the air-car window if we're not going too fast."

She went on to tell that part of the story, leaving out only that she had been piloting and that was why they'd been going so slowly. No one asked. Probably they figured she and Karl were doing some sort of sample survey. Not all SFS work was as glamorous as fighting fires.

"Was it Lionheart who led you to the others? Do you think he used that empathy or telepathy or whatever it is that they have?"

Again, the questioner was Anders, eager and wide-eyed. A few passing comments during the more general discussion had shown he really was pretty well-informed about treecats. Again, because it was him, Stephanie found herself answering maybe a little more freely than she might have otherwise.

"Lionheart did seem to sense them first," she said. "It's pretty clear treecats have means of communicating with each other that we don't understand. The empathy seems clear. However, it's possible that they have some manner of verbal communication we haven't figured out, as well."

She offered a winning smile to Kesia Guyen, the team's linguist. "Maybe you'll be able to figure out things we've missed."

Ms. Guyen looked both pleased and concerned. "Well, that's not going to be easy unless I have an opportunity to observe a colony or clan—at least some larger group—in action, and I believe that sort of thing is frowned upon these days."

Ranger Lethbridge cut in. "We have hours of recordings of the clan we helped out after the Ubel affair. Hours upon hours of material that has never been out of our archives. Lots of it is of sick treecats sleeping. Once the danger of infection was gone, knowing they're social creatures, we kept as many of them together as we could."

Dr. Hobbard chuckled. "It's seriously boring material. Definitely not for publication. However, if you want to watch it..."

Guyen nodded eagerly. "I'd love that. You'd be amazed at what you can learn from 'dull' stuff like that. They might have a gesture language to augment sound. Or they might be communicating in frequencies you didn't think to check."

Under the cover of the technical discussion of the recordings that followed, Stephanie sneaked a glance at Anders. To her embarrassment, she found he was looking right at her.

She knew she blushed up to the tops of her ears and felt relieved that her genotype hadn't mixed to make her as fair as him. The conversation swirled on around her, but for the first time since she had discovered the treecats, Stephanie Harrington found there was something at least as fascinating to occupy her attention.

ANDERS WAS THE ONLY ONE FROM THE ANTHROPO-logical team who was in when Stephanie Harrington commed the next day.

For someone who had been so cool and controlled speaking in front of a big group, she seemed more than a little nervous.

"I was wondering," she said, "if you—any of you, I mean—would like to come by our freehold. Dad thinks our patients are going to be moving on any day now, so this would be pretty much the last chance to see them. We could go for a hike, later, if you'd like."

"To where treecats live?" Anders asked excitedly.

Stephanie's expression grew stern. "No. None live near our freehold. A hike would be a good way to get a feeling for the local ecosystem."

"I'd like that," Anders replied, and was rewarded by seeing the stern expression melt away.

"Well, if you'd settle for just me," he continued, "I'd

really like to come see the 'cats and go for a hike. My dad and the rest of his crew are with Dr. Hobbard."

"That would be great!" Stephanie replied, her brown eyes shining.

They made arrangements for Anders to be picked up. On Urako, his home planet, he had a provisional air-car license, but that didn't extend to Sphinx. Anyhow, his dad and the team had taken the air van they'd rented.

It turned out, however, that Dr. Richard Harrington traveled all over this part of Sphinx as a result of his job. He was going to be in the vicinity of Twin Forks to see some sick herbivores and was happy to give Anders a lift back to the Harrington freehold in what he called the "Vet Van."

Dr. Richard—the form of address they compromised on when Anders admitted his dad would kill him if he addressed an adult he hardly knew by his first name—proved to be a relaxed and easy-going individual. Richard Harrington was of about average height. Like his daughter, his hair and eyes were brown, but several shades darker—except for those places where his hair was starting to show silver.

When he picked up Anders, Dr. Richard admitted to being in a particularly good mood because his patients were recovering quite nicely.

"We don't have many problems with parasites," he explained when Anders expressed interest. "Even within a terrestrial ecosystem, parasites rarely jump host species. However, as the Plague demonstrates all too well, microorganisms aren't nearly so picky. I think we've got this one beat. The infestation was the result of the owners cutting corners with dietary supplements and leaving the animals weaker than they should have been. Once I figured that out, they started to mend."

He went on for a bit about how poor diet created

vulnerabilities. Anders liked how Dr. Richard assumed Anders would understand him—and how when Anders did ask a question, he answered it as a specialist to a nonspecialist, rather than a grown-up to a kid. Anders was beginning to understand how Stephanie had gotten so comfortable talking to adults.

Eventually, Dr. Richard changed the subject. "I'm really glad you were free to come by, Anders. Stephanie has been in a foul mood ever since the SFS released that the fire a couple of days ago—the one where Right-Striped and Left-Striped were injured—was human-caused."

"It was?"

"Yeah. Some colonists by the name of Franchitti were behind it. Since they're First Wave descendants and one of the first groups to settle Sphinx, they own quite a lot of land. Apparently, one of the owners was doing some quick undergrowth clearance—the area's part of a large island in the Makara River, so he figured it was safe. Anyhow, the winds shifted when a front came in faster than expected and that's all she wrote."

Dr. Richard shrugged, the gesture eloquent as any words.

"Anyhow, Stephanie is completely pissed off. She can have a bit of a temper, especially when she thinks someone is a complete 'null'—'zorky,' as she would have said a few months ago. I think that term's out of favor now."

He chuckled, but the sound was affectionate, not in the least mocking.

Anders had noticed a few things. Now he decided to ask what could be an uncomfortable question.

"Dr. Richard, I noticed that although Stephanie was wearing a counter-grav unit at yesterday's meeting, she didn't have it turned on. She moved easily enough, though, even carrying Lionheart around."

Dr. Richard sighed. "I keep telling her that 'cat doesn't need to be carried and she's going to give herself scoliosis."

Anders forged ahead. He knew that asking someone straight out if he and his family were "genies" could be considered rude, but from his mother's political work he had also learned that "genie" did not immediately mean "monster," that, in fact, in some environments coming from a genetically modified background was a distinct advantage.

"I noticed you're wearing a counter-grav unit, but that it's also on 'off' ... How do you handle this gravity? I tried to go to sleep last night without my unit on and I felt like someone was sitting on my chest."

"So you're wondering how Steph and I manage," Dr. Richard said. He paused for thought, then gave another of those eloquent shrugs. "Well, if you decided to poke around, it would be easy enough to find out. All the members of our family have the genetic modifications designed for the Meyerdahl first wave. The greater bone density and more efficient muscle mass makes handling the higher gravity a lot easier for us. There are a couple of other changes that make it easier for us to handle the greater atmospheric pressure, too. In fact, the Meyerdahl modifications, combined with the fact that we paid our own way in, were two of the deciding factors in our application to colonize here on Sphinx being accepted. The other was that both my and Marjorie's specializations are in high demand on a colony world."

Anders nodded. "I was just curious. I mean, if there was a way I could get around without wearing this cursed counter-grav unit, I'd do it in a heartbeat. Why do you wear one if you don't need it?"

"The same reason Stephanie does when she's out. It's too late to go find one when you're about to have an accident. The counter-grav unit doesn't let me fly, but when one of my patients has decided to hide in an awkward place—like on top of a roof—it sure makes it easier to get to it."

Anders laughed, curiosity satisfied. He decided that good manners demanded he change the subject. "Tell me about your weirdest case—maybe one of those ones that ended up on a rooftop."

The answer came with a chuckle. "Just the weirdest one?"

Dr. Richard's stories entertained them the rest of the way to the Harrington freehold. Stephanie and Karl immediately came out to meet the arriving vehicle. Stephanie was carrying Lionheart, but put him down as soon as she saw her father raise a reprimanding eyebrow.

Anders thought, *She certainly doesn't look as if she's in a bad mood. Maybe Karl cheered her up, or maybe she gets over her moods as quickly as they hit her. If anyone looks grumpy, it's Karl.*

Ever the politician's son, he greeted his hosts with his warmest smile.

"Hi, Karl. Hi, Stephanie. Thanks for settling for me rather than the rest of the team."

A odd look flitted over Karl's face, but he settled into stoic impassivity so quickly Anders wondered if he'd imagined it.

Stephanie had given her dad a quick hug. Now she turned to Anders.

"You do realize this visit is all on the treecats' terms. If they seem nervous, or if Lionheart signals we shouldn't go any closer, then we stay back."

Anders nodded. "I understand. Absolutely."

Dr. Richard had grabbed a large case from the Vet Van. "Let me go out to the gazebo first. I checked Right-Striped's feet out this morning, but I might as well give them another going over. Like I said, I have a feeling the twins are going to move on pretty soon."

Stephanie nodded. "That's why I decided to call the anthropologists now, not wait."

Again an odd, sidelong look from Karl, a look that vanished as soon as he realized Anders had noticed, but which was decidedly unfriendly.

❖   ❖   ❖

Usually, Stephanie had to resist an urge to skip ahead of her dad, but today she found it easy to let him take the lead. Even her bad mood about the Franchitti fire seemed to have vanished when the Vet Van had touched down and she had seen for herself that Anders had really come.

The only thing blighting her good mood was Karl. Had he figured out that she had manipulated the situation so that Anders would be their only visitor from the anthropological expedition? He might well have.

After all, she thought, *Karl was there when Frank Jedrusinski happened to mention that Dr. Hobbard was taking the whole team to her local office in Yawata so that they could see some newer videos and examine her collection of treecat artifacts. It was a gamble calling, I know, but I did clear it with Mom and Dad first. I wonder why Karl is so annoyed? Maybe he doesn't think it's fair to take advantage of Right-Striped and Left-Striped like this.*

If she let herself, Stephanie had to admit that if the visitor had been anyone but Anders, she would have felt a bit uncomfortable about making the offer herself.

But Anders seems to really be interested in treecats. Unlike the rest of them, he doesn't have papers to publish or academic honors to win. His interest is pure.

Right-Striped was indeed doing much better. Stephanie felt her heart swell with pride for her dad as he carefully examined each of the treecat's six paws, paying particular attention to the rear two pairs. Stephanie, Karl, and Anders had stayed back about ten meters, but Lionheart had gone ahead with her dad. Stephanie knew Lionheart was offering comfort and reassurance to the two visiting 'cats, although she also thought that by now this was more routine than necessary.

"How are they, Dad?" Stephanie asked.

"I'll confirm my earlier assessment and say that I think these two are fully healed. They'll be a bit pink about the pads for a while, but the new skin is good and strong."

"So," Anders asked, "will you be giving them a lift back to where you found them?"

Stephanie shook her head. "We talked about it, but there's no real way to explain to them what we're doing, so, unless they ask, we'll let them do things their way."

Dad had been packing up his gear while they were talking and now left the gazebo. "I'm heading in. Let me know if you go anywhere, okay?"

Stephanie nodded. "I don't think we will for a while. As long as they'll put up with us, we want to spend some time with the treecats."

After Dad left, Lionheart reared up on his backmost pair of legs and signaled that the human visitors could come forward. Stephanie and Lionheart had worked out simple hand gestures for such situations within the first six T-months of their association. The signals were no more complicated than the commands that might be used in directing a herding dog—come on, stop, right, left, back up. The big difference was that in this case the "dog" used the gestures as often as did the "shepherd."

Stephanie thought that the ease with which Lionheart and Fisher had picked up and used these gestures was proof of their intelligence, but the hard-heads kept making comparisons to how dogs, horses, and other "companion animals" could learn to respond to human commands.

The three advanced, slowing when Lionheart signaled, moving to the right so that the wind would be at their backs and give Right-Striped and Left-Striped ample opportunity to take their scents. At last, about three meters from the gazebo, Lionheart signaled for them to stop.

"That was cool!" Anders said. "I saw some of the videos that Dr. Hobbard sent my dad but it's different to be up close and personal. Even if you—and Karl—hadn't been here to tell me what to do, I think I could have understood what Lionheart wanted."

Stephanie felt disproportionately pleased. She knew it was silly of her. Lionheart had worked out most of the signals himself, picking them up from her own body language, but somehow Anders' praise felt better than anything any of the rangers or scientists had said.

They stayed in the gazebo visiting with the treecats for quite a long time. Stephanie had thought Anders might get bored. After all, it wasn't like the three treecats were doing tricks or anything. They were just sitting watching the humans while the humans watched them. She suspected a lively conversation was going on between the 'cats, but if there was, no human would ever "hear" it.

After a while, Lionheart signaled that the humans should move on.

"I don't blame them," Karl said. "I mean, just how long would you want to be stared at?"

Stephanie suppressed a fleeting comment that if Anders was doing the staring, she could handle quite a bit of it.

Instead she said, "You guys want to go hiking? We could go back to the house and pack a picnic. I'm starved. Celery might be okay for the 'cats, but I want cake."

For a moment, Stephanie thought Karl was going to decline her offer. She felt guilty that her heart actually leapt at the possibility of having Anders to herself.

But after he glanced at his uni-link, Karl said, "I've got lots of time. Are we going to skip target practice? This is one of our usual days."

"We have a guest today," Stephanie countered, aware her voice sounded a little sharp.

Anders saved the day. "No problem. I read about how Stephanie used her handgun to deal with the hexapuma that went after Bolgeo. I've never fired one. Maybe you could teach me, Karl. You were the one who taught Stephanie, right?"

Karl nodded. "Me and Frank Lethbridge. How about we have that picnic first? You haven't seen how mean Stephanie gets when she misses a meal."

Karl grinned at her and she had to fight an urge to stick out her tongue. *That* certainly wouldn't impress Anders.

Karl went on. "After we eat and hike for a bit, then we could go to the shooting range we've set up here. That way Steph won't skip her lessons. Dr. Marjorie says she's gotten more and more undisciplined since she met Lionheart. She actually got an A-minus last term."

"Hey!" Stephanie protested. "That was in advanced spatial calculus."

The two boys laughed, but it wasn't an unfriendly sound. Stephanie found herself coloring, but she didn't feel bad at all.

✧   ✧   ✧

Climbs Quickly understood the utility of the thunder barkers with which Death Fang's Bane and Shadowed Sunlight regularly practiced, but that didn't mean he had to like them. Not only were they loud—even with the sound-blockers Death Fang's Bane carefully inserted into his ears—but they smelled bad.

Therefore, when there were signs that another such session was about to happen, Climbs Quickly absented himself and scampered over to the gazebo, where he found Left-Striped poking at Right-Striped's feet.

<*I tell you,*> Right-Striped protested indignantly, <*my feet feel fine. I am not hiding anything from you.*>

<*Healer does seem to have done a very good job,*> Left-Striped agreed.

Taking advantage of his brother's relative helplessness, he tickled his fingers along where the new skin remained tender and uncalloused. Right-Striped wriggled free, snorting with laughter, then pounced on his twin. The two wrestled for a few minutes, then sat up and gave Climbs Quickly their full attention.

<*I think you will be leaving soon,*> Climbs Quickly said. He carefully hid his disappointment. He was very happy living with Death Fang's Bane and her family, but he had very much enjoyed having other People nearby these last several days.

<*Yes. We think the time has come,*> Right-Striped agreed. <*My over-protective brother is finally convinced that I can walk on my own six feet again. It is a long journey, but with the supplies you have so kindly given us, we will be able to stay up in the trees and avoid the death fangs.*>

<*We are very grateful,*> Left-Striped added.

Climbs Quickly knew that by the standards of the two-legs, the twins were departing with hardly anything. However, each had a carry-net in which was wrapped some light, nourishing food—including sun-dried meat. In addition, they each had a few long pieces of cluster stalk. Despite the drought, there was ample water in the direction in which they were headed.

<*The Damp Ground clan needs us,*> Left-Striped said. <*There is always so much to do when a clan relocates. With the recent fire cutting us off from one area of hunting, the more hunters and scouts, the better.*>

Climbs Quickly could not disagree. Although he was sorry to see his new friends leave, he encouraged their intention, going with them for a ways, turning back only when he might otherwise be late for dinner. It wasn't as if he couldn't feed himself, or that Death Fang's Bane didn't know through their shared link that he was well, but he knew she would worry until he was back home.

He arrived to find that both Shadowed Sunlight and the new human—Bleached Fur, as he thought of him, not knowing his qualities well enough to give him a real name—had departed. Death Fang's Bane's mind-glow held a curious swirl of conflicting impulses. On the one hand, Climbs Quickly sensed a sorrow bordering on despondency. Mingled with this were contradictory spurts and sparks of what felt like joy or excitement. To further confuse the matter, outwardly, Death Fang's Bane was much her usual self.

That is, until Healer said something and Death Fang's Bane's wild emotional state exploded into something one step short of fury.

✧　　✧　　✧

Despite invitations to stay for dinner, both Karl and Anders said they had to get back home. Karl offered to drop Anders off. Since this meant Karl would have a longer trip home, the two boys left earlier than they otherwise might have done.

As Stephanie watched Karl's air car becoming a vanishing dot, she found herself wishing she was going with them. Well, not really with *them*. She wished she was going off with Anders.

If I had my provisional license, she thought as she trailed despondently in to do some of the lessons she'd let slide, *then I could have taken Anders to Twin Forks. We could have talked some more. Given how Karl kept snapping at him, I wonder if Anders will even want to hang out with me again. He might want to avoid any chance of seeing Karl.*

The thought made Stephanie so miserable that she actually messed up a couple of steps in a complicated calculus problem she was working on and had to go back and re-do them.

Of course, Karl was right, Stephanie thought, trying to be fair. *Anders was handling that gun unsafely—even if he had just seen it unloaded. I've never forgotten the story about that guy who shot a hole in his own wall while cleaning a gun he was sure was completely unloaded. Still... Karl was pretty harsh.*

Thankfully, Mom called Stephanie down to dinner soon after. Stephanie hurried down, determined that at least one of her obsessions would finally be addressed. Since she wasn't ready to talk about Anders, that meant asking her folks to schedule her provisional license test.

Lionheart had returned and was waiting on his stool by the table, eagerly eyeing the platter of roast that Mom had just set down. Since the gazebo had been empty of treecats on her return from the firing range, Stephanie had a pretty good idea where he had been. She thought he looked a little down, so she gave him an extra large helping of the roast, taking it from the rare center.

As Stephanie spooned a very large helping of mashed potatoes onto her plate and topped them with a sea of gravy, she waited impatiently for her parents to stop discussing some bit of local politics. Interrupting was not permitted in the Harrington household, maybe because Richard Harrington's job provided interruptions enough.

"And how was your day, Stephanie?" Mom asked. "It sounds as if it was rather busy."

Stephanie heard the subtext. *Don't forget. You promised when we let you sign up as a provisional ranger you wouldn't let your studies slide.*

She ignored this by answering the actual question.

"It was great! Anders Whittaker turned out to be the only one of the visiting anthropological team free, but he came out and saw the mirror twins. They left today, by the way."

Both her parents nodded and Stephanie went on. "I was thinking, my birthday is next week. To celebrate, I'd really love to go into town and get my provisional air-car license."

Unsaid was that while learner's permits could be acquired

over the net, provisional licenses required a hands-on test. The provisional license only allowed for flying only in visually safe conditions, but that was better than a learner's permit that required a licensed pilot in the vehicle.

Dad grinned. "Can't wait to get a bit more freedom, I see. As if hang gliding isn't enough. Well, you'll have to wait an extra day."

Mom nodded, also smiling. "Your dad is right. We've planned a birthday party for you. We were going to bring it up after dinner. We've already invited Scot, Irina, and, of course, Karl. Frank Lethbridge and Ainsley Jedrusinski are also going to drop by if they can. It's fire season, so they may not be able to get free. And we thought it would be nice if you invited some friends closer to your own age."

They waited a moment, as if expecting Stephanie to say something. When she didn't, Dad took over.

"The hang-gliding club meets tomorrow, so you can invite a few of the kids you like best. You don't have to invite all of them, but if you choose not to, be polite about how you do issue invitations."

"Maybe you could invite the boy who was here today," Mom added. "Andre, was it?"

"Anders!" Stephanie corrected.

She knew she sounded too severe, but she couldn't believe what she was hearing—and that they sounded so happy.

How could they be smiling like they'd just told her they were giving her a big treat, when they'd just told her that she couldn't get her provisional license on her birthday? Even if they didn't know about her jaunts with Karl, they had to know she'd been spending lots of simulator time to get ready.

Did this mean they weren't going to agree to the provisional license after all? Both of them thought she was spending too little time on her studies lately anyhow, never mind that she still got straight A's. Okay. An A minus. So her standing in the chess club had dropped a little, but did that matter when she was doing stuff so much more important than playing games?

Lionheart looked up from where he'd been messily devouring his slice of roast and "bleeked" very softly. Both Mom and Dad were staring at her. Stephanie strove to keep her temper.

"Anders," she said carefully, "probably wouldn't be able to come. He told me and Karl that his dad had set up some field tours over the next week or so."

In her head her thoughts swirled like things of their own: *That's right. Plan a party without telling me. Make me invite a bunch of blackholes when the one person I'd really like to be there is going to be off with a bunch of grown up scientists. His dad understands that Anders is nearly grown-up. Why are you suddenly treating me like a kid?*

She didn't say any of this, but maybe something of it showed in her eyes or the set of her chin. She felt Lionheart trying to get her to calm down, but while she usually welcomed his help, this time she found herself resenting it. Here was another person trying to keep her from having her own goals and opinions!

Mom said very gently. "Well, I'm sorry Anders won't be able to come, but there are still other people your age you could ask. We'd really like you to do this."

Dad added. "Stephanie, you know we know you're a remarkable young lady, but—and I admit it's partially our fault for bringing you to Sphinx just when you were ready to get involved with group programs back on Meyerdahl—since we've been here, other than Karl, you don't seem to have made any friends your own age."

"Even Karl's over a year older," Mom added. "And that's

only the difference in years. Emotionally, what Karl has been through has made him much older."

Normally, Stephanie would have jumped on this opportunity to learn more about Karl's background, but right now she just couldn't seem to care.

"I don't," she said, spacing the words so each came out like a slap, "like people my own age. They're boring. It's okay when we have something to do, like hang gliding, but having them over here would be horrible. Standing around talking would be hopeless. You don't expect us to play pin-the-tail-on-the-donkey, do you?"

Dad looked at Stephanie sternly. "Stephanie, don't you see? You're making our point for us. You're going to need to learn to get along with people—not only of your own age, but people you find boring or annoying or whatever. You can't go and be a hermit in the forest, not if you expect to do any good for anyone."

Stephanie shoved her plate away, appetite suddenly gone.

"Some birthday celebration," she said. "Instead of what I've been dreaming about, I get a socialization lesson."

Mom looked very sad. On some level, Stephanie regretted what she'd said, but she couldn't quite apologize. Dad still looked stern, which probably meant he was angry, but keeping his temper—he had one, too—under control.

"I can see," Dad said, "that we're past the point of discussion. We'll talk about both the party and learner's permit later."

"May I be excused?" Stephanie asked, stiffly polite. "I have studying to do."

"Of course."

As she pushed herself back from the table and hurried to her room, her dad's last words haunted her. *He said "learner's permit," not "provisional license." I can't get a license without their permission. Is he going to stop me, after all my hard work?*

Stephanie stormed into her room, stopping just short of slamming the door behind her. Instead of going to her computer, she flung herself on her bed. *What's wrong with them? Don't they like me anymore?*

She heard the door open and the soft *pad-pad* as Lionheart came in, shutting the door behind him. He thumped up on the bed next to her, but made no effort to touch her mood. She found herself wishing he would, even though a few minutes before the very idea had made her furious.

What's wrong, Stephanie thought forlornly, *with me?*

❖   ❖   ❖

Still troubled by the difficulties he had experienced when he had tried to help Death Fang's Bane earlier, when his two-leg settled into her studies and some of her emotional turmoil quieted, Climbs Quickly reached across the distance to see if he could touch the mind voice of his sister, Sings Truly.

Even before he had included cluster stalk as a routine element of his diet, Climbs Quickly had possessed a powerful mind voice for a male. Despite these advantages, he still needed the help of relays from roving hunters to send his message and receive the reply.

<You sound troubled, Climbs Quickly. You say Death Fang's Bane will soon be asleep? Come and meet me near the blue point trees close to where the lace leaf grows. Twig Weaver is coming to protect me. He has not forgotten that were it not for Death Fang's Bane he would be dead—or worse.>

With this reply, Climbs Quickly had to be content. He let Death Fang's Bane know he was going out. She hugged him tight and made mouth sounds in which he caught "Right-Striped" and "Left-Striped." Good, then. If she thought he was going to check on the twins, she would not worry.

Bleeking gentle reminder, he pointed toward her bed and was rewarded with a laugh—and a bright flicker in her mind-glow as well. She made more mouth sounds at him, none of which he understood, but the fussing tone was clear enough. She wanted him to go enjoy himself and not worry about her. She was fine.

The long summer nights were shortening, although the sky would hold an evening glow for a long while to come. Climbs Quickly scampered up the trunk of a nearby net-wood and worked his way through a route he had traveled many times before. Even as he kept alert for possible dangers—for although death fangs did not go up into the trees, a rotten branch could be as hazardous—he was aware of Death Fang's Bane's mind-glow. He knew when she stopped working and felt as she drifted off to sleep.

Eventually, Climbs Quickly came to the stand of blue point trees. Soon after, Sings Truly and Twig Weaver arrived. Both had brought carry nets with them. The seeds of the blue point tree were considered a delicacy among the People. Although it was early for many to be ripe, at this late stage the cones could be picked and stored. The seeds would continue ripening.

True-hands and hand-feet busy picking the cones, the three People fell into discussion. Twig Weaver offered to close himself from the discussion, but the siblings asked him to take part.

<*If you do not mind, that is,*> Climbs Quickly added. <*Your different experiences may give us some new wisdom.*>

Sings Truly, who as a memory singer had access to a huge volume of the shared experiences of the People, did not contradict her brother. Climbs Quickly had noticed that since she had become the clan's senior memory singer she had been more, rather than less, likely to invite the insights of others.

Perhaps, Climbs Quickly thought, *having seen the*

thoughts and stored memories of so many People, memories grown faint with distance and time, she has come to value the new more, rather than less.

That was an interesting thought, and he tucked it away for further consideration. For now, he needed to get what advice he could and then return to Death Fang's Bane. Now, of all times, he did not wish to be away from her.

It was very easy to explain to the others the source of his confusion. Although Climbs Quickly was becoming convinced that the two-legs were capable of communicating complicated ideas with their mouth sounds and the markings they made, still he pitied them. Mouth sounds must come in sequence. It had taken him some time to realize that the same sounds in a different order did not mean the same thing. He despaired of ever really understanding them.

Mind-speech, however, took many forms. Although one could "talk," framing thoughts in sequence, when an experience needed to be shared, there was no need to resort to this cumbersome form.

Now he showed Sings Truly and Twig Weaver what he had experienced from Death Fang's Bane that evening, presenting not only the impulses he had read from her mind-glow but the larger context of her interaction with her parents. He was even able to include his own interpretations of some of the mouth noises. These were mostly names, but he felt that even this little bit would clarify that the two-legs were intelligently communicating, not bellowing as the lake builders did when warning each other across the water.

For all the complexity, this sharing took very little time. He felt Sings Truly and Twig Weaver considering, weighing against their own experiences—and in the case of Sings Truly, against the experiences of many others.

Sings Truly said, *<I think that because your first meeting*

with Death Fang's Bane impressed you with her intel-
ligence...>

Twig Weaver did not so much interrupt as intersperse an image of how—despite his care—Climbs Quickly had found himself discovered by the young two-leg. Certainly, Death Fang's Bane (although, of course, she had been given no name then) had been clever to figure out how to set a snare he could not detect although he (and others of the People) had always been able to step over and around those set by her elders...

Sings Truly's thoughts went on, <*Because you have always thought her intelligent and resourceful, I think you often forget that she is very young. From what we can tell, she has not reached full maturity. Although her scent is close to that of an adult, there are differences. Indeed, when I look into the memories, I see that her scent now differs from her scent when you first met her. I think she is changing.*>

The thought startled Climbs Quickly. He was no memory singer, but he could summon some of his older memories. He compared them, tasted the memories that Sings Truly offered for his and Twig Weaver's inspection. The evidence was interesting. He offered them samples of his experiences with Death Fang's Bane over these last few days, choosing times when he had found her mind glow particularly confusing.

Twig Weaver said, <*I think what is happening is clear— although I do not fault you, since those who are closest do not always notice such things. Death Fang's Bane is changing from a child into an adult. Her scent shows that certain events—such as her encounter with Bleached Fur—makes certain scents change more wildly. Perhaps two-legs are like those creatures with seasonal breeding patterns. These often become very irrational when the need to breed is upon them.*>

Climbs Quickly considered. Certainly the interactions of

Death Fang's Bane and those of her peer group—especially some of the more aggressive ones—made sense if these were not only the results of hierarchical competition, but also maneuvering to breed. Didn't the female two-leg Death Fang's Bane disliked the most have a male who followed her attentively?

<You give me a great deal to consider,> Climbs Quickly said, filling the thought with gratitude. *<Sings Truly is correct. I do more often think of Death Fang's Bane as a long-time adult. Many of her actions of late make sense if I reconsider them as those of an almost-adult, testing her limits. Even her anger at her parents—who I know she loves and trusts—makes sense if she is not certain whether her impulses or theirs are wisest.>*

When Sings Truly replied, her mind-voice was shaded with the rueful notes of one who regularly tested established limits, sometimes limits that no one else even saw as limits until she pressed against them.

<So Death Fang's Bane will need more than comfort from you. I think she rejected the soothing you offered not because she did not need it, but because she needed to find out what was the right path even more. If you are to continue as her partner, you will also need to find new ways, permit her to err, even if those errors may cause her harm.>

Twig Weaver—who alone among them was pair-bonded and whose partner, Water Dancer, was nearly as strong-willed and innovative in her own way as Sings Truly—flirted his tail in a chuckle.

<As someday you may learn, permitting error is the way of any close partnership. However, you, Climbs Quickly, have challenges before you that none of the People has ever known. At least People can mind-speak, but for all the brightness of her mind-glow, Death Fang's Bane is mute and nearly deaf. You are the elder and, in this, must be the wiser as well.>

5

"OVER TO THE RIGHT," SAID RANGER JEDRUSINSKI, "you'll see the nest of a mated pair of condor owls."

Anders craned around—he was on the left side of the air van, in the backmost set of seats. His dad, sitting on the right, next to Ranger Jedrusinski, who was piloting, had the best view, but he didn't pay much attention. Anders wasn't surprised. Dad's specialization was material remains. This specialization was sometimes called ethno-archeology, because efforts were made to draw connections between past cultures and present.

Dr. Nez, who, despite his rank, had taken the other rearmost seat, specialized in living cultures, not things. To him, the other native life-forms on Sphinx were at least as important as the treecats themselves.

Now Dr. Nez grinned at Anders and pointed. "Look! Up there, near the top of that huge crown oak. Wow! That's a messy nest. I wonder if the condor owls build heavy for insulation in the winters?"

Dr. Nez leaned back so Anders could see past him. Gratefully, Anders shifted so he could get a good look. He'd never seen a Terran oak tree, except in pictures. He wondered if the person who'd named this tree had either. He supposed that the general shape was about right, but he didn't think that oak trees had those large arrowhead-shaped leaves. He didn't think any Terran oak had ever reached 80 meters in height, either.

Anders wondered why the plants were so large here, especially given that the gravity was higher than Terran normal. He'd have thought all the plants would be short and squat. He'd seen how humans born on Sphinx, even with access to counter-grav units and various therapies, tended to develop stockier builds. When Karl had taken Anders back to base, they'd gotten to talking about Urako in comparison to Sphinx. Karl had mentioned in passing that he had to take all sorts of supplements to assure strong bone growth.

The condor owls had built their nest in the upper third of the tree, taking advantage of the combination of an area where the trunk was heavy enough to be stable, but the branches were lighter, allowing for good launching points.

Ranger Jedrusinski brought the van around so all the passengers could get a good look at the nest.

Maybe she's figured out Dad isn't really interested, Anders thought. He moved so Dr. Nez could get a view from this angle.

Meanwhile, Ranger Jedrusinski was saying, "Despite the name given by early colonists on Sphinx, the condor owl is actually mammalian. It is covered with fine down, rather than feathers. Like most animals native to the planet, its structure is hexapedal. The front set of legs have become the wings, but it retains four strong legs, each of which has a very powerful set of talons."

"Am I correct," asked Dr. Emberly, the team xenobiologist, "in recalling that condor owls have been known to prey on treecats?"

"We've never witnessed such an event," Ranger Jedrusinski replied, "but the secondary evidence is pretty strong. We've found treecat bones in condor owl waste. This, of course, could be a result of scavenging on carrion. However, treecats shown what appeared to be a condor owl shadow take cover immediately. Certainly, the condor owls themselves should be capable of preying upon a treecat. They have extraordinarily keen vision and enough intelligence to realize that the picketwood serves as a highway for all sorts of creatures—treecats among them."

"But," protested Virgil Iwamoto, the lithics—or stone tool—specialist of the team, "treecats make stone tools. Doesn't that argue for an ability to defend themselves?"

"Treecat tool use," Ranger Jedrusinski replied, "seems to involve close-range tools used primarily for manipulating their environment. We haven't seen any evidence of bows and arrows, or even spear throwers. Unlike humans, treecats are excellently equipped by nature to hunt the creatures that are their usual prey. They show no ambition to take on creatures markedly larger than themselves, except in self-defense or defense of another of their kind."

Or Stephanie, Anders thought. He wondered what it would be like to find yourself being defended from a monster by a horde of treecats.

That morning, one of the other Forestry Service rangers had taken them to see a sort of "zoo" inhabited by native animals that, for one reason or another, needed care. Among these were captive hexapumas that were being prepared for release back into the wild. He didn't think "monster" was too strong a word for a creature over five meters long—without the tail, which added another 250 or so centimeters—that weighed as much as a horse.

Ranger Jedrusinski was wheeling them away from the crown oak that held the condor owl's nest. "At a meeting today, it was announced that a recently deserted treecat settlement had been located by SFS rangers inspecting the area after the Franchitti fire. We have just enough time to go by and look at it from the air."

This interested Dr. Whittaker.

"Is the settlement in a Forestry Service district or on private lands?" he asked.

Anders could swear his dad was already calculating contacting the land owners. If so, Ranger Jedrusinski's response must have dashed his hopes for finagling a way closer to the treecats.

"Oh, it's safely in a Forestry Service district," she said, obviously thinking Dr. Whittaker had wanted to be reassured that the treecats were safe. "The fire was on nearby privately held lands and, unfortunately, fire is no respecter of human boundaries."

"Ranger Jedrusinski," Anders asked. "I've been wondering. Just what is a Forestry Service district? Are they public lands? And are the treecats only protected if they're in a district?"

The ranger looked distinctly uncomfortable, but she didn't dodge his question.

"Forestry Service districts are lands that are actually owned by the Crown. We simply administer them. Currently, our policy is to preserve them as relatively pristine territories. This hasn't always made us popular with some local residents who feel that Crown lands should be exploited—they prefer words like 'utilized'—for human profit. As for the treecats...I don't think the Crown would like to hear of anyone mistreating *any* wildlife, but it's certainly a lot harder for us to enforce such policies on private lands."

Dr. Whittaker's interest in questions of land ownership

had vanished as soon as he learned he still had to deal with the SFS.

"Ranger Jedrusinski, will we have an opportunity to get out and take a closer look at the treecat colony site?"

"We'll just look today," Ranger Jedrusinski replied. "Maybe later. We'll want to observe and see if the treecats have actually abandoned it. Sometimes they leave for short periods of time. It's possible that the fire in that area led the inhabitants to temporarily relocate."

"I'm puzzled," said Kesia Guyen, the linguistics expert. "Why don't you know more about the treecats? Stephanie Harrington first encountered them in late 1518. I would think that in three years you would at least have major settlements marked."

Something in Ranger Jedrusinski's tone told Karl she'd answered this question a lot. "First of all, although Stephanie now admits to having first seen the treecat now called 'Lionheart' in late 1518, she didn't share the information immediately. It wasn't until March of 1519 that the rest of us were let in on the secret—and I wonder if we would have been then, except that Lionheart was so badly injured that he couldn't escape and his clan chose to stay and support him.

"That brings me to a point you can't overlook. Humans have been on Sphinx since 1422. We didn't see our first treecats until nearly a hundred years later. That means they chose to hide from us."

"But now you know they're there." Guyen's protest was phrased politely enough that Anders felt pretty certain she was showing off for Dad—after all, he was the boss. "Couldn't you do satellite surveys, use infrared to detect clusters that might indicate population density?"

Such options had been debated quite seriously when the research design for this mission was being put together. When he'd listened, Anders had thought the suggestions quite reasonable, so much so that he was surprised to hear Ranger Jedrusinski laugh in genuine amusement.

"It's wonderful to talk to someone who's as interested in treecats as some of us at SFS are. I wish the rest of Sphinx shared your priorities. The reality is that while most residents of Sphinx are delighted that such an interesting new species has been identified—sales of treecat toys do well with both locals and tourists—the fact is, treecats aren't considered very important."

"Not important?" Dr. Whittaker nearly bellowed the words. "A sentient species and not important?"

"You forget, sir, one of the reasons you and your team are here is to help decide if treecats are indeed sentient and, if so, to what extent. No one disagrees that they're tool users, but their lack of an apparent language remains a huge barrier to the acceptance of them as sentient."

"But the elaborate platforms they build..." Dr. Whittaker protested.

"I can name you a dozen species of birds on Terra alone," Ranger Jedrusinski replied, "that build nests as or more elaborate. Consider termite mounds or beehives or beaver dams—and those are only Terran examples."

Predictably, Iwamoto spoke in favor of his specialization. "What about the stone tools? Surely those show intelligence."

"Various Terran primates have been shown to make simple stone tools. Sea otters will carefully select and even reshape rocks they use for opening clams. Ursoid species on your own Urako, which no one claims are 'people,' make simple stone axes. Actually, we're placing a lot of hope on you in particular, Mr. Iwamoto. The stone tools—and the nets—are some of the best evidence of treecat intelligence we have—the sort that convince all but the most hard-headed."

"But what," persisted Guyen, perhaps miffed that tools

were being favored over language, "about using satellite look-down to map colonies?"

Ranger Jedrusinski sighed. "Sphinx is rich in wildlife—some of it quite large. Moreover, treecats are not the only native creatures to live in groups. Finally, quite simply, SFS doesn't merit much satellite time. Our primary mission is viewed as managing wild areas for the benefit of the colonists, not taking away resources that are needed for other things. Remember, this is a colony world. We simply don't have the infrastructure for what many consider luxuries."

"I read," Anders cut in, thinking someone should support the ranger, "how smaller thermal scanners can't penetrate the thick leafy canopy, so even if you could get the satellite time, it might not be of much use."

"There's that," Ranger Jedrusinski agreed cheerfully.

This question of technological options and priorities occupied the next leg of the journey. Anders half-listened—he'd heard a lot of similar discussions before, even between his mother and father about how government money "should" be spent. Instead, he studied the landscape, remembering the things Stephanie and Karl had taught him while they were hiking, about different trees and the zones in which they grew. He felt he was getting better at identifying different types.

Surely that was a grove of picketwood coming up. Those straight trunks were distinctive, even from a distance, even—maybe especially—from the air, where their odd connected patterns really stood out. With summer coming to an end—it could even be argued that the season was verging on autumn—a few rich, red leaves stood out among the green.

Anders had read that picketwood shed its leaves in autumn. He wondered if the treecats could stay as easily hidden in winter. Maybe that would be the time to try and map colonies or use thermal imaging technology.

He was about to suggest it, but then he remembered the length of the seasons on Sphinx. Winter wouldn't be here for fifteen months. By then, this expedition could be long gone.

He felt a little sad, then brightened. Maybe there would be a winter expedition. He'd be seventeen by then. If he studied hard, contributed something significant to this first expedition, maybe he could come back. Maybe, like Stephanie, he could serve as a sort of provisional ranger—or provisional grad assistant or something. Dad would never see him that way, but he bet Dr. Nez would.

When Ranger Jedrusinski brought them into the location of the abandoned treecat settlement, the buzz of excited conversation was general.

"This stand of picketwood borders on a more open area."

"Look! That platform is nearly new. Even from here, I can tell they've used a substantial amount of lace willow. That differs from the samples Dr. Hobbard showed us."

"That basket has quite a large hole in the bottom. I wonder if that's why they left it. Maybe it was ceremonially 'killed.'"

Anders could tell Dad was itching to get out and look around. When Ranger Jedrusinski was distracted answering Dr. Emberly's question about the probable source for a hank of fur pinned to a picketwood trunk, Anders saw Dad glance at the air van's directional readout, then make a few notes on his uni-link. Something about the way he then quickly leaned to take some pictures made Anders think Dad hoped no one had noticed.

After far too short a stay, Ranger Jedrusinski turned the air van in the direction of base. "Sorry, but I've got fire watch tomorrow morning at an hour when all of you will be snug in bed. I'll check with Chief Ranger Shelton about when we might come back. After all, you folks are going to be here some months yet. There's plenty of time."

If Ranger Jedrusinski had known Dr. Whittaker as well as Anders did, she might have worried about how placidly he took this departure. Certainly, Dr. Nez gave his long-time boss a curious look, but he didn't say anything.

When they got back to the ranger housing where they were staying, they found a message waiting.

"Hi. This is Marjorie Harrington. We're having a fifteenth-birthday celebration for Stephanie. We thought that if you're not in the field, Anders might like to come. Stephanie and Karl—who he's already met—will be here, but it will give him a chance to meet some of the other local kids his age, in case he ever gets tired of people who think of nothing but treecats. Anders certainly doesn't need to bring a present or anything, but I think Stephanie would be glad to have him here."

She ended with giving a date and time, and offering her private contact number.

Dr. Whittaker looked nearly as pleased as he had when he'd learned he'd won the competition to head the project to Sphinx.

"Good, boy," he said, pounding Anders between the shoulder blades. "If Dr. Harrington doesn't think her daughter is at least a little sweet on you, I'm no anthropologist. I'll certainly make sure we're available to get you to that party. Maybe I'll drop you off myself, just to show friendly... of course, I'll turn down any offer to stay. Don't want to cramp your style."

Whistling, Dr. Whittaker went off towards the shower. Anders, slowly stripping off his own field clothes, wondered why his own reaction to accepting the invitation was so mixed. After all, his father wasn't asking him to do anything worse than his mother did on a daily basis, right?

✧   ✧   ✧

Gritting her teeth, Stephanie let herself out of the air car, then tugged her black-and-orange hang glider out of the cargo compartment. Lionheart leapt lightly out after the glider. He, at least, was clearly looking forward to today's practice.

Stephanie wished that she was.

"Thanks for the ride, Dad," she said.

"Unless something goes wrong," Richard Harrington replied, "I'll be back to get you no later than an hour after practice ends. I'll com if I'll be late."

Stephanie nodded. "I brought my uni-link. If you're late, I'll go over to the café and do some homework."

She saw Dad swallow a comment. She knew he and Mom wished that she'd use time in town to visit with people her own age.

Well, she thought glumly as she waved good-bye to her father, shouldered the hang glider, and trotted off toward the practice field. *Today they'll get their wish. Damn birthday party . . .*

The late summer/early autumn weather was just about perfect for hang gliding, the winds light, with just enough variation to provide some challenge. Unlike those who had originally practiced this sport, Stephanie and her teammates had counter-grav units to make launching easier. So, instead of having to drop off a cliff or hope for a promising breeze, they could begin in an open field that air traffic control had isolated from any other vehicles.

But today, Stephanie thought, aware the image was just a bit melodramatic, *I feel as if I'm walking off a cliff just the same.*

"Bleek!" Lionheart commented, a note of reproof in his voice. At least, Stephanie thought she heard reproof. Lionheart might not be able to "talk," but he had a wide variety of verbalizations. These might not be "words" as such, but she'd learned to hear the differences between a "bleek" of excitement, of alarm, and, as this time, of disapproval.

She knew Lionheart knew she was nervous. All the way into town, the treecat had sat so he could wrap his tail around her neck—a gesture she knew was one of comfort. However, she'd felt no hint of him attempting to intrude into her emotions, to provide soothing and calming as he had from time to time.

I wonder if that means he thinks I'm up to dealing with this? The thought made her surprisingly cheerful.

They were close enough now for Stephanie to see that most of the club members had already arrived. When her dad and Mayor Sapristos had started the club, there had only been a few people interested, but it had grown quite a bit and even spawned an adult chapter. Initially, Stephanie had been one of the younger flyers, but now there were a fair number younger even than she'd been when she started. She liked that. She'd found that kids even a little younger than her didn't seem, well, as resentful of her as did kids her own age.

Topping the list of those kids Stephanie didn't get along with was Trudy Franchitti. Stephanie had already promised herself that she was going to avoid Trudy today. They hadn't met up since what the SFS informally called "the Franchitti fire" and Stephanie didn't trust herself to keep her temper if the subject came up.

Now that the club was larger, avoiding Trudy wouldn't be as tough. Moreover, after a few attempts to put them on the same team—in addition to solo flying practice, club meetings also featured team events like relay races— Mayor Sapristos had resigned himself to separating them.

Stephanie hadn't precisely been eavesdropping—was she to blame that so many grown-ups forgot that a kid apparently engrossed in reading might be listening as well?—when Mayor Sapristos had spoken with her dad.

"I know I agreed with you that even if Trudy and Stephanie were among our strongest flyers they might benefit from being on the same team. Problem is, what we've ended up with are four teams: the Red Team, the Blue Team, Team Stephanie, and Team Trudy. They won't pass to each other if they can help it. Trudy fouls Stephanie if she thinks she can get away with it. Stephanie doesn't quite go as far as fouling Trudy, but I've caught her stealing wind in a way that's more appropriate when done against a rival team."

Dad had sighed. "Better to put them on opposite teams then, where they won't ruin the fun for the rest of the kids. Pity, though. I'd hoped Stephanie was above that sort of thing."

Hearing that, Stephanie had flushed. She hoped no one had realized she heard. She hated disappointing her folks, but some of the other kids—especially Trudy and her gang—were such blackholes. Did Mayor Sapristos know that Stan Chang, Trudy's boyfriend, often came to practice high? Did he know that the reason Toby Mednick had screwed up so bad that time was because Stan and his good buddy Frank "Outta Focus" Câmara had pressured him into trying a hit of something?

She'd considered telling the mayor, so Stan could be kept away from Toby, but because she liked Toby, she hadn't done so. There would have been a blood test and Toby would have gotten seriously in trouble. His parents were super strict. The whole thing had been confusing, because Stephanie knew her parents would have said she should have told, that Toby could have been hurt.

She'd settled for keeping an eye on Toby. So far, his near accident seemed to have scared him from trying anything else dumb. As for Stan and Focus . . . Well, Stephanie just couldn't make herself care. They were belly lice and bullies. If they wanted to take theselves out of the gene pool by flying stoned, let them.

Toby was on Stephanie's guest list for the birthday party. He was only a few months younger than her, so she figured he fit that mysterious "peer" qualification. It seemed weird to Stephanie that age should matter so much. Trudy was almost a year older than her, but several sections behind in all their classes.

Don't be dense, Steph, she said to herself as she assembled her glider. *You know the reason Mom and Dad want you to invite kids your own age is precisely because you find that hardest. Think of this as a test, just like in math or literature.*

That thought buoyed her up. All she had to do was think about social skills as if they were another subject—like social studies. Hadn't people once studied such things very seriously? Things like etiquette or the complex hierarchical systems of the ancient Japanese—traces of which still existed in their forms of personal address.

Stephanie grinned, wishing Karl was around so she could share her insight. He'd laugh, patting her on the head like he did his little sisters, Nadia and Anastasia. She wondered what Anders would think of her insight. As the son of an anthropologist, he probably had already thought of such things. Still, maybe she could ask him sometime.

The thought of Anders was the final thing Stephanie needed to give her spirit wings. She strapped herself and Lionheart (who had his own harness) into the hang glider and made her way over to where the rest of the club was assembling. She even managed to make "small talk" with a couple of the other kids.

Solo practice, especially acrobatics and targeting, went really well. A new girl in the club, Jessica Pheriss, was really good at some of the more complicated moves. Stephanie might have considered asking Jessica for some tips, but Jessica had firmly attached herself to the Trudy Franchitti faction and that made her off-limits.

Anyhow, anyone too dumb to see through Trudy was probably too dumb to teach anything. Jessica probably performed her maneuvers by instinct, like a Meyerdahl tree-bat flying in fog.

After solo acrobatics, Mayor Sapristos had arranged for a relay race. Stephanie set Lionheart down for this. It was one thing to have her solo performance affected by the treecat's extra bulk, but she didn't think it was fair to the rest of the team. Lionheart didn't mind, especially when she gave him a stalk of celery. He scampered up a nearby spike thorn, deftly avoiding the ten-centimeter-long thorns in his quest for a perch from which he could both enjoy his snack and watch the race.

There was a close moment when Focus Câmara closed in on Christine Schroeder, nearly snagging his wing with hers as he tried to intercept the flag Chet Pontier had tossed to Christine. Christine went into a sharp dive, saving her wing and grabbing the flag in a move that set the audience (hang-gliding club practice often drew onlookers, especially on days with warm, pleasant weather like this one) into loud cheers. After much maneuvering and a near drop of the flag when they handed off, Stephanie's Blue Team won the race.

After the race, Focus hardly stopped long enough to listen to Mayor Sapristos' post-game analysis, probably figuring—rightly—that he wasn't going to come in for much praise. He stayed long enough for manners, but instead of joining the usual chatter that followed a club meeting, he motioned toward town with a toss of his head.

"Hey, Stan, Becky, Trudy, c'mon. Let's go grab something to eat. Somebody else can teach the bitty kiddies how to fold their wings."

Since Stephanie was busy helping one of the littler club members do just that, she knew the taunt was intended at least partially for her. She knew she was supposed to feel bad that she hadn't been asked along, but she didn't care. The only thing that stung was knowing he'd wanted to hurt her.

Finishing with her "bitty," Stephanie looked around. There was Toby, talking with Chet and Christine. She hurried over, knowing that her folks would take no excuses if she didn't make at least a few invitations in person rather than over the net.

Etiquette, Stephanie reminded herself. *Just another class.*

"Hi," she said, feeling suddenly shy. "Uh. Great move, Christine. I wish I'd been close enough to help."

Christine, a tall, willowy girl almost a year older than Stephanie, whose fair hair was cut short in a crest that reminded Stephanie of some sort of exotic bird, grinned.

"I wasn't sure I could do it," she said, "but Focus makes me so mad. Ever since I turned him down, he's been out to get even. As if I didn't know he only asked me out because Becky was sick with some flu. Jerk!"

Stephanie, who had never been asked out by anyone, felt a momentary flicker of envy. She'd thought that maybe her figure—or lack of one—was the problem, but Christine was no more curvaceous. Of course, Christine was taller . . .

Stephanie spoke quickly, before she could lose her nerve. "Listen, my fifteenth birthday is coming up. My folks are . . . I mean, they insist . . . Anyhow, they're having a party. Fifteenth birthdays are really big on Meyerdahl. Something to do with the mixed German and Spanish heritage."

She realized she was babbling. Christine was smiling. Chet looked as if he was trying to swallow a laugh. Only Toby looked as serious as she felt. She realized that was because he probably was wondering if he was going to be included.

"Anyhow, I was wondering if you guys would come.

If my dad doesn't have any emergency calls, we're going to have hang gliding first. Later, there's going to be a formal dinner, with some other people."

She waited to be turned down, but Christine nodded. "That sounds like fun. I've never been to a Meyerdahl party, but I've heard they're great. Give me the date and time, and I'll check with my mom."

"Me, too," Chet said. "I don't have a tuxedo, though. My folks say I'm growing too fast for the investment. Would just nice clothes do? I mean, you did say 'formal.'"

Stephanie nodded. "Not *that* formal. Just dress up, sit down, like that. Not a picnic or buffet."

She was turning to make sure Toby knew he was included in the invitation when she realized that what she'd taken for a group of three—Toby, Christine, and Chet—had actually been four. Jessica Pherris had been standing where the height of the others, combined with the partially folded hang gliders, had hidden her from Stephanie.

Stephanie wrestled for a moment with her worse self, but, remembering how Frank's deliberate "not-inviting" had stung, she knew she didn't want to act the same.

"Toby, Jessica," she said, "you'll come, too, won't you? I mean, if you're free."

Toby glowed. Jessica, perhaps having noticed Stephanie's hesitation, paused.

"I'll check with my folks," she said. "We're new to Sphinx, new to the whole Star Kingdom, actually. What's formal wear here?"

Christine laughed. "On Manticore proper it would be a tuxedo, but this is a colony planet. Stephanie's folks will probably be fine with anything other than your kick-arounds."

Stephanie hurried to second this. "My folks just wanted to make clear this wasn't just a hang-gliding outing. They love to cook. I think they're planning a whole banquet built around symbolic foods."

Jessica looked relieved. "Okay. Hey, thanks. That's nice of you. Listen, I've got to run. I promised my mom I'd help her with her garden."

That sounded interesting, but before Stephanie could ask more, Jessica had dashed off. Only after she was gone and Stephanie was collecting Lionheart from the spike-thorn tree did she remember something.

Frank hadn't invited Jessica to go with him and the others, either. She'd thought Jessica and Trudy were tight, but neither Trudy nor Becky had asked her to come along.

Of course, Stephanie thought as she walked over to where she'd promised to meet her dad, *they were two guys, two girls. Maybe Becky and Trudy didn't want the competition. Jessica's almost as well-developed as Trudy, though she doesn't show it off the same way. Maybe Becky doesn't want her around Frank. Christine implied . . .*

Her brain spun as she tried to work out all these per-mutations. Calculus, she decided, was easier than human relations, a whole lot easier.

From where he scampered along beside her, Lionheart responded with a heartfelt, "Bleek!"

✧   ✧   ✧

The days leading up to Stephanie's birthday went very well. Even with her doubts, Stephanie couldn't help but be excited. Back on Meyerdahl, especially when Stephanie had been really small, birthdays had always been a big deal. She'd been ten, almost eleven when they'd moved to Sphinx, and that greater age, combined with separation from their usual circle of friends and family, *and* the fact that both her parents had been really, really busy had led to birthdays becoming family celebrations.

She'd been on Sphinx for almost a third of her life now,

and had almost forgotten the big fuss Meyerdahl made at fifteen. The celebration was heavily influenced by the ancient Spanish *quinceañera*, with the emphasis being on reaching adulthood, rather than marriageability. However, a good many of Meyerdahl's original colonists had been of German extraction. Like many of those who left their homeland, they kept to old traditions more faithfully than did those they had left behind. Germans, as Stephanie confirmed when she double-checked one of her mother's passing comments on the net, had actually invented the individual birthday celebration, complete with cake and candles.

Over the last few days, several of her parents' conversations had broken off when Stephanie had come into the room. Having no desire to ruin any planned surprise, she'd even taken to making sure she whistled or talked to Lionheart so they'd have warning.

Then, on very day of the party, the whole thing was nearly ruined. Over a mid-morning snack, meant to hold them all until lunch, Marjorie Harrington turned to Stephanie.

"I hope you don't mind, dear, but I invited another couple of people to your party."

"Oh?" Stephanie managed around a full mouth.

"First, I was delivering some autumn squash plants to one of the holdings and I saw a girl I recognized from your hang-gliding club. She looked so lonely, sitting there by herself, that I asked if she would like to come to your birthday party."

Richard Harrington asked, "Which holding was this?"

"The Franchitti holding. The girl's name is Trudy." Marjorie saw the twin looks of surprise on her husband and daughter's face and misunderstood. "I'm not crazy about that family in general and I know a Franchitti was responsible for the recent fire, but I didn't think this girl could be blamed."

Stephanie's appetite vanished and she put her sandwich down.

"Trudy Franchitti is coming here. Oh, happy, happy birthday to me..."

"Stephanie!" Marjorie Harrington was shocked.

Richard Harrington cut in. "Stephanie and Trudy don't get along. Never have."

Marjorie Harrington blinked. "I had no idea."

"You wouldn't," Stephanie said. "You never pay attention to what I say. I told you that the kids here were utter and complete nulls. You just decide I'm poorly socialized. Now I'm going to have to put up with Trudy and her constantly reminding everyone that her father was among the first native born children on Sphinx. Happy, happy..."

"Stephanie!" The snap in Richard Harrington's voice made it clear he thought his daughter had overstepped. "Don't speak to your mother that way. Maybe if you talked to *her* more often she'd have a better understanding. Instead, you universally condemn everyone as zorks and nulls. I only know how you feel about Trudy because I coach the hang-gliding club when I can—and because Mayor Sapristos told me that he ended up putting the two of you on separate teams because you wouldn't play nice together."

Stephanie ground her teeth at the phrase "play nice," but she could see her dad was really peeved. She knew he loved her, but he loved her mom, too, and hated when they butted heads. Besides, technically, the description was accurate—at least on Trudy's side.

Richard Harrington continued. "Stephanie, one of the reasons fifteenth birthdays are a big deal—not just on Meyerdahl, but in a lot of cultures—is that especially in pre-tech civilizations, they marked the beginning of adulthood. I suppose your challenge on this birthday will be to act like an adult...even if Trudy, who is older than you, does not."

He quirked the corner of his mouth in a little smile. "She certainly does act adult in some ways, but I must agree, she is a zip in the brains department."

Marjorie Harrington took a deep breath. "And I apologize, Stephanie. I should have asked first. I suppose my 'warm fuzzies' over this whole birthday celebration got ahead of me."

Stephanie knew what was expected. Even though butterflies were churning around the bits of sandwich she'd eaten, she managed.

"Thanks, Mom. That's nice of you to say. I'll do my best. Honest." She couldn't resist adding, "But really, Trudy is a perfect example of evolution in reverse."

"I'll take your word for it," Marjorie Harrington hesitated. "I hope I haven't screwed up again, but remember I said I'd invited some 'people.'"

Stephanie nodded, thinking, *Please, please, please not Stan or Frank...I could handle Becky, but not Stan or Frank...*

"It's not another girl," Marjorie Harrington went on and Stephanie's heart sank further. "It's Anders Whittaker. His dad will be dropping him off sometime between hang gliding and dinner."

Stephanie wouldn't have believed the butterflies in her gut could get any worse, but now they were dancing and interweaving, this time in a happy bouncing dance.

"Anders?"

"I thought you and Karl got along with him," Mom said, looking really anxious now. "I mean, you seemed to that day he came by to see the treecats."

"Oh, Mom!" Stephanie wanted to hug her, but restrained herself. After all, she wasn't quite sure why the idea of Anders coming was so great, but it absolutely was. She settled for bouncing in her chair and reaching for her neglected sandwich. "He's razor sharp. Definitely *not* a null wit."

"Or a zork?" Mom said, the teasing note in her voice not quite hiding her tension.

"Definitely not a zork," Stephanie assured her.

She grinned and bit into her sandwich. Then a thought hit her that started a new set of butterflies up to join the others.

Anders was coming. Anders, who definitely *wasn't* all the things she usually despised in Trudy's crowd. Anders, who was actually good-looking and smart and had that great way of listening so you felt he really understood.

And this time he'd probably not even talk to her except to say "Happy Birthday." Trudy would be there, and the guys always noticed Trudy. And Jessica, who was nearly as shapely. And Christine, who had lots of guys asking her out.

Anders was coming. But probably he wouldn't notice her at all...

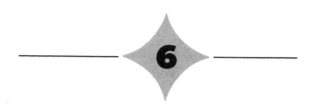

SINCE HE WASN'T TAKING PART IN THE HANG GLIDING, Anders arrived at Stephanie's birthday party dressed for dinner. His dad had meditated on renting Anders a tuxedo, so he'd be in local fashion, but had decided against it.

"You have good dress clothes with you already. I know I protested when your mother insisted we pack an outfit, but she was right. You can't prepare after the fact."

Dr. Whittaker himself was dressed for a day in the field—part of his "I'm just dropping the boy off before getting back to work" routine.

Dr. Marjorie met them as they landed. After greetings were exchanged, she gestured in the direction of the sky, where brightly colored hang gliders could be seen darting and hovering like dragonflies.

"The hang-gliding party got off the ground a bit late," she said. "A couple of the guests misunderstood and came dressed for dinner, then had to change."

She looked at Anders and smiled. "You look wonderful. Is that traditional formal wear for your planet?"

Anders nodded. "My mom picked it out," he said. "The color, too, I mean. We don't all need to wear tunics in tan trimmed with green. It is pretty usual for the trousers to echo the trim, though."

"I like the combination," Dr. Marjorie said, leading the Whittakers from the landing pad to a shaded area mid-point between the house and the flying field, where stood a long table arrayed with a tasteful variety of finger foods. "I understand that at one point on Old Terra, men all wore black to formal occasions. They must have looked like a bunch of rusty old crows."

She gestured toward the food. "Please, help yourselves. This is just a bridge to hold us until dinner. The rest of the dinner guests should show up fairly soon."

Anders noticed that the spread featured a wide array of very interesting-looking fruits and vegetables. He picked up one that resembled a star fruit, except this one was a dark indigo blue, rather than the more usual golden-yellow.

"Is this your work?" he asked, remembering Dr. Marjorie was a specialist in plant genetics.

"It is," she said, "a cross between a purple berry Richard noted the treecats eat and some Terran plants. It's rather tart, but completely safe. As you may know, humans can eat a wide variety of the native plants on Sphinx. They don't contain all the necessary nutrients, but if you know your foraging, you could survive for a while."

"Rather as treecats can eat human food," Dr. Whittaker said, "and sometimes thrive. Still, do you find yourself needing to give Lionheart supplements?"

"I think we would," Dr. Marjorie said, "if he only ate human foods. However, Richard insists that Lionheart do some of his own foraging. Lionheart doesn't seem to mind. In fact, he seems to enjoy hunting. Still, his attitude may be different when winter rolls around again."

The conversation drifted to treecat eating habits in the wild. Dr. Marjorie didn't claim to be an expert, but admitted that since early 1519, when Lionheart had come to live with them, she had both observed what he chose to eat (in addition to celery) and tried out various of her hybrids on him.

"He likes that purple star Anders noticed," she commented. "Not as much as celery, but quite a bit."

Eventually, the hang gliders began dropping out of the air one by one. Dr. Whittaker took this as his cue to get going, although it was obvious to Anders that he had really enjoyed talking with Dr. Marjorie.

After waving good-bye to his dad, Anders drifted over to where the hang gliders were coming in for landing.

Dr. Marjorie walked with him. "Stephanie's glider is the one with the orange-and-black striped wings. We gave her one with that pattern after she smashed up her first Sphinx model and she's kept the theme since. She calls them all the Flying Tiger and numbers them. Very methodical, our Steph."

Stephanie seemed to be taking her time landing, so Anders took the opportunity to observe the other flyers. He found Karl beneath a cobalt-and-white glider coming in for a slightly clumsy landing on the far side of the field.

Already landed, closer to where Anders stood, was a dark-complexioned boy about Stephanie's age, his silky, dark curls tousled by the wind, his bright brown eyes laughing as he struggled to get the wings of his yellow-and-brown glider stowed.

Another boy, a year or so older, swooped in next to him, neatly tucking his scarlet wings as if he was some sort of human hawk. Anders guessed that this boy had used counter-grav assist at the very end, but that didn't make it any less a neat trick. The younger boy obviously agreed, calling out, "Nice landing, Chet! You've got to teach me that one."

"You bet, Toby," Chet said. "Look at Christine. She's going to do me one better."

He pointed up toward where a long-bodied, slimly built girl—either a genie like Stephanie or a newcomer to Sphinx—was sweeping through the sky, her steel-blue-and-white hang glider moving through an elegant swirling pattern as it descended.

Rather like one half of a DNA spiral, Anders thought. *I wonder if two really good flyers could make that into a full pattern?*

He had his answer in a moment. Another glider, this one patterned in shades of green that evoked a fanciful collage of springtime leaves, echoed Christine's pattern. The pilot—a girl, obviously, from the curves in her coverall—never came in low enough to risk fouling Christine's wings, but nonetheless managed to make Anders "see" the other glider's earlier progress. The illusion was so vivid that he found himself rubbing his eyes, checking for a tracer.

Chet said enthusiastically to Toby, "Jessica was a super addition to the club. I'm glad she came today. Steph's a great flyer, but a soloist by nature. Christine loves tandem work."

Toby nodded wistful enthusiasm.

"Someday," he said, his tone that of a young knight making a vow, "I'm going to be as good at the three of them combined!"

Christine touched ground and folded her wings, shrugging out of her harness so that she could rush over and offer Jessica a squeeze, squealing with excitement.

"That was *so* hexy! Like ballet or something. We've got to practice it more."

Jessica shrugged out of her leaf-patterned glider and

returned Christine's hug. "I'd like that, but later. I don't know about you, but I'm starved!"

As she spoke, Jessica tugged off a close-fitting cap that matched her coveralls, revealing exuberantly untidy masses of long, curly light auburn hair.

When Christine pulled off her cap, she immediately began to comb her much shorter white-blond hair into a style rather like a cockatoo's crest. Her eyes proved to be ice-blue. The light hair and eyes made a marvelous contrast to the sandalwood hues of her complexion. Anders spent an enjoyable moment contemplating this delightful proof that female beauty could come in such contrasting packages.

"I'm starved, too," Christine agreed. "I'm sure Stephanie's folks will have laid out plenty of food, but we should wait for Stephanie, don't you think? I mean, this is her party."

"Absolutely," Jessica agreed. "Only she and Trudy are still up. I think they're having another go at the bulls-eye target."

Trudy must be the owner of the pale pink polka-dotted glider. It had seemed to Anders' untutored eye that she and Stephanie were competing for who would stay up longest. Then he realized the situation was more subtle. Both were aiming to land within a large target laid out in an open field. While Stephanie was apparently merely trying to hit center, Trudy was actually impeding Stephanie's descent. Her moves were subtle, but Anders figured if he could tell, so could the rest of the club members.

"There they go again," Toby said, his tone one of long-suffering. "I wonder why Trudy is even here. I mean, Stephanie can't stand her."

"The social mystery of the century," Chet agreed in the tones of a veteran newsie. "It's like the Monarchists inviting the Levelers to tea."

At that moment, the pattern of dodge and feint above

changed. Stephanie broke hard right. When Trudy moved to block her, Stephanie swirled higher, cut over Trudy to the left, then dove. If Chet's dive had resembled that of a hunting hawk, Stephanie's looked like an orange-and-black brick hurtling toward the ground.

A scream sounded from nearer to the house. Glancing back, Anders saw a man with flaming red hair beginning to run forward. Dr. Marjorie stood stock still next to a heavyset woman with brown hair who, from her open mouth, was probably the source of the scream. Despite the adult panicking, there was no doubt in Anders' mind that Stephanie was in complete control of the situation.

Well above the ground, Stephanie pulled out of her plummeting dive, caught a slowing air current, and came swirling in for a landing, her feet touching lightly in the very center of the black target placed on the meadow grass. Immediately, with what Anders guessed was proper etiquette in such games, she moved out of the way of the other flyer, and strode toward the gathered party, still wearing her glider harness.

Strapped in behind her, Lionheart was chittering away. Anders had listened to enough hours of recorded treecat sounds to guess that the 'cat was scolding his human.

Above, moving more like a butterfly than a hawk, Trudy came in for an elegant landing of her own, also touching down on the bull's-eye's center, but after Stephanie's daredevil maneuver or Christine and Jessica's ballet, her demo failed to be at all impressive. Most of the club members had run over to tease Stephanie about how she'd nearly not made it to fifteen and a day...

Only Dr. Richard, standing to the side, his strong features just a bit too fixed, seemed less than enthusiastic about Stephanie's performance.

No. Make that two who looked less than happy. Karl Zivonik, his glider slung so he could carry it over one powerful shoulder, shared Stephanie's father's lack of enthusiasm for Stephanie's risky acrobatics. Equally obviously, neither of them was going to call Stephanie on the incident—today.

For her part, after unstrapping Lionheart, Stephanie stowed the Flying Tiger, accepting compliments with just the right balance of pleasure and enthusiasm. If she and Trudy had indeed been involved in some sort of private joust, no one would have known it from her.

Trudy, on the other hand, looked more than a little miffed. Like Jessica, she had worn her hair under a cap. Now she pulled the cap off, combing out thick, dark tresses whose sausage curl certainly owed as much to art as to nature. Pretending to be completely absorbed in her primping, Trudy's brilliant violet-blue eyes scanned the group.

When she noticed Anders, he could have sworn those eyes flashed. Anders was aware he was attractive. His mother had made certain he had no illusions on that point, saying that ignorance would just leave him vulnerable. He'd even had his share of what she insisted on calling "puppy loves"—girls who called him up and left messages on his uni-link. But the look Trudy gave him as she sauntered over toward him was almost hungry.

"Hel-lo!" Trudy said, pulling the word out into several syllables. "And who might you be, and where have you been all my life?"

She'd thrown her shoulders back, raising her right hand to toy with the closure on her flight-suit, ostensibly because she was warm—out on the field, Anders could see that Toby and Chet had already divested themselves of their suits—but in actuality to draw attention to what she clearly thought of as irresistible assets.

Those bouncing breasts were quite remarkable, especially on someone who was probably not much more than sixteen, but Anders thought the approach rather simplistic—and even sort of sad. What a pity she had to offer herself as if she was some sort of appetizer. Anders realized, though, that he must have been more distracted than he wanted to admit because the question still hung in the air between them.

"I'm Anders Whittaker," he said. "I'm new to Sphinx. My father's in charge of a team of xenoanthropologists here from Urako to study the treecats."

Trudy clearly had to think about what that might mean to her. After consideration, she apparently decided that just because Dr. Whittaker was here to study the treecats, that didn't mean Anders was interested in them.

"How deadly for you," she purred, coming up next to him and somehow slipping an arm through his. "Your father really must talk to my father and brothers on the subject. After all, a balanced view is important, isn't it?"

"Indeed it is," came the voice of Dr. Richard from behind them. "However, Anders has been very politely waiting for the rest of you before getting something to eat. Here's the plan. Grab a snack from the buffet, then go in and change. Oh! Save some room for dinner. We've made some very special dishes."

The mention of food caused a general rush, in the course of which Anders managed to get free from Trudy. He made his way over to Stephanie just as they all reached the buffet.

"Happy Birthday!" he said. "That was quite a landing."

"I think Dad's going to have my ears," Stephanie said, forcing a laugh. "Lionheart has already chewed me out. I'm not supposed to do things like that."

Anders shrugged. "Hey . . . It looked terrifying, but I never thought you were in trouble. Can you tell me what's what on the buffet? I haven't been on Sphinx long enough to know the local delicacies."

Stephanie giggled. Not a contrived girlish giggle, just a laugh that invited him to share a joke. "You won't find a lot of this stuff anywhere else. Some is Meyerdahl-influenced. Some are my mom and dad's creations. They both love to cook."

Christine, who had been spreading something orange and pink on a cracker, halted in mid-motion. "Creations in her kitchen or her lab?"

Marjorie Harrington laughed. "Kitchen and lab—but all the stuff from the lab has been cleared for human consumption. You probably have most of it in your cooler at home."

Christine bit into the cracker and looked blissed-out. "Not this. Definitely not this. Can I have the recipe?"

Chatter became general after that. Anders had more than Stephanie helping him select treats to try. All the hang-glider club members vied to get him to try river-roe and ice-potato paste, toasted near-pine nuts, and other oddities.

Adults were arriving now. Anders was delighted to meet Scott MacDallan and Fisher, "his" treecat. MacDallan proved to be the red-haired man he'd seen rushing toward what had seemed like Stephanie's inevitable crash—not a big surprise, since he was a medical doctor. The stocky woman with brown hair proved to be both Scott's wife and Karl's aunt, Irina Kisaevna, a very nice woman. Ranger Lethbridge came, making apologies for his partner, Ranger Jedrusinski, and saying that he couldn't stay for dinner.

"We drew straws for fire watch," he said, "and she lost. I've promised to bring her a dry crust or two for consolation."

"We can do better than that," Stephanie promised, and immediately started piling a plate with finger foods to set aside. "Mom won't want me to cut the cake yet, but I'll bring you both some tomorrow."

One by one, the members of the hang-gliding club emerged, each dressed in some interesting variation on formal wear. Karl, it turned out, actually owned a tuxedo, and looked very dashing in it. Toby's outfit consisted of flowing robes made from a pale golden fabric that set off his dark skin and flowing black hair to perfection. He seemed momentarily shy about his attire until Christine and Jessica started gushing about how they wished Star Kingdom clothes were as elegant. Chet wore something less flashy, but still quite respectable.

The girls all looked pretty good, Anders thought. Trudy—predictably, he thought, although he'd only known her for something like an hour—wore a pink-and-lavender gown with both slit seams on the sides *and* a plunging neckline. She claimed it was an ancestral costume from Old Earth itself.

Christine and Stephanie both wore slacks and blouses, a simpler variation on the Star Kingdom tuxedo. The cummerbunds showed off trim waists and made an asset of their relative lack of busts. Jessica emerged arrayed in frothy layers of silk and taffeta in pale yellow and green touched with hints of white lace.

"It's actually my mom's," she explained shyly. "Neo-Victorian was all the rage on our last planet."

Talking about clothing inevitably led to discussion of birthday customs. Toby admitted that his culture didn't even celebrate birthdays.

"We celebrate Saint's Days instead. Mine is Saint Tobias."

Christine, Chet, Karl, and Trudy all proved to have been born on Sphinx.

"My father was one of the first children born on Sphinx," Trudy boasted. "For a while, his birthday was practically a planetary holiday."

"There were problems with childbirth initially," Scott MacDallan agreed. "The heavier gravity and air pressure made it difficult for women to carry to term. However, now, between nanotherapies and wider use of counter-gravity, more and more pregnancies are successful."

Karl added, "I remember when Scott was delivering my little brother Lev. A treecat showed up at the door all beat up. Scott ended up going to the rescue."

"And leaving your mother to suffer?" Trudy sounded genuinely shocked.

"It wasn't quite like that," Scott MacDallan said. He might have explained further, but Irina called to him from the house.

"Scott! We need a surgeon to carve the roast."

Most of the adults seemed to take this as a summons to dinner but, perhaps because Stephanie stayed outside, perhaps because there was still finger food, the younger guests lingered near the appetizers.

Trudy took a step toward Stephanie, but her gaze rested on the males in the group.

"There's an important Star Kingdom tradition we haven't followed for our birthday girl's special day," Trudy said, her voice filled with teasing laughter. "She hasn't had her spankings. . . ."

Something in the way Trudy said "spankings" made Anders feel she'd said something a lot more risqué. Maybe it was the way she winked at him when she said it.

"In my family," Trudy continued, "the guys hold the birthday girl and then the girls give the whacks—one for each year. If she can take it without crying out, then she'll be lucky all year."

"My family doesn't do that," Christine protested.

Karl looked uncomfortable, so Anders was willing to bet that his family practiced some variation of the rite. Chet was shifting restlessly from foot to foot. Clearly, Trudy might be overselling her point, but she wasn't flat-out lying.

"Well, you may have been born here," Trudy said to Christine, "but your family is relatively new. Mine is tough, pioneer stock. We don't have any use for wimps and pansies. I'm sure Stephanie doesn't either. After all, she goes around slaying hexapumas with her bare hands, if we're to believe the stories."

Stephanie looked both angry and somehow trapped. Lionheart pressed against her leg, his ears canted in concern. Anders could see that Stephanie didn't want to be taken as anything less than tough, but the idea of being held down and hit on didn't appeal either.

Trudy smiled silkily. "So, Stephanie. Are you up to showing you're a real Sphinxian girl?"

At that moment, Dr. Richard came to the door. "Are you all waiting for individual invitations? Soup's on!"

"Saved by the bell..." Trudy murmured softly. "But then our Stephanie is always getting saved, isn't she? What a lucky girl."

No one replied, but more than one pair of eyes strayed to where Lionheart, his scars and mutilations all too evident, testified to the price of Stephanie's "luck."

Anders noticed that Stephanie was the one who looked the longest.

✧   ✧   ✧

As dinner progressed, Stephanie realized she was enjoying her birthday party more than she had thought possible. Yeah... Trudy was there, but so were Chet, Christine, Toby, and Karl. Jessica had surprised Stephanie by not sucking up to Trudy (who had already been there when Jessica arrived), but by making herself part of the general crowd. And, best of all, Anders was there.

The weather for hang gliding had been great. Her folks had given her one of their gifts early—a modified harness that made Lionheart's flight experience safer, while at the same time allowing Stephanie to "trim" the treecat's weight more efficiently.

She'd used it to pull off the spectacular dive that had

gotten her around Trudy. She was still flushed by the
exhilarating experience, enough that she just might have
taken her "spanks" if Dad's call to dinner hadn't saved
her the humiliation. Right then, she'd felt like she could
take anything.

Or *was* it the hang gliding that had her so high?
Stephanie tried not to make her interest too obvious, but
Mom had seated Anders Whittaker across the table from
her, just one seat over. He looked really, really good in
the green-and-cream tunic and trousers he wore, but even
more admirable—because he couldn't help being hot—he
was doing a great job holding his own in a conversation
with a bunch of near strangers.

Stephanie had been given a great excuse to look at
Anders a lot during the first course. This featured extra-long
noodles in a sesame-oil sauce served over near-lettuce, a
leafy plant native to Sphinx that tasted like Romaine lettuce
with a light hint of onion. The taste combination was one
of Stephanie's favorites, but the extra-long noodles were a
birthday tradition on the Harrington side of the family.

"You need to eat the noodles without cutting them,"
Richard Harrington explained as he expertly demonstrated
how to twirl them around paired chopsticks. "The long
noodles are symbolic of long life, so you don't want to
cut the noodles in case you cut off your own life! We've
provided a variety of tools, so give it a try."

Everyone did, with lots of giggles and a few protests
when a noodle seemed to develop a life of its own.
Stephanie wished she was sitting next to Anders, so she
could demonstrate, but watching him—he proved to be a
dab hand with chopsticks—was nearly as good. He had
great lips. She found herself wondering what they'd be
like to kiss.

As the noodle plates were cleared away, Irina turned
to Anders.

"Dr. Hobbard," Irina said, "has already interviewed Scott and Stephanie, who are the only living humans to have been adopted by treecats. She took advantage of the proximity of the two treecats Richard kept here for rehab after that business with Bolgeo to collect even more information. What does your father hope to add?"

Stephanie thought a lesser person than Anders would have been offended by the aggressive note that underlay the question. Stephanie knew she probably would have been, since it implied that the xenoanthropological team had nothing new to offer.

Irina was a really sweet person, but she knew how wearing being continually cross-examined could be, and she was protective of both Scott and Fisher—and probably of Stephanie and Lionheart, too. Clearly, she saw the arrival of Dr. Whittaker as more trouble for her favorite people.

However, Anders didn't show the least sign of being offended by the question. He began by telling a bit about each of the specialists his father had brought with him, going on to explain how each individual would contribute something new to human understanding of treecats.

"Dr. Hobbard," Anders concluded, "has and had other responsibilities than the treecats. She's Chair of the Anthropology Department at Landing University on Manticore, for one. Although she does have xenoanthropological experience, it would be too much to expect her also to be a linguistics expert like Ms. Guyen or a specialist in anthroarcheology like my dad."

Trudy's voice, polite as could be, added when Anders paused, "My dad says the fact that Dr. Hobbard is associated with Landing University makes her biased. He says that Dr. Hobbard has too much invested in *wanting* Sphinx—and that means the Star Kingdom—to be the place where another intelligent life-form is discovered. Dad says that one reason he agreed to an outside team being sent in was because he felt a team from another system wouldn't share that bias and so could look at the issues more clearly."

The ways Trudy inflected "he agreed" implied that without Jordan Franchitti's approval, no such team would have been permitted to as much as get a sniff of a treecat.

Stephanie saw a couple of the adults smile slightly at Trudy's confident assertion that Sphinx politics revolved around her dad, but she didn't think what Trudy said was at all funny. Trudy might have an inflated idea of her dad's importance, but even a few months working with the SFS had shown her how much influence the First Families—especially those like the Franchittis, that held enormous amounts of land—wielded.

Trudy directed the gaze of her big violet-blue eyes on Anders. "Your dad's unbiased, isn't he? He isn't going to make any pronouncements about treecat intelligence without speaking to all sorts of people—not just the ones who already keep treecats as pets."

At the word "pets," Stephanie stiffened. She started to say something, but Lionheart tugged gently on her ear, drawing her attention to where Scott MacDallan was very, very slightly shaking his head "no."

Anders looked appropriately serious. "My dad is unbiased. Sure, Dad would like to be head author on the report that announces to the universe that humanity has located another intelligent species, but he's also aware that he'd look like an idiot if he made a premature judgement. Even before humanity left Terra, humans wanted to believe they shared the universe with other intelligences. More often than not, those who declared that we did found themselves mocked."

"I guess," Trudy responded, "that would be interesting, but even if the treecats are intelligent, well, they're not ever going to be like us, are they? I mean, I've heard they use tools, but I don't call a broken-off bit of rock a 'knife'—no matter what label Dr. Hobbard and the SFS have put on it in a museum."

"Humans," Scott MacDallan said very gently, "started out with stone knives. Treecats make nets, too, remember. And they build dens up in the trees."

Trudy shrugged, setting her assets jiggling provocatively. "My brother says those nets aren't real tools. He says he's seen spiderwebs more complicated than those 'nets.' Heck, he says that near-beavers make more complicated dams than any treecat 'house' he's seen."

No one answered. Perhaps taking silence for agreement, Trudy turned her attention back to Anders. Stephanie felt sure that Trudy thought that if she could win Anders over, he would influence Dr. Whittaker in favor of her point of view.

"I'm not saying that treecats aren't really interesting and clever. I'd love to have one as a..." This time Trudy stopped before actually using the ill-advised word "pet," and amended it. "Companion. I think treecats are marvelous, really marvelous. But they're not humans and that's just how it is."

More silence. Stephanie thought she knew exactly what was going on in the minds of those gathered around the long dining room table. The adults—all of whom except her mom and dad thought Trudy must be Stephanie's friend or she wouldn't have been invited to the party— were reluctant to argue and so ruin Stephanie's fun. The kids, all of whom labored under no such illusion, were too polite to want to start a fight. Nonetheless, from the way his broad shoulders were shifting under his tuxedo jacket, Karl was definitely about to say something, and whatever he said wouldn't be in agreement with Trudy.

Stephanie guessed what Trudy would say to any opinion of Karl's ... Something like, "Oh!" Giggle. Giggle. Flutter of eyelashes. Bounce of assets. "But you're Stephanie's special friend. Of course you'd say that..."

Trudy might even say "you're Stephanie's boyfriend," and then what would Anders think?

I mean, I can't go to him later and say, "Listen, Karl's not really my boyfriend, no matter what Trudy said. I mean, he's my buddy, but he's not my boyfriend, and I want you to know this because..."

Feeling herself about to become embarrassed over a conversation that hadn't even happened, Stephanie spoke into the uncomfortable silence. She had meant to take anything Trudy said with stoic silence, so her mom wouldn't feel bad about inviting Trudy, but this was getting serious!

She spoke in her sweetest, most reasonable tone of voice, the one she'd perfected in what seemed like millions of interviews. "Trudy, does 'just how it is' mean that even if Dr. Whittaker's study ends up showing that treecats aren't 'intelligent' or 'sentient' or whatever term they decide to use, you don't think treecats have any rights? They were here on Sphinx before us. This is their only planet."

Trudy laughed, a loud, completely genuine laugh that was worse than any mockery could be.

"Oh, come on, Stephanie. I'd never take you for a hypocrite. Look at this house you're living in! Do you think the trees that got cut down to make it wouldn't have preferred to keep living? What about all the birds and beasts that lost their homes so your family could have this great big house—and greenhouses and vehicle hangars and gazebos. You're not telling me you're going to take up living in a tent so you minimize your ecological footprint? If you do, remind me not to come visit you in the winter!"

Stephanie found herself fumbling to explain. The problem was, Trudy clearly thought that the treecats didn't have any more right than did a tree. And how could

Stephanie explain that there *were* times she did feel bad when she considered the majestic crown oaks, near-pines, and rock trees that had died so that the space in which her family's home now stood could be cleared? Trudy would probably laugh so hard that Scott would need to give her a tranquilizer to calm her down.

To Stephanie's surprise, it was neither Karl nor one of her adult friends who spoke out, but Jessica Pheriss.

"Don't be a moron, Trudy. Don't you see? You're making Stephanie's point for her—or at least the Forestry Service's point. Responsible settlers must pay attention to the local ecology. That protocol has been followed from the start of settlement here. I read speculations that one of the reasons humans didn't find treecats sooner was because early biological surveys showed that picketwood trees might look like groves, but they're actually one huge tree. Treecats—as I'm sure you know—prefer picketwood over other types of trees for their colonies, but since clearing picketwood was so destructive of a segment of the local ecosystem, humans tended to stay clear of them—and so the treecats stayed hidden."

"So..." Trudy sneered. "This means what?"

"So this means," Jessica continued speaking slowly, almost, but not quite, as if to a very small child, "that from the very start, colonization on Sphinx has been done with an awareness of the local ecology. That policy isn't going to change. If the treecats are ruled sentient, that awareness will be adapted. I mean, we can't just move in on the local residents."

Trudy rolled her eyes. "Wow, Jessica, you already know so much, and your family just got here. Well, let me tell you this. Humans, not treecats, are the ones who vote in the assembly. My dad and his friends aren't going to let a bunch of cute mini-hexapumas be used to get around their rights."

Jessica's intervention had given Stephanie a chance to organize her thoughts. Now she spoke up, striving with all her might to be reasonable when what she wanted to do was shout something like, "You moron! Maybe if Dr. Whittaker proves treecats are sentient, then they will get a vote. What would you do then?"

Instead, she said calmly. "Trudy, I can send you files and files about what happens when humans start forgetting that we're only one part of the local ecosystem—one part that can be destructive all out of proportion."

"Fizz on the files," Trudy said, laughing dismissively. "Like I want to spend my time reading propaganda written by people who are only interested in taking away the rights of serious land-holders."

At this point, Marjorie Harrington interrupted, using her best "mom" voice, the one that held the snap of a starship commander beneath its reasonable tones.

"I can see we have some quite varied opinions here. Perhaps we should stop before we ruin our appetites for dessert? I've made both chocolate cake and tanapple pie. I thought we'd move into the living room for dessert."

The Mom Voice—or maybe the prospect of dessert—stopped the debate, but Stephanie didn't think Trudy's mind had been changed one bit. In the general movement to clear away dishes and move into the living room, she noticed Trudy moving over to talk to Anders. From the way Trudy was pressing close to him, she, at least, hadn't given up her campaign.

"Ultra-stonishing," said Jessica, speaking very quietly, but so the kids closest could hear. "Is Trudy obvious or what? I wonder if I should take a picture or two and e-mail them anonymously to Stan..."

She was grinning mischievously, but Stephanie didn't doubt she'd do it.

"Don't," Chet said. He wasn't grinning. "Stan isn't nice.

I mean, really isn't nice. Trudy's family seems to like to play with fire."

Christine nodded. "Yeah. Listen, Steph. You were great there. I mean, I've seen you lose it a whole lot more at practice when Trudy gets dumb. This was a lot nastier than blocking your glider."

Toby bounced in agreement. "You *were* great. I thought we were going to see you use Trudy's head to mash the ice potatoes."

Stephanie laughed. "My folks would have killed me. They take hospitality seriously—and so do I. I saw Karl carrying the tanapple pie out. I hope you'll try it. It's his Aunt Irina's recipe. It's seriously wonderful, sour at first, but with a sweet note."

"Kinda like Steph herself," Chet said, grinning. "Right, Christine?"

"Absolutely," Christine said.

"Bleek!" agreed Lionheart, scampering ahead to where a tray of celery had been put out for his and Fisher's dessert. "Bleek! Bleek!"

STEPHANIE SLID INTO THE PILOT'S SEAT OF THE GOV-
ernment air car, belted herself in, and took a quick minute
to familiarize herself with the control panel while Ms.
Schwartz, the test administrator—a wiry woman whose
jaded expression said she'd seen it all and expected to
see worse—got in on the other side.

"Whenever you're ready," Ms. Schwartz said, position-
ing her uni-link so she could take notes. "We'll start
with the vehicle on automatic. Then, if you pass the first
part of the test, we'll go through the same areas with
the air car on manual so you can attempt to qualify
for a provisional license. The route should be coming
up on the HUD."

Stephanie noted where a neat shocking-green line was
taking form on the heads-up display and nodded. She
checked right and left, as well as behind and above, before
taking the air car out of its parking space and into the
streets of Twin Forks.

Last night at the party, word had somehow gotten out that Stephanie planned on taking her test today. Everyone still there—Trudy, thank goodness, had left—had regaled Stephanie with stories about how the test administrators delighted in taking off points for the most minor infractions—one of which included relying on the HUD to the exclusion of visual checks.

The course the shocking-green line guided Stephanie through included piloting at various elevations and through both urban and rural conditions. Stephanie had only limited real experience with street-level piloting, but she'd put in so many hours on the sims that she had to remind herself that this time it was for real.

Eventually, she brought the air car back to their starting point.

"You've a perfect score so far," Ms. Schwartz said, managing to sound both pleased and miffed. "Are you sure you want to try the manual test? If you fail, you'll lose even your learner's permit. You can't retest for another three T-months."

Stephanie had thought the penalty was ridiculous, but now, considering Trudy and her blackhole friends, Stephanie thought she understood. Cockiness—especially when someone was handling something as potentially lethal as an air car—was not to be encouraged.

"I'm sure I want to try, ma'am," Stephanie said.

"Then switch to manual," the administrator replied, reaching forward to activate something on her override panel, "and follow the line."

The second pass went smoothly until they were outside of Twin Forks. As they were passing over one of the many streams that fed the Mankara River, a freak squall blew up. Solid as the air car was, the vehicle bucked enough to rattle Stephanie's teeth. Ms. Schwartz gasped aloud and leaned toward her override panel.

Here, Stephanie's hours of hang gliding, as well as those spent practicing with Karl, paid off. Before Ms. Schwartz could activate the override, Stephanie had compensated for the turbulence, anticipated where the wind was headed, and moved the car into smooth air without diverting too far off the pre-ordained route. As soon as she judged weather conditions were safe, Stephanie brought the air car back on course and finished the test route.

Ms. Schwartz said nothing until the air car touched down outside of the government center and Stephanie had performed the shut-down routine in perfect order. Then she leaned over and clapped Stephanie on the shoulder.

"Good job, Ms. Harrington," Ms. Schwartz said, beaming. "I'd heard you had a cool head. I'm glad the stories were true."

"Does that mean I passed?"

"With a perfect score. I'll be sending the results in to headquarters, and the official license should be on record before it's time for you to fly home." Ms. Schwartz gave an impish grin. "Be sure to ask your father to let you pilot."

Stephanie grinned back. She knew her dad would, just as she knew he'd be nervous about actually letting her be in charge. Even the best parents were funny that way.

Because Lionheart had come into town with them, and treecats weren't allowed inside without special permission, the doctors Harrington had waited outside the administration building for Stephanie.

"Lionheart has been 'bleek bleeking' in obvious glee since you brought the air car back from the second pass," Mom said, laughing as Stephanie ran up to them, "so don't bother to tell us you passed. We know!"

"This calls for a celebration," Dad added. "I've called Eric Flint and reserved a table for us at the Red Letter Café. Fortunately, they're open for late lunch."

The Red Letter Café was one the businesses that had pioneered a "treecat friendly" policy. That—and the fact that it served desserts to die for in very large portions—made it a favorite of the Harrington clan. After they'd stuffed themselves with both lunch and enormous ice-cream concoctions, Stephanie looked at her parents.

"Dad, Mom, the woman who gave me my test said that I should ask you if I could fly home. Please?"

Richard Harrington sighed theatrically. "Well, at least I'll die well-fed. Why don't you go bring the car around? I know we usually walk here in town, but maybe you'll get pulled over and I'll be spared a terrifying ride."

Giggling, Stephanie leapt to her feet and motioned to Lionheart.

"Not this time," Mom said. "Let's have your maiden voyage be with as few distractions as possible, all right?"

Stephanie didn't protest. Lionheart was rather soggy, since his idea of a terrific dessert involved shredding massive amounts of celery. If he stayed with her folks, he'd have a chance to mop up.

They'd parked over near the administrative center, but Stephanie didn't mind the walk. In fact, it was all she could do not to skip. She was considering comming Karl and sharing the good news when she heard familiar voices coming from near a couple of businesses that had already closed for the day.

She couldn't see the speakers—they must be around back—or make out what was being said, but one voice definitely belonged to Stan Chang, Trudy's beau and someone Stephanie disliked, if possible, even more than she did Trudy. Another was Stan's good buddy, Focus Câmara. Normally, Stephanie would have just hoped they wouldn't see her, but as she drew closer, she heard Toby Mednick speak.

"No, guys, really. I can't. I'm late already."

"Awe, c'mon, Toby," Focus said. "If you're already late, then what does it matter if you're later?"

"But, guys..."

Toby's voice held notes of defeat rather than protest. Stephanie knew the prudent thing would be to keep going or at least get some backup, but remembering how Stan and Focus had gotten Toby into trouble at least once already, she couldn't. Not only was Toby younger than her, but—remembering how much fun they'd had at her party the day before—Toby was her *friend*. Stephanie had gotten so used to thinking of herself as friendless—at least when it came to kids her own age—that the thought hit her with almost physical force. But it was true. Toby was her friend and she could no more leave him in the lurch than she could Karl...or Lionheart.

Again, Stephanie considered comming for help, but something in the tone of the voices made her think there wasn't any time to waste.

Stan was saying, "You know, Toby, from how you're acting, you'd think you didn't want to be pals with us. Here we're offering to share some really expensive, really good stuff with you and you act like we're trying to give you dog shit. Now, here, take just a little, then you won't care how late you are. You'll be flying without a glider."

"Well..." Toby was saying when Stephanie peeked around the corner.

The three boys were standing in a little garden behind the shops. Toby was backed up against a round table, and Stan was all but shoving an amber-colored capsule toward his face. Focus hulked to one side, blocking Toby's avenue of escape.

Thinking fast, Stephanie considered her options.

Should I confront them directly? Stan did back down that time last year, but what if he didn't this time? And exactly how would that solve anything? All that would happen is that Toby would probably get beat up next time they got him alone... and I'd have to watch my back. No. There has to be another way.

An idea hit her. It wasn't the best, maybe, but Toby was already reaching for the capsule. Feigning a delight she didn't feel, Stephanie rounded the corner at a run, talking as fast as she could.

"Toby! Is that you? Toby! I did it! I passed!"

The three boys stared at her, Stan and Focus in astonishment, Toby in something like awe and amazement. He wasn't so startled that he didn't catch her hint.

"You did! Steph, that's absolutely hexy!" He looked at the Stan and Focus, both of whom were now openly gaping. "Did you hear, guys? Stephanie just passed her air-car test. Did you get the provisional license?"

"I did," she said, not bothering to hide her pleasure. She turned and beamed at Stan and Focus. "I heard Toby's voice and I just *had* to tell someone. I'm so glad you guys are here, too. Great news, huh?"

She grabbed Focus by both hands and swung him around as if they were dancing—incidentally creating an opening for Toby. Focus stumbled. His skin was so clammy that Stephanie had to resist an impulse to drop his hands as if they were a couple of dead fish. Clearly, he was already a bit "outta focus."

Flabbergasted at the interruption, Stan had dropped the arm that held the amber capsule, cupping his hand around it protectively. Stephanie wouldn't be surprised if Stan had already sampled its twin or something like it because he was clearly having trouble processing the changed situation.

On the other hand, it might be just because Stan wasn't very smart. But he was very mean. As much fun as it was seeing them gawping, it was time she and Toby got out of this too-quiet corner and onto a more public street.

"My folks said I could fly us home," Stephanie babbled, "and I'm going to get the air car from over at government central. Want to come with me?"

She made the invitation general, but wasn't surprised to see the two older boys shake their heads. The last thing they'd want was to do was go over by government central—which housed the police—in their currently impaired condition.

"I'd love to," Toby said. "Bye, fellows. See you in the sky."

Toby and Stephanie hurried out of the small park with perhaps a little too much haste for good manners, but Stephanie wasn't going to let the older boys reconsider letting them go.

Toby didn't say anything until they were well clear of the other two. When he spoke, his voice was tight. "You must think I'm as much of a blackhole as those two."

"No. I think you were in a bad spot, that's all. I thought you were staying clear of them."

"I was," Toby said, "but my dad asked me to take a late delivery over to that boutique before it closed. The owner was just leaving, but she opened up, then made me wait. Focus's dad owns the eatery next door. I think he and Stan do some cleaning up after hours. I guess he and Stan saw me coming in, because when I came out with the boutique owner, they called me over, saying they had some news about the club. I couldn't say no without it seeming strange to Ms. Bond, then, well..."

"I get it," Stephanie said, and she did.

"I was so glad when you came six-legging it around the corner," Toby went on. "I owe you, big time."

Stephanie grinned at him. "Hey, no problem. I mean, what are friends for?"

✧   ✧   ✧

Climbs Quickly slipped out the window into the autumn night. The day following the big party had been very busy. Despite the activity of the day, Climbs Quickly found himself unable to settle in to sleep. Change was in the air—and not just because of the events in Death Fang's Bane's life. The seasons were stirring.

Stretching out his body in an easy, ground-covering lope, Climbs Quickly made his way a distance from the houses. When he came to a particularly stately golden-leaf that had become one of his favorite lookouts, he left the ground. Scampering high up along the trunk, he came out above most of the leafy canopy. Then Climbs Quickly spread his whiskers and let the wind fingers tickle his fur.

Closing his leaf-green eyes to slits, the treecat let ears and nose keep watch while he concentrated on more subtle, less easily read signs.

Yes. The weather was changing. Up here, away from where all the two-legs' machines and enormous nests created interference, he could feel it more certainly. The winds were moving with purpose, yet the restless clouds they carried were not heavy with the rain the land craved, but thin and starved. There was a friction in the air, a prickly sensation that made his fur feel itchy.

Fire weather. Every treecat knew of it. It didn't happen every season's turning, nor every hand of turnings, but once felt it was not to be forgotten. When Climbs Quickly had been half his current age, such fire weather had come. Bolts of blue and white light had forked from the skies, too often striking trees like this very golden-leaf, trees that might seem to flourish but which felt brittle beneath the claws from lack of moisture.

His ears caught a swoosh of faint noise far closer than the uneasy crackle of the building storms. Hunkering close to the branch he had chosen for his perch, Climbs

Quickly caught the shadow of a death-wing passing over him, two sets of claws spread to grasp at the exposed treecat, downy wings spread wide so that it might glide without making any more sound than absolutely necessary.

But Climbs Quickly was no adventurous kitten and he had chosen this watch stand well. A branch protected him from above, while not interfering too greatly with the wind currents he had sought to read. Even so, death-wings were too dangerous to taunt. He had confirmed what he had already suspected—his current uneasiness had only a little to do with Death Fang's Bane and her rioting emotions, but was tied into something far more primal. He scampered down to safer levels, considering what he had learned.

The changing from summer into autumn always brought storms, as cooler air argued with warmer. However, this season those storms would not bring much moisture. Instead, they would bring destruction. Destruction the elders always told them was needed for the forests to be healthy, but destruction nonetheless.

Memories of fleeing masses of the People racing ahead of the hungry tongues of flame, of the mind-screams of those who could not run fast enough, of mothers who would not leave their kittens, these and more flooded into Climbs Quickly and made his heart beat fast.

Fire weather was coming and with it blazes that would make the one from which they had rescued Right-Striped and Left-Striped seem little more than the contained blaze the two-legs lit to warm their dens in winter.

Fire weather.

He ran back to where Death Fang's Bane slept, wishing it were possible to run from knowledge as simply as one fled a death-wing.

✧　　✧　　✧

Anders hadn't meant to eavesdrop. He'd been in the bathroom hanging his robe on the hook behind the door when his father and Dr. Nez had come into the suite.

The two men were in the middle of a conversation that was one step away from being an argument. If either had even glanced at the bathroom door, they would have seen it was ajar and therefore assumed the bathroom wasn't in use, that the suite was obviously empty.

If they had come in a few minutes before or a few minutes after, the suite *would* have been empty. That morning, Anders had not elected to go with the team to another of their interminable meetings. Instead, Anders had—with his dad's enthusiastic encouragement—taken up an invitation from Stephanie to go with her and Karl on a hike. Jessica Pherris and Toby Mednick had joined them.

Jessica clearly liked the outdoors and seemed quite interested in the local plants. Toby's reasons for joining them were a little more complex. After watching the dynamics, Anders was pretty sure Toby had a crush on Stephanie—or if not a proper crush, at least a major case of hero worship. The way he'd hovered near her, asking questions about everything from the ecology of the Copperwall Mountains to the handgun she wore in a businesslike holster, gave him away.

Amusingly, Stephanie seemed completely unaware of how Toby felt. For someone who could be so sophisticated when talking to adults, she was amazingly naive in other areas.

It had been a good day. Anders had come back to shower and change. He was then going to grab his reader, head down to the dining room, and, over a heavy snack, download some files Stephanie had sent him on the local ecology. One of these was an SFS ranger guide that wasn't usually circulated. Another was an unpublished manuscript of her mother's.

Stephanie had gotten permission to loan him both, she assured Anders, "But it might be better if you don't pass them on to any of your dad's staff without checking first."

Now he stood behind the bathroom door, wishing that the first words out of Dr. Nez's mouth hadn't made it pretty much impossible for him to step out and let them know he was there.

"I wouldn't say this in front of the rest of the team," Dr. Nez said, "but I feel I must say to you that I don't approve of your plans, not in the least. You're violating the trust that both the SFS and Dr. Hobbard have invested in us—and for what reason? So we can see a site a few weeks earlier than we might otherwise."

Dr. Whittaker put on his "more in sorrow than anger" expression, one Anders knew all too well. His dad never yelled at anyone if he thought he could make them feel guilty instead. Dr. Nez had to know that, too, since he'd been Dad's grad assistant for years before he got his own degree.

"Langston," Dr. Whittaker said gently. "I don't see this as a violation of trust. You heard me ask Dr. Hobbard today whether we were free to take a look at public lands, as long as we didn't bother treecat colonies. She said that was fine."

"You implied," Dr. Nez said implacably, "that we wanted a chance to examine a picketwood grove or two, so we would have baseline data about how they develop without the influence—or contaminating factor—of treecat dwellings. You didn't say anything about planning to go to that abandoned nesting site."

"True," Dr. Whittaker smiled. "Sometimes it is easier to ask forgiveness than permission. You've heard the arguments at some of these meetings. For a while there, I thought we were going to be blocked even from reviewing the tapes made by the SFS of the recovering and relocated treecats. That Jordan Franchitti is pretty canny. His argument that the actions and reactions of a 'captive population' might bias our interpretations of a wild population was very convincing."

"You have a point," Dr. Nez said reluctantly. "Still, I'd be happier if we weren't being so 'creative' in our interpretation of Dr. Hobbard's permissions."

"Langston," Dr. Whittaker said, "I would agree but for one very important consideration. Every day we wait, the physical artifacts on that site are deteriorating. I want to get pictures before they do. I'd remove items if I didn't think that *would* create trouble. However, fresh images, temperature and moisture readings, as well as investigations of fecal materials before they fully deteriorate, are all things that must be done sooner, rather than later."

Anders couldn't see Dr. Nez's expression, but he must have looked at least somewhat persuaded, because Dad's voice warmed.

"I see you understand. Moreover, although the data are scarce—humans haven't known about treecats very long and so haven't had enough cycles of the longer Sphinxian year to confirm initial impressions—there are indications that treecats do most of their migration in the summer and early autumn."

"Because," Dr. Nez added as if thinking aloud, "those are the times when there are surplus resources. Winter travel is further complicated by snow. Spring—especially early spring—is a lean time. What you're saying is that if we don't look at this site, we might not locate another so fresh for an entire Sphinxian year. Couldn't we bring that up to Dr. Hobbard and have her ask the SFS for permission? Surely they'd see our desire is only reasonable."

"Dr. Hobbard would," Dad said. "She's an anthropologist. I'm not so certain about the SFS. They're overly protective of the treecats—even if our confirming the species' obvious intelligence is the best protection the 'cats could have. The Forestry Service is also over-reacting to this 'fire season.' I can't believe how much of their staff is simply sitting around waiting for a fire. I actually resent it when I think about how pre-Bolgeo researchers were given such accommodation—even though they hadn't been hand-picked as our team has been."

"You can't really blame the Forestry Service for their priorities," Dr. Nez protested. "They get their funding from the human citizens. They need to show they're doing something for human interests—not just for the native ecology."

"An ecology," Dad countered, "that many of the locals would just as soon do without. I've had a couple of very good chats with Marjorie Harrington when I've dropped Anders by the Harrington place. She admits to having no trouble getting funding because everyone wants her to develop hybrids that will enable humans to have all the comforts of home here on a colony planet."

"Humans are funny that way," Dr. Nez agreed. "Over and over again, they go to new planets, then try to make them just like the places they left behind."

Dr. Whittaker nodded. "Now, Langston, if you're uncomfortable with my plans, I'll offer you an 'out.' I don't plan for this to be a long jaunt. If you or any other member of the team feel uncomfortable with my intentions, then you can stay behind. You, especially, won't have any problems justifying that. Xenobiology and exotic botany are not your specializations."

Anders knew none of the other team members would refuse to go. Both Kesia Guyen and Virgil Iwamoto required Dr. Whittaker's approval before they could take that final step forward to the grand day when they could put Ph.D. after their names. Dr. Emberly *was* an xenobiologist and would not miss this opportunity.

Dr. Nez knew this too. There was a note of resignation in his voice when he next spoke.

"I'll consider your offer, Bradford," he said, "but I think I'll come along. I'm no less eager than you to see a newly abandoned treecat settlement. I simply wish we could go about it more directly."

"So do I," said Dad, "but when it's a matter of etiquette or science, science must always come first."

And where it's a matter of making sure you don't go overboard in your enthusiasm for science, Anders thought, *I guess I'm the only one who doesn't have his career to worry about, so I'd better make sure I go along, too.*

✧   ✧   ✧

Stephanie's wild excitement over getting her provisional license (rather than the dreaded learner's permit) was somewhat dampened when it became clear that Mom and Dad planned to let matters go on much as before. The Harringtons owned three vehicles. One was Dad's Vet Van—equipped not only with a portable lab, but with what amounted to a complete surgery. Mom had recently traded in her sedan for another tailored van, this one equipped with racks to hold plants of various sizes and shapes. Stephanie had hoped the family air car would be hers to use.

Stephanie had, in moments of fantasy, even imagined that her birthday gift would include an air car of her very own. She'd known that was unlikely, but both Chet and Trudy had cars of their own, and they didn't even live as far away from Twin Forks as the Harringtons did. She'd felt a slight letdown when, a few days after she had passed the air-car license test, no car materialized.

A couple days after she got her license, Dad had said at breakfast, "I'm actually available to coach at hang-glider practice today. I don't think you have Forestry Service duty, either. So, if I don't have any emergency calls, we should have a nice relaxed time."

"I don't have ranger duty," Stephanie replied, "but SFS is really stretched thin with fire-watch. I was thinking if I could get out to the ranger station, I could free someone up. Maybe I should take the car and fly over after practice?"

Richard Harrington flashed a quick grin that told Stephanie without words that he saw through her ruse.

"I don't think so. You tend to get carried away when you get involved with your SFS work. Remember, legally, your license is only good when conditions are visually safe: dawn to dusk, and no bad weather."

Stephanie knew better than to try to get around Dad when he had that look. Better to wait and see what other approaches she could come up with.

Dynamics within the hang-gliding club had changed in the couple of days since Stephanie's birthday party. Trudy had been heard to say quite loudly—obviously not caring that Dad was close enough to hear—that the only reason she'd gone to that boring party was that her folks hadn't wanted to offend the doctors Harrington.

"They're so necessary, you know," she drawled to Becky Morowitz. "I mean, vets and botanists.... We must be polite."

Stephanie had felt Lionheart pressing against her leg, offering support if needed, but she was surprised at how little Trudy's comments bothered her.

Anders told us when he went hiking the other day that he had thought Trudy was a complete zip. I knew he wasn't dumb enough to get blinded by her physical charms. I wish he hang glided...I bet he'd look like an angel against the sky.

Another change was that Jessica Pheriss was definitely "out" of the Trudy circle. She came in for more than a few catty comments, mostly about her clothes. Stephanie had never noticed before, but Jessica did seem to have a more limited wardrobe than the rest of them.

I guess if I even noticed, I thought she didn't choose to vary what she wore for hang gliding—and most of the time, I've seen her in her flight coveralls anyhow.

To say Jessica was indifferent to the teasing would have been wrong. Her cheeks burned when Frank Câmara made a particularly nasty comment about how Jessica had to wash her panties each night or go without—and implying that he had first-hand knowledge to confirm.

However, Jessica ignored the comments and went on chatting with Christine and Chet—who were, now that Stephanie bothered to notice, definitely on the way to being a "couple"—as if someone else was being grilled.

I wonder, Stephanie thought as she adjusted her counter-grav and spread her wings to take advantage of a rising air-current, *who the zip really is—all the rest of them or me for being so deliberately blind?*

"Bleek," said Lionheart softly from his new harness, but whether his comment was in reaction to her thoughtful mood or in anticipation of the coming flight, Stephanie couldn't know. The warmth that came through their link made her pretty sure she was being teased.

Later on, Richard Harrington came trotting across the field to where Stephanie and the other members of the Blue Team were discussing their strategies for the obstacle course relay race that would end the day.

"Steph, I just got a call. The Lins' herd is showing signs of something nasty. I can't wait. I hate to pull you from practice, but Mayor Sapristos says he has a meeting this evening, and your mother is hours away working on planting a field of that new range-barley hybrid she's been working on."

Stephanie knew her dad already had the Vet Van

with him—he never went much of anywhere without it, which was why she'd thought her using the family air car wasn't unreasonable. However, this was not the time to try and score points.

Dad was really worried. The Lins' herd was crucial to the future of Sphinx's dairy industry. On such a heavily forested planet, grazers didn't flourish—there simply wasn't enough open land. The Lins' capri-cows were a new strain of browsers, based largely on goats, but with genes that enabled them to give creamy milk that didn't pick up the flavors of the strong-tasting leaves of the native plants.

Immediately, Stephanie started shrugging out of her glider, but before she could get more than a few straps undone, Jessica Pheriss cut in.

"Dr. Harrington," Jessica said very politely, "I have my folks' car. I'm supposed to do some grocery shopping after practice, but if you don't mind my doing that, then dropping the stuff off, I could take Stephanie back."

"Your parents won't mind?" Richard said.

"I'll call," Jessica said, taking out a uni-link that Stephanie—with her new insights into Jessica's probable economic level—realized was an older, refurbished model. "Right away."

In less time than it would have taken Stephanie to stow her glider, Jessica had confirmed that it was fine if she took Stephanie home—as long as she dropped off the groceries first. Richard Harrington thanked her and, after giving Stephanie an abstracted kiss on the forehead, hurried off to do his best for the Lins' capri-cows.

The Blue Team lost the relay race by a few points. However, Stephanie didn't feel too bad about it. Trudy and Stan had pulled a few moves that were definitely outside of the rule book. To Stephanie, at least, that made their victory pretty hollow. From the look on Mayor Sapristos' face as he did his post-game analysis, he agreed, but didn't feel he had enough evidence to register a complaint.

"I'm parked over there," Jessica said when they'd finished going over the game with their teammates. She indicated a strip off to one side, partially sheltered by some particularly thick spike-thorn bushes.

When they reached the vehicle, Stephanie guessed that Jessica had chosen the parking space deliberately, so as not to draw attention to the air car. It wasn't a wreck. In fact, when Jessica started it up, the engine caught smoothly. But even an effort at a plaid pattern couldn't disguise that the seats were patched with fabric-tape. And nothing would ever hide that it was definitely an older model.

Jessica fitted their two hang gliders into the trunk with an ease that spoke of lots of similar experience.

"We'll stow the groceries in the backseat," she said. There was a forced casualness to her words that told Stephanie she was embarrassed.

"You're lucky to be allowed to fly the family car," Stephanie said as she got in on the passenger side. "I know I only got my provisional license a couple of days ago, but nothing's changed at home."

Jessica brought them around smoothly. Stephanie had always figured they were close in age, but now she wondered if Jessica was actually a bit older.

"You're a really good pilot," she said. "I mean, you fly like you've been doing this for years."

Jessica laughed, but there was something painful underneath the sound. "I have been. Trebuchet, the last system we lived in, had a much lower age requirement. My folks both work and I had to do a lot of the routine piloting, like today. Then my mom got me a job where she was working. Trebuchet is known for a remarkable number of plants with proven medicinal properties. However, some of them have to be harvested by hand. They're just too fragile for anything else. I went to some really out-of-the way places on that job."

"By yourself?" Stephanie asked.

"Oh, no!" Jessica laughed. "I took a couple of my younger brothers and sisters. They could help with the picking, but they weren't old enough to pilot."

She sighed as she brought them down by a big warehouse Stephanie had seen but never been in. It didn't look in the least like a grocery store. When they went inside, she realized it wasn't. Instead, it was a storehouse for damaged goods. Jessica's mother had apparently already done most of the purchasing over the net, but Jessica negotiated for a couple of boxes of ice-potatoes that were going brown around the edges.

Stephanie frowned to herself as she helped load the groceries into the car. She'd seen her mother throw out vegetables in a lot better condition than these, but then the Harringtons did have extensive greenhouses. Maybe she was a bit spoiled by all that bounty.

"Mom's going to be thrilled with these," Jessica said as she loaded the boxes of ice-potatoes. "We've planted near-lettuce. The house we're renting has a good stand of near-pine with the nuts coming on, but we haven't been here long enough to get anything like ice-potatoes in."

Stephanie tried to think of something to say, but she simply was too honest to rejoice in partially-rotted vegetables. As she got into the air car, she finally found what she hoped was a safe comment.

"How will you cook them?"

"Mashed," Jessica said, as she set the car to rise and entered in navigation coordinates. "We'll cut out the bad parts first, of course. Mom uses almond oil instead of butter to bring out the natural nutty taste of the ice-potatoes themselves."

"We use sesame oil for the same reason," Stephanie said. She wanted to be a good guest—after all, Jessica was doing her a favor—but she really didn't know what was polite to say. "Were you born in the Trebuchet system?"

Jessica shook her head, sending ripples through her masses of curly light-auburn hair. "No, in the van Mook system. But we didn't stay there long. We moved to the Sankar, Tasmania, and Madeleine systems. And we moved a lot on the planets, too. My dad..."

She paused, then sighed. "You might as well hear it from me. Trudy's sure to bring it up one way or another. My dad is what might be politely called a drifter. He's not a bad man. He doesn't get drunk or stoned or anything— at least not more than most people. But he's a dreamer. There's always something better over the next hill, on the next planet, in the next system."

"And your mom?" Stephanie asked.

"She's... Well, I think at first she wasn't much different from dad except that she was interested in different things in these new places. She really loves plants—animals, too, but plants are her thing. She always hates leaving her gardens, but she comforts herself with the idea that she's leaving something beautiful behind her. And, then, she's also lured by the idea of what new thing she'll find."

"I should have known that," Stephanie said, "from the way she chooses to cook ice-potatoes. Lots of recipes are for how to make them taste more like Terran spuds. She appreciates the difference. But you said 'at first.' What changed?"

"Us," Jessica said. "Me and my siblings. I'm the oldest of seven."

"Wow..." Stephanie said. "I think that's even bigger than Karl's family. And your family keeps moving at that size? I'd think liner fees would be prohibitive."

"They are," Jessica agreed, "but Dad's learned a lot as a

drifter. He's a real jack-of-all-trades and often gets a job aboard—nothing involving engines or anything, but as a steward or porter. Mom is always in demand on liners because she's a wizard with hydroponics. I even had a job on our last trip, assistant in the kiddie entertainment lounge. I think I'm going to swear off kids..."

She laughed when she said this, but Stephanie didn't doubt there was a grain of truth in the words. She remembered the entertainment lounges on the liner her family had taken from Meyerdahl to Sphinx. The relentless cheerfulness had driven her to their family's cabin where at least she could read in peace. The adult lounges had almost been worse. No one seemed to value quiet or conversation.

Jessica went on. "When Mom heard about the incentives for settlers who would come to Sphinx, she talked my dad into coming here. We're zero-balancers, so we don't own any land or anything. In fact, the house we're renting is owned by the Franchittis. That's how I met Trudy. She was really nice at first, even loaned me a hang-gliding rig she wasn't using when she learned I knew how to glide. But lately...I don't like Stan. I think he's a bad influence, not just on Trudy, but on the planet. I don't like even breathing the same air as him."

Stephanie nodded. "Stan's come to practice high more than once. I don't know why Mayor Sapristos doesn't call him on it."

"Because," Jessica said with a cynicism that told Stephanie volumes about her life, "Stan is connected. Not only is his family friends with the Franchittis, but they have connections back on Manticore. If my dad smokes a little too much wonder weed and is late to work, then he gets his pay docked, but if Stan takes something a whole lot stronger, he's going to have to crash his glider before Mayor Sapristos does anything. Part of being mayor is knowing how people expect to be treated."

Stephanie wanted to disagree. After all, she liked Mayor Sapristos and he was one of her dad's closer friends. But she couldn't. In the four T-years she'd been living on Sphinx, she'd learned a lot about the social and political hierarchy. It would be nice if a relatively newly opened colony world was egalitarian, but so far as she could tell the truth was that such environments attracted the ambitious, and the ambitious often wanted recognition and power as much or more than they wanted new lands or a chance to discover.

"There's my house," Jessica said, pointing and bringing the air car in for a smooth landing. "And my mom coming out to meet us with some of the kids."

Ms. Pherris proved to be a very nice lady. She invited Stephanie and Lionheart in for a tumbler of a sweet-tart punch made with the flowers of a plant related to spike thorn. Stephanie loved it, but Lionheart clearly would have preferred something else.

"I checked, and both flowers and fruit were listed as edible," Ms. Pheriss said, "but too sour to be really enjoyable. Well, that sort of thing is a challenge to me and we have hedges of the stuff on the property."

On the way home, Stephanie tapped out a quick message to her mom and dad, asking if Jessica could stay for dinner.

"She has a full license, so she'll have no problem getting home."

The reply was almost instantaneous. "Definitely!"

Dad didn't make it back for dinner. The situation with the Lins' capri-cows was still critical, so he was planning to camp out in the Vet Van while waiting to learn whether the medications he had given had worked.

Over dinner, Stephanie encouraged Jessica to talk about her mother's interest in plants. As Stephanie had hoped, Marjorie Harrington, who had frequently bemoaned the fact that she had trouble getting assistants who were not either overqualified (and thus tried to run the show for her) or underqualified (and so ruined delicate experiments) was immediately interested.

"You say she's working, though," Mom said.

Jessica nodded. "In child care. The advantage is she doesn't need to pay to leave the little ones anywhere. The job lets her keep them with her. That's useful, since Nathan is still nursing."

Mom looked thoughtful, and by the time Jessica had to leave—"I usually try to be home to help wash up the kids and stuff some of them to bed"—a plan was clearly in the works.

After seeing Jessica off, Stephanie went into the kitchen to help clean up.

"Thanks for letting Jessica come at such short notice, Mom."

Marjorie hugged her. "I'm proud of you for taking initiative."

Stephanie grinned. "I guess not all the kids here are total losses. Jessica is interesting. I bet she'd be almost up to my study levels if her family hadn't had to move so much."

Quickly, hoping she wasn't betraying a confidence, Stephanie shared what Jessica had told her about her father and the Pheriss family's many moves.

"Mom," she concluded, "even if things don't work out when you interview Ms. Pheriss, I was wondering. Jessica was really glad today to buy some ice potatoes you would have tossed on the compost. Could we, I mean, when you cull the greenhouse, could I take some of the stuff over to the Pheriss house?"

Marjorie Harrington nodded, but her expression was serious.

"Charity is a difficult matter, Steph. Sometimes it

backfires—like my trying to be nice to that horrible Trudy."

Stephanie nodded. "I understand. We might hurt the Pheriss' feelings. Still, sometimes good comes out of even that sort of thing. I mean, if Trudy hadn't come to the party and been such a know-it-all, I might not have found out that Jessica had a mind of her own. Even if she'd been friendly at the party, I would have thought it was just because she was a guest, but when she spoke out that way..."

"Good point. We won't know unless we try, but let's be cautious about how we go about it. It will be easy enough if Ms. Pherris works out as an assistant. I can just tell her to help herself—that there's too much for three humans and one treecat."

"Bleek!" protested Lionheart, although his comment could have been because Stephanie was pulling a casserole dish away before he'd completely scoured the cheese and meat sauce off the ceramic.

"Well, then," Stephanie said. "I'll just have to hope Ms. Pheriss is qualified."

Snuggled under the covers that night, listening to the night noises through the open window, Stephanie watched Lionheart scamper out. She hoped he wasn't too lonely for other treecats. Now that she was making human friends, it seemed even more important that her best friend not be deprived of similar companionship.

"You okay, Lionheart?" she called after him.

"Bleek," he assured her, his warmth and affection flowing back to her stronger than any sound. "Bleek. Bleek. Bleek."

She had to hope those sounds meant, "Yes. Absolutely and unquestionably, yes." not, "I'm miserably lonely, but I'll stick by you."

WHEN GETTING READY FOR THE EXPEDITION TO THE abandoned treecat site, Anders made certain to pack his reader as well as several changes of socks. He had gone on some of his dad's field trips before and usually he was allowed to help, but none of those trips had ever been as important as this one. For all he knew, his assisting might be considered a contamination of data or something.

But maybe not, he thought. *Dacey Emberly is coming along, but then she's on the books as an official scientific illustrator. Poor Peony Rose . . . I know she was counting on helping Virgil on this project, but her morning sickness is pretty bad.*

He grinned, remembering the look of astonishment and delight that had lit Virgil Iwamoto's bearded features when he'd announced to the team over dinner just a few nights ago that his wife's recent bouts of illness were not some form of flu, as everyone had expected, but were because she was pregnant.

"Peony Rose didn't renew her implant after we were married," Virgil had explained shyly, "because we planned on starting a family. The med-tech told her that it would probably take months before her cycles re-established, especially with the stress of travel, but it seems her body had other ideas."

Congratulations had gone around, but later Anders had heard his father grumbling that Peony Rose really could have chosen a better time, since he'd planned to make her a crew chief. Now, if they got permission to excavate a site, he'd probably need to hire someone local. Virgil couldn't be expected to handle the lithics analysis—so crucial at this early stage when stone tools would be one of the most important means of judging the complexity of treecat culture—and also coordinate the laborers Dr. Whittaker hoped to hire.

Dad's thinking weeks ahead, of course, Anders thought, *but that's like him. This project means more to him than anything.*

John Qin, Kesia Guyen's husband, hadn't been coming on these jaunts. His interest in treecats was mostly because *she* was interested. His passion was interstellar trade. He'd been taking meeting after meeting since their arrival, trying both to get an idea of what the colonists of Sphinx needed and what the Star Kingdom would allow to be imported.

So it was a group of seven who got into the air van early that morning: Dr. Whittaker, Dr. Nez, Dr. Emberly, Dacey Emberly, Kesia Guyen, and Virgil Iwamoto. Since the ostensible reason for the trip was to visit a variety of picketwood groves north of Twin Forks, they had loaded up with ladders, slings, and other gear related to arboreal investigation.

Counter-grav units were great for getting up and down, but none of the crew was particularly skilled in doing work while floating in mid-air. Besides, such activities did put a drain on the power sources. While those could be charged from the air-van, the broadcast power didn't reach if one went out of range.

In addition to this gear, they'd packed a lot more field gear—including a selection of envelopes and boxes into which smaller samples could be put. This told Anders that, even if Dr. Whittaker said that most of their work would be in the nature of a photographic survey, he wasn't about to risk losing some choice artifact.

So what happens if the site isn't really abandoned? Anders thought. *What if what the treecats have done is more like moving to winter quarters after summering somewhere else? When Mom and Dad close our cabin in the mountains for the winter, we leave all sorts of stuff behind. If someone took that, we'd figure they were stealing. Why shouldn't the treecats feel the same?*

Anders wanted to ask his dad about this ethical fine point, but he knew that Dr. Whittaker would simply brush it off by denying that he intended to take anything, so why did it matter? Dad knew perfectly well that once they were in the field, Anders wouldn't embarrass him in front of his crew. Not embarrassing either of his parents—especially his mother, who, as a politician, lived in the public eye—was something Anders had been trained in since he started to walk and talk.

I'll ask Dr. Nez, Anders thought. *He likes questions like that. I guess that's why he's a cultural anthropologist, rather than an ethno-archeologist like Dad.*

Dr. Whittaker chose to fly them himself. He departed in the direction of the first stand of picketwood they were scheduled to investigate, then, when they were far from any of the settlements, he dipped down below the tree line, punched up the map program, and entered the coordinates for the abandoned treecat settlement which Ranger Jedrusinski had shown them.

This looped them around back south, all the way to the south side of the Makara River, hundreds of kilometers from their assigned locations.

Even with the need to navigate around the trees, they made good time. As in many first-growth forests, the under story was relatively clear. Fire activity cleared away the snags, dead grasses, leaves, shrubs, and other low-level detritus, scarring the trunks of the more massive trees, but often stimulating growth. More flammable trees— like the near-pines from which Stephanie and Karl had rescued Right-Striped and Left-Striped—actually needed fire activity to clear away weaker trees and break the hulls on their seeds.

Still, Anders thought, looking up at the sky when the air-van passed through a small clearing, *I'm glad to see it's a nice day, not a trace of storm clouds in the sky.*

Dr. Whittaker took them up a little higher when they arrived near the site so they could make certain no one else was around, but he was careful to stay below the elevation of some nearby crown oaks. These provided them with sufficient cover to survey the picketwood grove and its surroundings, since picketwood averaged between thirty-five and forty-five meters in height, while crown oak regularly reached eighty meters.

"There's a nice landing spot over there," Dr. Whittaker said. "Level and still relatively green, but far enough from the picketwood that our landing won't hurt valuable artifacts."

Dr. Calida Emberly had pulled out a pair of binoculars and was surveying the area. "I don't see any signs of use," she began. "Maybe we should take a closer look before landing."

Dr. Whittaker shrugged. "Let's not look a gift horse in the mouth. You know, the Forestry Service's fanatical interest in fire watch and control has gotten me thinking.

How do treecats deal with forest fire? They certainly haven't survived by waiting for Stephanie Harrington to come rescue them from burning trees."

He laughed at his joke, politely echoed by Guyen and Iwamoto.

"Seriously," Dad continued. "I think one of the ways we can judge whether or not treecats are intelligent would be to look for evidence of fire control features near their dwelling areas; cleared areas like this one could be just such evidence."

On that triumphant note, he brought the air van down. The surface underfoot was thick with a springy vegetation. Dr. Emberly bent to clip a sample.

"It reminds me of wild portulaca," she said. "I wonder if this also has a mat structure?"

Despite her silver-gray hair, her excitement made her seem girlish. Anders remembered how many new discoveries awaited science on Sphinx. Marjorie Harrington had mentioned that probably fewer than fifty percent of the plants had been typed: "And most of those we have identified fall into broad categories," she'd said. "It will be decades, maybe centuries before we recognize sub-species and the environmental cues they evolved in response to."

"Is that really important?" Anders had asked, not to challenge, but because he'd never really thought about plants.

"Absolutely!" Dr. Marjorie had responded. "We can learn about the life-cycle of the planet that way, anticipate, perhaps, seasonal variations and prepare for them. It's all too usual for new arrivals to a planet to assume that what they see when they first arrive is 'normal,' but it's just as likely that landfall might have been made during a time of drought or flooding. Plants can tell us far more."

She'd had a lot more to say, but most of it had gone right over Anders' head. What he had come away from that talk with was a realization that—despite mobile humanity's tendency to give preference to creatures that move—the vegetative world was a whole lot more than backdrop.

Dr. Emberly was tugging at the edge of one of her "portulacas."

"Look, Anders. They do form a mat, a pretty thick one. I wouldn't be surprised to discover that these 'plants' are actually one plant. In a heavily forested environment like this one, there would be a real survival advantage to being able to stretch."

"Like picketwood," Anders said, "only this does it sideways more than up and down."

"Interesting comparison," Dr. Emberly said, taking a note. "I must check if Dr. Harrington has written anything about that."

Bradford Whittaker's voice bellowed across the open area. "Dr. Emberly! I've located some bones. I'd like your opinion regarding their source."

Dr. Emberly, who, after all, was a xenozoologist as well as a xenobotanist, hurried to go look.

Dr. Nez called to Anders. "I'm going to walk around the immediate area. Want to join me?"

Anders hurried over, happy to be needed. "What are we looking for?"

Langston Nez made a sweeping gesture with one arm. "I want to see if we can work out just how much of this grove the treecats were actively using. Your father's thought about fire-control features is an interesting one. If the treecats are intelligent—as most of us think they are—then they should have done something."

"What can they do?" Anders asked. "They don't have machines to pump water or anything. They certainly can't fly in trained crews or dump hundreds of gallons of water mixed with fire suppressant chemicals."

"I can tell you've been listening to the SFS rangers," Dr. Nez said with a chuckle.

"Well, fire control is their favorite topic these days," Anders said. "I heard that Chief Ranger Shelton was preparing an educational broadcast about the costs of fighting even a smallish fire like the Franchitti fire. He's hoping that those who can't be convinced to value the wild lands for themselves will think of fire control as a way to prevent a tax increase."

"It's a good approach," Dr. Nez said. "As an anthropologist, I have to agree that more people are motivated by self-interest than by altruism."

Thinking of his dad, Anders silently agreed.

They spent the next couple of hours working on their range estimate. As they did so, they listened to the chatter on their private uni-link channel. The bones Dr. Whittaker had found proved to be fish bones, lots of them. Anders knew that his dad—despite his claims to the contrary—would be taking samples. Well, hopefully the treecats didn't think fish bones were sacred or something.

Virgil Iwamoto had found a couple of areas where lithics scatter indicated the treecats had been in the habit of making their stone tools. These "workshops" had him almost unreasonably excited.

"It proves the treecats didn't just whack off a chunk of stone as needed for a job. These areas indicate that they probably had specialists, perhaps older 'cats, past their best hunting days, who continued to contribute to the community in this fashion."

"And if they have one type of specialist," Dr. Nez added, "they might have others. Weavers, perhaps? We know they make nets. I wonder if we can find evidence of a weaving 'shop.'"

"I saw some lace willow near where we left the van," Dr. Emberly supplied. "We should check to see if there's evidence of a workshop near there. Of course, they could have chosen to move their materials elsewhere."

"Still," Dr. Nez replied, "it's a logical place to check. Thanks for the information. Anders and I will go take a look."

He reset his uni-link to "listen" mode and frowned. "Lace willow. Why does that bother me? Well, let's go and take a look."

Anders had been reading about local plants in the SFS guide Stephanie had given him out of self-defense, after he'd gone hiking with Stephanie, Karl, Jessica, and Toby, and had learned that even Jessica—who was relatively new to the planet—knew more than he did about common plant types.

"Lace willow lives mostly near waterways or marshy areas," Anders recited. "It is relatively low-growing and bushy—at least for Sphinx, where really huge seems to be the size of most plants. It's interesting because its leaves are pierced as an insect-trapping mechanism."

Dr. Nez started trotting.

"Waterways and marshy areas," he repeated. "Open green spaces on a planet that has been experiencing drought. Fish bones..."

He started running. Anders, catching his urgency even before he figured out the reason why, pounded alongside him. They were closer than the rest of the team to where the air van had been parked, which was doubtless why Dr. Nez didn't immediately call for assistance. The other reason, Anders intuitively knew, was Dr. Whittaker himself. Dr. Whittaker was in the midst of grand discoveries and would not want to be interrupted for anything other than a full-blown emergency.

They reached the bouncy area covered with what Dr. Emberly had informally dubbed "mat-portulaca." Was it Anders' imagination, or did his feet sink just a little as he ran?

Arriving at the van, they saw disaster in progress. The

air van had sunk into the ground. Already the lower portions of the doors were covered. Anders could see the ooze moving up even as he watched.

"He parked on a bog," Dr. Nez said, his tone as fierce as any profanity. "On a *bog!*"

He activated his uni-link. "We've got a problem here. The van is sinking, seems we accidentally parked on wetlands. Dr. Whittaker, I think you'd better call for help."

There was a longer pause than absolutely necessary, then Dr. Whittaker's voice came back. "Sinking? How deep is it?"

Anders could imagine the course of his father's thoughts. Did they need to call for help? Maybe they could get the van out themselves. If they called for help, then the Forestry Service and Dr. Hobbard would know they'd been bending the rules.

"The bottoms of the doors are covered," Dr. Nez shot back. "That means all the heavier parts are already under. I know we brought rope, but it's a lot to expect seven people to pull out a vehicle."

"Get inside and see if the engine will still run," Dr. Whittaker snapped. "We'll be there in a few minutes."

Dr. Nez rolled his eyes. "It's worth my job if I make the call, Anders, but if you do..."

He trailed off, not asking, and began picking his way over the ground nearer to the van.

Anders watched Dr. Nez's progress while he activated his uni-link, trying to think of a solution that wouldn't be directly disobedient to his father, yet would get them help. He agreed with Dr. Nez. There was no way seven people—one of them an old lady—were going to pull the van out of the bog.

Stephanie! he thought. *I'll call Stephanie, tell her what's going on, and she'll call the SFS. Even if they get here too late to save the van, we're going to need a ride out.*

Keeping an eye on Dr. Nez, who was using a branch as a makeshift crowbar in an attempt to force the van's door, Anders requested the uni-link connect him with Stephanie Harrington.

"Cannot connect at this time," the device replied. "Unable to sync with planetary net."

"Huh?" Anders tried again, this time hand-keying in the information. The response was the same. He spoke into the device again. "Get me SFS headquarters."

"Cannot connect at this time," came the reply. "Unable to sync with planetary net."

The chatter of excited voices told Anders that others were coming. Glancing over, he saw Virgil Iwamoto and his dad in the lead. Kesia Guyen and Dr. Emberly weren't far behind. Dacey Emberly, a sketch pad still held in one hand, was looking anxiously after.

Dr. Whittaker thundered up. "Did you get the door open?"

"Electronic lock is jammed," Dr. Nez said, his voice tight with effort. "I think the sensor is blocked. The override is on the inside."

He didn't ask if Dr. Whittaker had called for help. Anders wondered how much he had overheard of Anders' attempts to use the uni-link.

Dr. Whittaker assessed the situation. "You're not going to manage to pry it open," he said. "Anders, run fast and grab a stone or something else hard. Maybe we can break a window."

Virgil said, "I have a rock hammer with me."

Anders dropped back a few paces to give the others room. Dr. Emberly had her uni-link out. Clearly, she'd assessed the situation for herself and didn't fear Dr. Whittaker's wrath. Anders felt relieved—until he saw a puzzled expression spread over her hawk-nosed countenance and her fingers move to input a command.

"Not working?" he asked softly. "Mine wouldn't either. It's strange. These should be fine. Dad ordered new models for the whole expedition."

Behind them, there was a sound of breaking crystoplast.

"Got it!" Virgil crowed.

Anders looked. Virgil had bashed a hole through one of the large front windows and was now enlarging the opening with his hammer.

"Bradford!" Dr. Emberly called, her lack of formality a sign of her urgency—while working, Dr. Whittaker always insisted on titles. "My uni-link isn't working."

"Mine either," said Kesia Guyen, her tone slightly embarrassed, as if hoping she wasn't going to get yelled at for violating the tacit communication ban.

Dr. Whittaker frowned. "We'll use the com unit in the van. Are you through yet, Virgil?"

Iwamoto pulled back. "I've got a good-sized hole."

"Fine. Let me through. I'll call for aid. I'm sure..."

What Dad was sure of, he didn't say, but Anders would have bet the entirety of the tuition fund his grandparents had set up for him that it had something to do with what his mom called "spin control"—putting the best slant on a bad situation.

Dr. Whittaker was not a small man. When he set his bulk on the front of the van, what they all should have expected happened. The front of the van tilted forward, the nose of the craft vanishing beneath the wet ground within moments, the hole in the front window sliding under almost before Dr. Whittaker could pull himself free.

"Marshes," Dr. Emberly said, her tone acid, "often contain air pockets as well as damp soil and water. I'm guessing that when a great deal of weight was suddenly added, the nose encountered one of those. Take care..."

The van had stopped sliding forward as soon as Dr.

Whittaker jumped back and now resumed its slower sinking, nose down. Com unit down. There would be no calling for help that way.

"Virgil, give me the hammer," Dr. Nez said. "We've got to smash one of the rear windows and pull out some of the luggage and food. It may take a while for rescue to reach us."

Virgil nodded, but he didn't release his tool. Instead, he bashed at the rear window with all of his strength. The words that slipped from his lips revealed the reason for the violence of his attack on the innocent piece of crystoplast.

"Peony Rose is going to worry," he said, in a staccato cadence. "Has everyone tried their uni-links?"

Everyone had, even old Dacey Emberly, who had remained back by the picketwood. The failure of the uni-links was a mystery to be delved into later. Right now, they had to get out as many supplies as possible.

Dr. Whittaker had learned the hard way that his bulk was of no advantage in this situation. Dr. Nez moved up and almost pushed Virgil to one side.

"I'll go in," he said. "I'm smaller than you. Give me a boost."

Kesia Guyen worked her way forward.

"I'm smaller," she said, her voice tight.

Dr. Nez already had his head through the hole in the crystoplast, but his voice came back clearly as he pulled himself into the van. "Shorter, maybe. We can argue later on who weighs more. Anyhow, you and Virgil have people waiting for you..."

"That doesn't matter," Kesia said, her voice rising, then breaking. "We don't need tents or anything. It's not worth the risk!"

"Really," Dr. Nez was handing out packages as fast as he could. "How long before rescue comes? We're going to need water purification at least, a med kit. Dacey's medications..."

Anders joined the line relaying materials back. Dacey had come out to join them. Now her voice, suddenly quavery and old as it had never been before, said, "I think the van's sinking faster! Langston, you've got to get out of there!"

Virgil Iwamoto clearly agreed with her assessment, because the next time Langston Nez's hands emerged through the hole with a package, he grabbed him by the wrists.

"Somebody," Virgil shouted, "help me get a hold on him!"

"It's sinking!" came Dacey's shrill scream. "Oh, bright stars! It's sinking!"

Dr. Whittaker shoved forward, almost knocking Kesia Guyen onto her round rump, and joined Virgil. There wasn't much room, but both men managed to get a hold on Langston Nez and hauled with all their might. However, even as they did so, the bog gasped and gulped, taking into itself the huge bulk of the van as if it was nothing more than a bug.

Anders stood transfixed in horror as Dad and Virgil were pulled forward by the suction, falling to their knees as they strove to keep their hold on the man who had just been buried alive.

Behind him, someone was sobbing—Kesia, from the sound. Anders flung himself forward and began scrabbling like a dog in the mud, throwing out great gobs of the wet, sticky stuff in an effort to break the sucking hold. On the other side of where Dad and Virgil maintained their life-and-death grip, he saw Calida Emberly also digging, her silver hair streaked with mud. Then Kesia Guyen—still sobbing—joined them in their efforts.

Water that reeked of rotting vegetation seeped down Anders' sleeves. Gritty mud sanded his fingers raw, but Anders kept digging. Was it his imagination or was the sucking pull weakening?

Slowly, horribly slowly, first Dad, then Virgil began

to rock back on their heels. For an agonizing moment, Anders thought that meant they had lost their hold on Dr. Nez. He began to dig more frantically, slime and filth splashing into his face. If they'd given up, he wasn't going to. He'd dig to the planet's core if he had to, if that was the only way to bring Dr. Nez up from this sudden grave.

Feeling himself tiring, Anders fueled his frantic digging with memories of Dr. Nez—no, Langston, at this moment only the human being called Langston—and his many kindnesses, not just on this trip but over the years when he'd been Dad's assistant. They weren't going to leave him here, a body in the mud of an alien world. They weren't! They weren't!

Then Virgil gasped. "He's coming up. We've got him!"

Dr. Whittaker said nothing, only grunted with effort, straining to get his feet under him so he could use his full strength and height to pull the buried man free of the grasping muck. He flung himself upwards, bringing Langston Nez, sleek with mud, hanging like a dead man, into the air and light.

"Is he breathing?" Dacey asked.

Exhausted by their efforts, Dad and Virgil had fallen to their knees. Anders half-rolled, half-crawled to look at Langston Nez. Wiping his hands on the seat of his trousers, he cleared mud from the drowned man's nose and mouth, then held his ear low against lips and chest. He'd taken life-saving only the term before. Now he went through the check routine.

"He's breathing," he said. The ground beneath him shuddered. "But we've got to get out of here or we're down going after the van!"

"You and I will carry Langston," Dr. Emberly said. "Mother, help Kesia get the supplies that haven't already been relayed to solid ground. It may be enough for Virgil and Bradford to move themselves."

Anders obeyed. Dr. Emberly was about his own height. When she took Langston's feet, Anders raised the mud-covered man's head and shoulders. The unconscious man might not be overly tall, but covered with mud and soaking wet, he was astonishingly heavy.

Dr. Emberly reached and checked the controls on Dr. Nez's counter-grav unit.

"Ruined," she said. "These are basic units, not meant to be sunk in the mud."

She stripped off her own unit and wrapped it around Dr. Nez, then adjusted the dial. "Go! He's light enough for one person to move now. I'll get myself back to shore."

Anders obeyed, but remembering how he had felt the couple of times he'd tried to move around Sphinx's 1.35 gravity without his unit, he could only admire the older woman for her tenacity.

Eventually, they got themselves and their gear to what they now all thought of as "shore." Kesia located a fresh-water spring near the lace willows, and brought back water. With this, Anders carefully cleared Langston's mouth and nose, periodically turning him and thumping him gently on the back in the hope that he would cough up any mud that had lodged in his lungs. However, although Dr. Nez's heart beat and he was breathing, that breath came shallow and rasping.

In the background, Anders heard someone say something about "oxygen starvation" and "brain damage," but he wasn't giving up. Dr. Emberly reclaimed her counter-grav belt and went to assist in setting up camp. Dacey Emberly came over to join Anders.

"I'm going to give Langston my belt," she said softly, "but don't tell Calida. She'll worry. My heart isn't what it used to be, but I'm sure I'll be fine if I sit quietly. That poor man doesn't need to fight the gravity along with everything else."

Anders forced a smile. He didn't know when he'd last

felt so tired, but for some reason the image of Stephanie Harrington kept coming to him. She'd saved Lionheart from the hexapuma *after*, not before, she'd broken her arm, seriously banged up her knee, and cracked a bunch of ribs when her hang glider had crashed in that storm. If Stephanie could do that, surely he could keep going when all he'd done was move some mud.

Inspired by this, he got Dr. Nez comfortable, then, leaving him under Dacey Emberly's watch, he went to see what he could do to help with setting up camp. He found Dad—more or less clean now—arguing with Dr. Emberly.

"I think you're overdoing it. Yes, we're out of communication with base. Yes, we won't be expected back until tomorrow—we were set to camp tonight, but eventually someone will come looking."

"And where will they search?" came Dr. Emberly's icy reply. "At various picketwood groves to the north—not here. I seem to recall you 'overlooked' telling them about your intention to stop here."

Dad was temporarily silenced, then he said, "When they can't find us, they'll search for the air van. The crash beacon will bring them right to us."

Anders—tired, fed-up, angry that Dad had taken time to change and get clean while others tried to help Langston, while poor old Dacey was sitting carefully over there so her counter-grav unit could be used to ease the injured man's suffering—lost control. Forgetting everything he'd ever been taught about not embarrassing his parents in public, he exploded.

"Crash beacon! Crash beacon? There isn't going to be any crash beacon. We didn't crash. You landed us very neatly, right on the edge of a bog. The van sank very slowly. There was no crash to set the beacon off. No one is going to be able to find us because no one knows where to look—and it's all your fault!"

"WHAT DO YOU MEAN, 'THEY'RE MISSING'?" STEPHANIE
exclaimed.

Karl frowned. "I mean exactly what I said, Steph. You
know Frank and Ainsley are both close friends of Uncle
Scott. Well, they stopped by yesterday to update him on
someone he'd treated for them—a hiker who slipped and
broke a leg."

I don't care about any stupid hiker, Stephanie thought.
Is Anders missing?

"Then Frank went on to say, 'I wish there was some
way we could ask everyone who leaves town to wear a
tracking beacon. Chief Ranger Shelton hasn't made an
official announcement, but those off-planet anthropologists may have gone missing.'

"I came in then," Karl went on. "I mean, this had
to be Anders' group, and I've gotten to like him. First
I confirmed whether or not Anders was with his dad's
team. He was."

A faint flicker of hope died in Stephanie's breast. "Go on."

"Then I got what details they'd give me—but I had to swear that I wouldn't tell anyone but you. I think," Karl grinned, "they knew you'd kill me if I didn't tell you."

Stephanie rolled her eyes. "Go on, Karl, or I'll do worse than kill you."

"Okay. Here's the short form. Four days ago, Dr. Whittaker logged that he and his crew—which included Anders and that older lady, the painter, Dacey Emberly—were going to view several picketwood groves north of Twin Forks, ones that, as far as anyone knows, have not been used by treecats. They were covering a wide region, since the idea was to lay in data about picketwood groves for later comparison to treecat dwellings.

"The trip was supposed to take two full days. That is, they would be back at their base on the evening of the second day. That evening, Peony Rose Iwamoto and Jon Qin—spouses of two of the crew members—commed Dr. Hobbard to ask if she knew where Dr. Whittaker's crew was. Apparently, they'd tried to com the team and had not been able to make contact. These two were a little worried, but not panicked, since they weren't certain how complete the Sphinx com-net is."

"It bugs me," Stephanie said, trying to sound normal, "how off-worlders seem to assume that because this is a colony planet, we're primitive or something."

"Yeah. Well, Dr. Hobbard said some stuff that calmed their worries, but she also got in touch with Chief Ranger Shelton. She went right to the top, because she didn't want the newsies to get a hold of this and embarrass the Forestry Service."

"Nice of her," Stephanie said, but even her high opinion of Dr. Hobbard couldn't stop a building sense of apprehension. "You say they were reported missing after only two days, but they've been missing four? What's happened since?"

Karl raised a hand on which four fingers were extended, then folded down the first two. "Okay. Here's the end of Day Two. Chief Ranger Shelton wouldn't have been too worried, but he didn't like the fact that the anthropologists hadn't answered their uni-links. He himself went to the picketwood grove that should have been their last stop, but they weren't there. There wasn't any sign they'd been there.

"Without making a huge fuss, he couldn't send search teams out—these areas were in different ecological zones, but still within a 'night' time zone, and sending out search parties would have raised the exact sort of fuss Dr. Hobbard hoped to avoid."

Stephanie wanted to protest—after all, this was *Anders* they were talking about—but she forced herself to be rational.

"I suppose," she said, "that Chief Ranger Shelton thought it was possible the anthropologists decided to go back to one of the other areas or something. Did they have camping gear with them?"

"They did. They planned to camp the one night rather than return to base." Karl folded down his third finger. "On Day Three, Chief Ranger Shelton got a few tight-lipped rangers to check the various sites Dr. Whittaker had noted the team was going to inspect. They did. Again, there was no hint they'd ever been there. Seven people, even if trying for minimal impact, should have left something trained eyes could find."

Karl folded down his fourth finger. "That takes us to today—Day Four. SFS is expanding the search now, checking along the flight path the anthropologists would have taken going out to the first site, then between the sites. They're figuring that the air van must have gone down somewhere in there."

"They think the van crashed?" Stephanie said. "No. That wouldn't work. If the van crashed, then a beacon would have gone off immediately. I bet even the junker Jessica pilots has a crash beacon—and it's really old model."

Karl nodded. "I asked about that. Frank said they're operating on the theory that the van didn't crash. They're figuring that the team landed it safely, but somehow did something to disable the van so they couldn't take off again."

"What would they do that would disable the van and its com-unit?" Stephanie protested. "And their uni-links?"

Karl grinned, but it was a tired grin. "'You get your Sherlock Holmes badge,' to quote what Frank said when I asked the same questions. No one knows what could have happened to the com-unit—although there has been speculation that the van suffered a complete electronics failure. However, we do have a solution to the Mystery of the Uni-Links."

"Oh?"

"Both Peony Rose Iwamoto and John Qin had uni-links to match those being used by Dr. Whittaker's crew. Chief Ranger Shelton had these checked over. Turns out that Dr. Whittaker's crew is using units manufactured off-world. The operating system worked fine when it only needed to mesh with the local com-net. However, it's all wrong for longer distances. Basically, it won't link to the correct programs in the communication satellites. The crew had experienced a few minor problems already, but since they were mostly communicating with members of their own team who were local, maybe making a few calls to SFS personnel and Dr. Hobbard, they worked around them."

"Let me guess," Stephanie said. "The anthropologists probably figured the problem had nothing to do with their uni-links, but everything to do with the primitive systems on this colony world of ours. Right?"

Karl gave a rueful sigh. "I didn't ask, but I bet you're

right. It would explain why the two family members didn't think it completely odd when they couldn't reach the team. Communications blackouts would have been a familiar problem."

"If they'd been here just a little longer," Stephanie said, "they would have realized something was wrong. Anders was starting to hang out with us.... All it would have taken was him trying to com his dad and not getting through and us telling him it wasn't normal..."

"Irina's always quoting some old poem about how the saddest words are 'it might have been,'" Karl interrupted her. "Fact is, Dr. Whittaker took his crew out—and something happened. Since it's unlikely that he went somewhere other than the areas he indicated—I mean, they wouldn't be so stupid as to risk SFS goodwill by going to look for Lionheart's clan or something—the search is concentrating on the region north of Twin Forks, up to the foothills of the Copperwall Mountains."

Already considering herself part of the search, Stephanie called up a map on her uni-link.

"The search isn't going to be easy," she said, holding the uni-link out so Karl could look at the map with her. "There's some rough terrain in there."

"Yeah," Karl agreed. "That's actually why the anthropological team chose the area in the first place. Because of the rise and fall of the mountains there—and that large river—there are a lot of ecosystems represented in a relatively compact area. Problem is, while the map shows the area as a couple hundred square kilometers, when you take into account all the dips and rises, what the search parties need to deal with is actually closer to twice or three times as much area."

"Including a river," Stephanie said. She pulled up details on it. "Large and fast-moving. You don't think they landed the van in the river somehow?"

Karl's expression became grim. "I don't think even the most absent-minded scientist could do that, but if they did, the end result isn't worth thinking about. They'd be gone and no one would find them, not in a million years."

✧　　✧　　✧

Climbs Quickly tasted the spike of anxiety and fear in Death Fang's Bane's mind-glow as Shadowed Sunlight talked. He felt his usual bud of frustration since none of the mouth noises gave him any indication of what the problem was. Once or twice, he heard the sound "Anders"—a sound which he thought applied to the bright-haired young male his two-leg was so interested in. However, since she often made this noise lately, Climbs Quickly couldn't be certain that Bleached Fur was involved in whatever the problem might be.

As he was trying to piece together what might be wrong, Death Fang's Bane's newest friend, Windswept—as Climbs Quickly had dubbed the girl, both in tribute to her physical appearance and the changeable surges of her bright mind-glow—came trotting over to join Shadowed Sunlight and Death Fang's Bane. The wild-haired girl had visited Death Fang's Bane quite a bit lately, as had a female Climbs Quickly was fairly certain was Windswept's mother.

Although Windswept could not read mind-glows, the new arrival was apparently aware of the tension. She asked a question. In reply, both Death Fang's Bane and Shadowed Sunlight began talking rapidly, their mouth noises overlapping each other in a manner that Climbs Quickly wondered if anyone ever found confusing. However, whatever was being said, one thing became clear: whatever was wrong was centered on Bleached Fur. Death Fang's Bane's mind-glow as she explained matters to Windswept became shaded with a level of dread that was distinctly unsettling.

Climbs Quickly was certain this feeling was rooted in something real, not in those wild surges of emotion that filled Death Fang's Bane whenever the young man was near. For one thing, Shadowed Sunlight and Windswept were also both disturbed.

Climbs Quickly was not in the least surprised when Death Fang's Bane turned to him. Most of her mouth noises as she spoke to him were incomprehensible, but he caught two he recognized: "Go" and "Anders." These, combined with the urgency in her mind-glow, were all he needed to know.

They were going to do something about this "Anders" problem, and his two-leg wanted him along.

"Bleek!" Climbs Quickly replied, scampering ahead in the direction of Shadowed Sunlight's air car. "Bleek! Bleek!"

✧   ✧   ✧

For Anders, the days since the crash had been a blur of cascading emergencies. Once the crew had accepted that they couldn't hope for rescue any earlier than two or three days from now, there had been a round of blame-slinging.

Anders knew his own angry explosion had triggered this, so he felt guilty when Dr. Whittaker diverted the issue by tossing around some blame of his own.

"And, why," Dr. Whittaker said to the air in his best "professor questioning the class" tone, "aren't our uni-links working?"

He glowered generally, but it was Virgil Iwamoto who wilted. As junior member of the crew, he had been responsible for assembling much of the gear.

"We did notice a few problems before," he began hesitantly, "but they didn't seem to matter much, since we'd have the on-vehicle unit."

That had been the wrong thing to say. Dr. Whittaker

hadn't been married for nearly twenty years to a politician without knowing that disapproval worked far more efficiently than anger in reining in subordinates. He ignored the question of the vehicle and focused on the uni-links.

"You should have looked into having the problem fixed or substituted units purchased as soon as the problem first showed," he stated in a manner that brooked no argument—and how could Virgil argue? What Dr. Whittaker said was correct.

Then came the question of where to set up their camp. They weren't high enough in the Copperwall Mountains for peak bears to be a problem, but the highly adaptable hexapumas could not be ignored—especially since their only weapons were utilitarian vibro-blades and a single tranq rifle with only one clip of darts. That meant setting up camp in the trees, and *that*, as far as Dr. Whittaker was concerned, meant finding a location that would not contaminate his beloved site.

Again, arguing was useless. There was no overlooking the fact that when they were found, Dr. Whittaker was going to have a certain amount of fast-talking to do if the expedition's relationship with the SFS was to be salvaged. Damage to the treecat site would only complicate matters.

Valuable time was spent while they surveyed the area until they located a stand of yellow rock trees that didn't seem to have been used by the treecats. However, the anthropologists' insistence on not contaminating the site made setting up camp more difficult. While the network of branches and nodal trunks made picketwood ideal for what Kesia flippantly termed "treehouse building," the straight-trunked rock trees were less well-suited.

Eventually, however, they located a stand of younger trees, many of which retained horizontal limbs at a relatively "low" seven or so meters from the ground. At least rock trees—called such for the extreme hardness and density of their wood—were strong enough that even a young one could hold a fair amount of weight.

Transporting their gear and erecting the camping shelters at that height above the ground introduced the next problem.

"I just looked at my counter-grav unit," Virgil said. "The read-out seems lower than it should be."

His tone was hesitant. Anders didn't blame him, given that Dr. Whittaker seemed set on making Virgil the scapegoat for any and all problems having to do with equipment. He'd already been reprimanded for only arranging for enough food for their planned jaunt and because the box containing the tea Dr. Whittaker favored, along with a few other luxury goods, hadn't been among those removed from the sinking van.

There was a moment's hesitation while everyone else checked their units. All, to varying degrees, were exhausted below the level they should have been. Dr. Whittaker's was the closest to normal. He somehow seemed to think this made him virtuous.

"Perhaps you damaged the unit," he began, "with all that jumping about in the bog..."

Dr. Emberly cut him off.

"The source of the problem is obvious," she said crisply. "At our usual rate of use, these units are good for about thirty-three hours. However, since we've been using them to lighten our loads while we make camp, we're burning more power. Usually, that wouldn't be an issue, since broadcast power from the van would have recharged the units as we used them, but that isn't available."

And, Anders added in silent, vicious commentary, *since Dad has mostly been standing around, giving orders and not doing much hauling, he hasn't burned as much power as some of us.*

Anders' own unit's read-out was about the same as

Virgil's. He tried to remember the conversion factor. Details escaped him, but he did remember that at minimum power use—which reduced gravity by about twenty-five percent—the counter-grav units were good for right on forty-eight hours. Since they already had been using them at a higher setting—Sphinx's gravity was one Terran normal, plus an additional third or so—they had been drawing power to counter an extra fifteen percent. That was why the units were good for about thirty-three hours, rather than the full forty-eight, since increasing counter-grav above the minimum drew power at a higher rate of use.

And over the last couple of hours, Anders thought, *we've been acting as if this is an inexhaustible resource, when it's anything but...*

"Do we have any power packs?" Kesia asked anxiously.

"We have a few," Virgil replied. "We don't have anywhere near enough for us to continue at normal use without our completely running out."

"So," Dr. Emberly said, making an adjustment to her own unit, "we need to decrease use immediately. We have ladders, so we'll use them. All of us who are healthy and strong should see if we can decrease to minimum usage levels."

Anders spoke up. "Dr. Emberly, you mentioned 'healthy.' I noticed that your mother has taken off her unit so that Dr. Nez could use it. She can't keep doing that or we're going to have two patients, not just one."

As soon as they'd gotten the first platform and shelter up, Dr. Nez had been moved to safety, with Dacey Emberly accompanying him as nurse. At first she'd taken her sketchbook out, but the last few times he'd been up, Anders had noticed she was sitting very still, moving only to periodically check on Langston Nez.

Kesia Guyen said, "I agree with Anders. Dacey's looking a bit blue around the lips. Does she have a heart condition?"

"She does," Dr. Emberly said, a thin line appearing between her brows. "Nothing so bad that she couldn't go on this trip, but that's one of the things she takes medication for. Any chance we can get Langston's unit working, even a bit?"

"I could take a look at it," Kesia said. "John's good with gadgets and I've learned a trick or two, but I can't offer a lot of hope. The type of units we're using aren't meant to be submerged and then cemented with mud."

Setting up their camp took most of the rest of the day. That night, they ate lightly, but at least water wasn't an issue. The same swamp that had eaten the air van gave as much water as they needed, and the purification unit Virgil had selected was efficient and used minimal power—a model intended not for luxury camping, but for disaster situations.

Since he slept with his counter-grav unit off to conserve power, Anders might not have slept well if he hadn't been exhausted. The next morning, he awoke, not precisely refreshed, but feeling better. It had been agreed that anyone who would be moving around could set their counter-grav units for the minimum power drain. That meant he only had to deal with fifteen percent extra gravity. After a night at thirty-five percent extra, Anders felt as if he could fly.

"I've a guide book here," he said, holding up his reader. "Stephanie also gave me some articles her mother wrote. I thought that maybe I could do some foraging."

Dr. Emberly looked interested. "Is that guidebook the Forestry Service issue? I kept meaning to ask for one, just out of curiosity. If you'll accept an assistant, I'd like to join you."

"Is this foraging really necessary?" Dr. Whittaker grumbled.

A big man, he was clearly not happy about having to function with his usual weight increased. Anders could have sworn he'd seen Dad raise the power level on his counter-grav unit above the agreed-upon minimum a few times. Only a heated intervention on the part of Dr. Emberly had made certain that two of the spare power packs had gone to Dr. Nez and Dacey.

Miraculously, Kesia had managed to get the damaged unit working, but it would not counter gravity above a twenty-five percent reduction, and used quite a bit of power to do so. A schedule had been worked out where Dacey traded units with Dr. Nez, so that each of them had time at normal gravity.

Dr. Nez remained unconscious, his breathing labored. Since none of them had medical training above first aid, they couldn't diagnose what was wrong.

But he probably breathed in some mud, Anders thought, *and the particles are inflaming his lungs. He's probably well on the way to pneumonia. As it is, he's lucky all of us were so dosed up on antivirals and antibacterials before coming here that he's resistant to infection. Dacey keeps Langston's lips moist, but we can't get him to drink more than an occasional swallow, so he's getting dehydrated, too.*

"Is foraging necessary?" Dr. Emberly repeated Dr. Whittaker's question and then answered it herself. Not for the first time, Anders was glad that there was one member of the crew who wasn't intimidated by his father. "Yes, it is. I know you're hoping we'll be rescued quickly, but I assert that is an unrealistically optimistic position. We won't even be missed until tonight. I doubt any serious search will be mounted until the next morning—and then all they're going to find is that we're not where we said we'd be."

Dr. Whittaker looked weary, but Anders wasn't sure that he wasn't playacting at remorse. By now, he didn't trust his dad's intentions. That doubt increased with Dr. Whittaker's next words.

"I see. Since we lack extra food supplies..." Here Dad

paused to glower at Virgil, "Then I suppose we must plan for the worst. However, since some of us lack either an SFS guidebook or your skills as a xenobiologist, perhaps we can carry on with the job we came here to do."

"You mean inspect the treecat areas?" Kesia sounded astonished.

"Why not?" Dr. Whittaker said. "You're a linguist, but you do have some training in basic field methods. You can photograph and record. Best of all, if we use ladders or record from ground level, we can conserve the power on our counter-grav units."

"Well," Dr. Emberly said reluctantly. "You do have a point. We can't have people getting poisoned because they eat native plants that aren't compatible with our metabolisms. Anders and I will make foraging our department."

Oddly enough, while foraging, they learned quite a bit about the treecats. This group of treecats hadn't precisely been farmers, but there was evidence that they did encourage plants they liked. One of their first finds was a recovering patch of near-lettuce.

"Probably harvested before they moved," Dr. Emberly commented as she carefully clipped off the edible leaves, "but with the roots left to send up fresh growth. We'll do the same."

They found some near-pine a short distance away. Survey through binoculars showed some ripening nuts near the top. After consideration, Dr. Emberly decided that they would expend enough extra power on one counter-grav unit so they could harvest some of the thumb-sized nuts. The trees were branchless for the lower third of their height, so climbing wasn't an option.

"We're going to need the calories," she said to Anders. "You go up. You're more agile. Remember, only pick the pods that are turning a dark reddish brown. Drop them down and I'll gather them."

Anders agreed, not admitting even to himself how good it felt to be lighter. Dutifully, however, once he'd gotten into the branches, he turned the counter-grav unit back to minimum and kept it that way until he was ready to climb down. Then, well aware that broken bones would inconvenience them more than a drained battery pack, he turned the counter-grav unit back to normal gravity for his descent.

The SFS guidebook proved useful for other things than plants. It told them which animals were edible. The anthropologists weren't set for hunting, but Dr. Emberly knew how to make fish traps.

"Lace willow will work," she said, showing Anders what parts of the plant to cut. "However, I don't have much hope of catching anything. The treecats probably fished out this area. I wouldn't be surprised if that's part of the reason they moved on. In a year with normal rainfall, the swamp would be replenished by rain, but now it's relying on whatever ground seep there is. We haven't seen much sign of near-otter or near-beaver. It's possible near-beavers might have originally created this wetland long ago."

If it hadn't been for the desperate nature of their situation, Anders would have enjoyed the outing. However, when they returned to camp, laden with their gleaning, and found Dr. Whittaker gloating over some stone tools and broken baskets, while on a bedroll, Dr. Nez wheezed for every breath, what Anders felt most strongly was a sense that everything was all wrong.

And I want to make it right, he thought, clenching his fists in desperation. *I want to make it* right.

✧   ✧   ✧

Stephanie, Karl, and Jessica were permitted to join the search for Dr. Whittaker and his crew, but only if they all swore they wouldn't say anything about the situation.

"I'll keep the secret," Jessica said, holding her hand up in a timeless gesture dating back to ancient courtrooms, "but I'll admit that I don't quite understand why. When I was living in the Tasmania system, a little girl went missing in the foothills of some mountains. Not only did the local police send out teams, they recruited everyone who was willing to help. It was one of the volunteers—my dad—who found the kid, too . . ."

Chief Ranger Shelton gave a tired smile. "Asking for volunteers would be a sensible course of action to take in most cases, but this isn't one."

He held up his fingers and started ticking off points.

So that's where Karl picked up that mannerism, Stephanie thought, swallowing a wholly inappropriate giggle—a giggle she knew was born of the tension coiling and uncoiling in her gut.

"First of all, it's fire season," Chief Ranger Shelton said. "With the drought conditions, the risk is higher than usual. As Stephanie and Karl can tell you, most fires—on other worlds, at least—are started by human action. Here on Sphinx we don't have enough people yet for that to be the case, but the more people you have wandering around, the more likely you're going to have somebody careless doing the wandering. As much as we want to find Dr. Whittaker and the others, we don't want to be responsible for scattering potential fire sources all over the landscape.

"Second, although those of us at SFS have welcomed these off-planet scientists and their insights, our feelings are not universal. There are many here on Sphinx who view them as intruders. Worse, Dr. Hobbard tells me that not all of the intellectual community even here in the Star Kingdom was delighted about the decision to bring in out-of-system specialists, no matter how carefully they were chosen.

"Third—and rather selfishly, as I'll be the first to admit— if the news becomes general that these people slipped SFS supervision so easily, we're going to come in for a lot of criticism. Already SFS is not the most popular body on the planet. We spend too much time telling people not to do things they want to do. We protect resources many colonists prefer to see as limitless. These people would just love an excuse to criticize us further.

"Fourth," Chief Ranger Shelton's expression turned very serious, "there's the question of why Dr. Whittaker and his crew apparently never arrived at their first scheduled destination. Did their accident happen before they could arrive or did they have some other agenda? We're operating on the assumption that either the accident occurred first or that, for some reason that doubtless will make perfect sense when we hear it, they changed the order in which they were going to view the sites and neglected to tell us. They may not have thought it necessary. After all, they were cleared to visit all of those areas. In any case, for some reason they went to another site first—and the accident occurred then."

Karl nodded, "Which is why they haven't been found yet. The area is too spread out."

"Exactly," Chief Ranger Shelton replied. He turned to Jessica. "Does that clarify why we're not calling in a larger group?"

She nodded, very somber. "I promise I won't say anything, not even to my parents. I've told my mom that I'm going to tag along with Stephanie and Karl on their SFS probationary ranger rounds. That's true enough, right?"

"Right." Chief Ranger Shelton indicated a segment of a holomap that dominated one portion of the table. "This is where we're sending you in. Cover as much ground as you can as carefully as you can from the air, landing only if you think there's a good reason. Dr. Whittaker's vehicle was a boxy air van, capable of carrying a lot of people and gear. At least we're not looking for shreds of a lighter-than-air craft. Report if you find anything worth landing to inspect. Good luck."

"We'll do our best," Stephanie promised, then they hurried out.

They were taking Karl's car, so he slid into the pilot's seat. Stephanie took the front passenger seat, while Jessica got in the back, behind Karl.

"So I can cover that side while you pilot. I wish they could have given us some sort of fancy scanner array."

Stephanie replied, "They've already done what they can with satellite downlook and such. No hot-spots or the like to indicate a crash. In a way, we're lucky it's fire season, so the SFS already has extra satellite time allocated."

Lionheart perched in Stephanie's lap, placing his "hands" on the side of the door and looking down. For once, he didn't "bleek" to have the window opened.

I guess, Stephanie thought, *he's figured out this isn't a time for the wind in his fur. I wonder if he's just looking out because that's what he always does or because he knows we're looking for Anders and his dad and the others. Whatever, I'm glad to have him here.*

She was no less glad when the search was called at twilight and despair as black as the gathering night filled her. Climbs Quickly stood on his hind legs and stroked her cheek with his true-hand, then leapt into the backseat to wrap his tail around Jessica and nuzzle her downturned face. Since Karl was piloting, the treecat settled for patting him lightly on one shoulder before getting back into Stephanie's lap.

Jessica's voice came disembodied from the back of the air car. "You don't think they're all dead, do you? I can't believe there could have been an accident that huge without some sign."

Unless they crashed in the river, Stephanie thought. *Unless they were somehow sabotaged. Chief Ranger Shelton mentioned that not everyone was happy Dr. Whittaker was here, but would they go to such lengths?*

Once she wouldn't have had such thoughts, but that was before Dr. Ubel had sabotaged Arvin Erhardt's air car just to get rid of an inconvenient witness. Or before she herself had held a gun on Tennessee Bolgeo, knowing she would shoot him if he didn't stop what he was doing. Before she had seen what Bolgeo was willing to do to creatures he, at least, didn't seem to doubt were sentient.

Karl spoke reassuringly. "Tomorrow they plan to expand the range of the search. We already have our assignment—that ravine we saw today, but couldn't go down into without spending more time than we should."

But by the next morning, everything had changed.

10

AS THE SECOND DAY OF THEIR EXILE DREW TO A CLOSE, Anders was aware of a growing sense of expectation among the crew. He thought it was unduly optimistic—they wouldn't even be missed until that night—but he knew that both Virgil and Kesia hoped their spouses would alert the authorities.

Anders realized, too, that his own activities had certainly added to this sense that rescue was certain to come quickly. After helping Dr. Emberly with checking the fish traps and more foraging, he'd asked to be excused.

"It's not that I'm not interested, Dr. Emberly," he said, looking at the four rather strange-looking "fish" they'd taken from the traps. It was a good thing the SFS guidebook assured them this species was edible, because based on appearance alone, Anders would have had serious doubts. "But I have some ideas how we might make it easier for us to be found."

"Why don't you just call me Calida," she suggested. "It seems ridiculous to use titles while we're all stranded here."

"Because my dad wouldn't like it," Anders replied promptly. "But if you don't mind, I'll call you Doctor Calida."

"Done," she said. "Now, what is it you have in mind?"

After listening to Anders outline his plans, Dr. Calida had agreed. "But be careful up in the trees."

Figuring that talking to Dr. Calida counted as asking permission, Anders avoided talking to his father. Dr. Whittaker—Dad had glowered when any of his underlings had addressed him by anything except this title—was behaving really strangely. Not only was he insisting on maintaining the academic hierarchy, but he was carrying on with his fieldwork as if nothing else was important.

When Anders had questioned him about this, privately, so as not to cause any embarrassment, Dad had smiled fondly and all but patted him on the head.

"You go ahead and play at camping adventure if you'd like," he said, his tone so warm and affectionate that Anders wondered if he somehow imagined they were on holiday at their mountain cabin. "I'm here to work and so are the others. We're learning a great deal. Dr. Emberly has already recorded some fascinating evidence that the treecats may be in transition from a purely hunter-gatherer lifestyle to one with elements of agriculture. She wouldn't have had the opportunity to learn this without our current situation. Even if we'd waited only a few weeks for permission to come here, much of the evidence—such as those patches of near-lettuce—would have grown beyond the point where we could record the treecats' use of them."

Anders could tell he wasn't going to get through, so he went on with his plans, embarrassingly aware that there *was* a certain adventure story quality to them.

Experimentation had shown that for someone of his weight, walking on the surface of the bog was relatively safe—as long as he didn't stick his foot on one of those areas where only a thin screen of vegetation covered the sucking mud beneath. Dr. Calida had explained that in more normal situations traversing the bog would not have been as safe.

"I'm guessing," she said, "that in addition to the wetlands providing the treecats with drinking water, an interesting variety of useful plants, and fresh fish, the bog also provided a natural moat. A creature as heavy as a hexapuma would think twice or even three times before crossing that area. The risk of getting trapped would be too great."

After consulting his SFS guide book to make certain he would not be exposing himself to any toxic saps, Anders cut a quantity of undergrowth from the edges of the bog in which the air-van had sunk. This he dragged out onto the bog itself and arranged it on a slight rise in a large X pattern. He was very careful where he stepped, but even so, his shoes—the only pair he had brought with him—got thoroughly muddy, and he had reason to be glad that he'd packed extra socks.

He was also reassured to know that Dacey Emberly was keeping watch on him from her perch in the treetops. The elderly painter might be less than active, but she was earning the gratitude of the expedition. Not only was she tending to the unconscious Langston Nez, but she minded the pots simmering on the cookstove—fresh food could not be prepared as quickly as the camping staples Anders had been familiar with before this. She also had assigned herself the role of watch—not only for aerial traffic, of which there was depressingly little, but also for ground-level hazards.

"I don't know much about Sphinx," Dacey said, "but

I haven't associated with a xenobiologist all these years without learning that water always draws the wild things. Though that area's dry for a bog, it's still plenty wet to provide drinking water."

When Anders expressed concern that despite his efforts to place it safely, his brushwood X would simply doom another vehicle to land and sink, Dacey had chuckled.

"Don't you worry about that. I've been spotting wood rats—and even a smaller critter or two Calida tells me might not yet be in the official zoological record. I got pictures, even!" She turned serious. "Honestly, I'm not going to miss something the size of an air car. If one comes here, I'm going to holler so loud that, first, they don't fail to know we're here, and, second, they set down somewhere else."

Making the X, especially under the demands of fifteen percent added gravity, wore Anders out thoroughly enough that he didn't get on to the next part of his plan until the third day. That day, after once again helping Dr. Calida with the foraging, then helping Dacey with cleaning and turning the still unconscious Langston Nez, Anders set off on a slow climb to the top of one of the highest of the picketwood trees.

He'd had to argue with his father about this part of his plan—not because Dr. Whittaker was worried about Anders falling, but because he was concerned about contamination of the treecat habitat. In the end, Anders won, but only when he promised that the blazing he planned to do would not be permanent. That meant he'd need to carry even the post for the flag he planned to erect with him—adding to both his weight and to the awkwardness of his climb. At least the "flag" itself would not be too heavy.

Most of what Langston Nez had tossed out of the sinking van had been gear brought along for the expedition, rather than the personal property of the crew. Dr. Whittaker had not stopped grumbling that his goodie bag had gone to the bottom, but at least the bag containing his and Anders' clothing had made it out. Poor Virgil didn't have even a change of clothes until Anders gave him some. Neither of the Emberlys' clothes bags had made it out, but Langston had made a point of making sure that the small satchel in which Dacey kept her medications—along with her painting supplies and camera—had been among the first he retrieved.

That meant all three women were at least partially dressed out of Kesia Guyen's rather flashy wardrobe. Happily, Kesia was very full-figured, so although her clothing hung loosely on the two Emberly women, it did fit. Now Kesia's bag supplied what Anders needed for his treetop expedition.

"Good thing I like scarves," she said, pulling out half a dozen, "and that they roll up so small I always keep a supply tucked in my travel bag."

She'd grinned at him. "Nothing like a scarf to change your appearance when you're short on other clothes. I bet your mama knows that."

Now some of those scarves were stuffed into the front of Anders' shirt as he began his laborious climb toward the top of the picketwood, the flagpole he'd shaped from a sapling lace willow strapped to his back and hanging down behind like a tail.

Here and there, as he climbed, Anders saw evidence of the treecats' past use of the tree. He might have been defeated in one place where sometime in the distant past a branch had broken off, leaving no hand- or footholds, but he used a vibro-blade to cut himself toeholds.

More than once during that climb, Anders wished he could switch on his counter-grav unit. It would have carried him to his destination much more quickly—and if he had lost his grip, his fall would have been of much lesser consequence. However, he didn't do so. Already he was regretting the extra power he'd used when picking near-pine pods with Dr. Calida. Dacey kept watch over the stack of power packets, but even with setting the counter-grav units at minimum, that stack was diminishing rapidly.

Soon, Anders thought, *someone is going to have to go without. It can't be Langston or Dacey. Why do I think Dad's going to have excuses why it can't be him? I'm guessing Virgil will volunteer. He's still feeling stupidly guilty over the problem with the uni-links—even though Dad's as much to blame. Or maybe Dad will suggest that since I'm not a "real" part of the expedition, I can do without. Maybe he'd even be right.*

When he reached the top of the picketwood tree, Anders braced himself and began tying the scarves into long, brilliantly colored streamers at the narrow end of his pole. Then, holding short lengths of rope in his mouth, he lashed the flagpole into place. He'd practiced this part when he was lower down, but he hadn't counted on the steady press of the wind that tried to wrestle the length of lace willow from his hands.

The streamers snapped in the occasional cross-draft, one stinging him across his face like a whip. Eventually, however, he got the flagpole into place. When he did, the scarves—most of which were at least a meter wide—billowed out and flew, defiant slashes of unnatural color against the Sphinxian sky.

He stayed up at the top of the picketwood for a while, watching, hoping, he knew against hope, to see some air car that he could wave down. But the sky remained empty, and once again Anders found himself regretting an SFS policy that restricted use not only of some wild lands, but of the airspace above them.

At last Anders made his slow, careful way down. That evening over a dinner that included some interesting results of Dr. Calida's foraging combined with the last of their supplies, speculation was rife as to when they would be located.

"Tomorrow, certainly," Dr. Whittaker said. "Last night we didn't report in as planned. Certainly, some searching was done today. Indeed, I'm surprised we haven't been located already."

His tone was disapproving, as if with an entire planet to search, the SFS should have homed in on them at once. No one reminded Dr. Whittaker that the SFS had no idea where to look, but from the expressions on various faces, Anders was certain he was not the only one who remembered.

❖   ❖   ❖

Despite Dr. Whittaker's confident assertions, the fourth day of their castaway existence passed without their being found. On the fifth day, morale was distinctly low.

On the third day, Kesia Guyen had done her part to solve the question of who had access to the increasingly diminished supply of power packs for the counter-grav units by refusing to have anything more to do with surveying the remnants of the treecat community.

"I do have training in fieldwork," she said, "but my primary skills are linguistic. I've had it with climbing trees, knowing I'll bust my butt—or something a lot less well-padded—if I fall. I'm going to go sit with Dacey and turn my belt unit off unless I absolutely need to move."

Anders watched in trepidation as Dr. Whittaker—he just couldn't think of him as "Dad" when he got this way— ballooned up like a ship's captain facing incipient mutiny.

Then Langston Nez coughed. The injured man had been doing more of this. The stuff coming up his throat didn't look good: thick, viscous, and the color of mud. Anders tried to believe that it was good that some of this stuff was coming out, but it was hard to convince himself. Langston only had a low-grade fever, the sort even a minor system irritation like an allergy could cause. Nonetheless, his cheeks were hollow and his eyes—which occasionally fluttered open, but never seemed to see them—were sunken.

"Perhaps," Dr. Whittaker said, "that is a good choice, Kesia. Dacey has been doing triple duty. Maybe if the two of you work together, you'd be able to get a bit more liquid into Langston. Water is more important than food for survival."

Dr. Calida continued her researches, but since these supplied the bulk of their food, no one suggested she stop. Anders had assigned himself as her assistant, but to do his part to preserve power for the counter-grav units, he always slept (or tried to) with his unit turned off. There was no more soaring aloft lighter than his surroundings to pick nuts or seed pods.

Breakfast that morning was slim: small portions of a grilled fish-thing mixed with a strong-tasting fungus. The fungus smelled like old boots, but actually tasted sort of buttery. Marjorie Harrington's notes commented that it was full of protein, though the entry ended, "Unless we can breed a variation that eliminates the odor but not the nutritional value, this fungus is likely to be—like the durian fruit of Old Terra—only appreciated by gourmets."

Choking down his portion, Anders had to agree.

When they returned for lunch—bringing with them the strange array of plants that would be all they had for dinner unless the new location to which they'd moved the fish traps proved a lucky one—they found Dr. Whittaker in full rant.

"What I can't understand," he said, "is why no one has

thought to look for us here! Surely, Ranger Jedrusinski must recall she showed us this place. By now—we've been missing for five days."

"Three," mouthed Kesia, who was becoming distinctly mutinous.

In spite of the linguist's constant jokes about how John was going to love her newly slimmed self, it was clear that Kesia worried how he was taking her being missing. Apparently, John Qin hadn't gotten where he had in business without having a strong sense of what was due to him and his.

Virgil's situation was worse because—unlike Kesia who, maybe because of her husband's relatively well-to-do station, had decided she could defy Dr. Whittaker—Virgil clearly felt his dependence strongly. Doubtless he was all too aware of the impending baby and knew this was not a time for him to go looking for work.

Even when twilight forced them in from their field work, Virgil would sit cataloging artifacts or photo-images by the light of one of the low-power light units with which they were fortunately well-supplied. Virgil rarely mentioned Peony Rose, but Anders had seen how frequently he glanced at her picture on his uni-link when he thought no one was looking.

I heard Dacey and Kesia talking. The first trimester is the riskiest time for a pregnancy. Morning sickness can just be the body adjusting, but Dacey said sometimes it means the body's having trouble keeping the baby. Virgil's got to know this. He must be mad with worry.

Now, as Dr. Whittaker continued his harangue against the SFS in general and Ranger Jedrusinski in particular, Anders could see that Kesia was about to get herself into trouble. He couldn't let her do that. She'd done more than Dad to make certain they were comfortable. She was the one who had fixed Langston's counter-grav unit. She was the one who told stories at night, when they were all worn out but needed something to feed the soul as well as the body before they could sleep. Now she was helping with Langston, cleaning him and nursing water into him with infinite patience.

Anders couldn't let Kesia say anything that would irrevocably ruin her chances at academic advancement—or worse, create a situation in which she might have to bring his dad up against some sort of review board to prove her rights. That wouldn't help either of them. Academics could be as touchy as the military about hierarchies—and the rules were a lot less clear-cut.

"Dad," Anders said, speaking over whatever Kesia had been about to say. "You're wrong and you know you are. I was along that day, don't forget. Ranger Jedrusinski took us to dozens of places related to treecats in one way or another."

"Yes. But this was the only real site. Surely, if she used her pea brain for something other than keeping lists of rules and regulations, she would remember this very important area and think to direct the search there."

"She'd also remember," Anders said, hands on hips, chin thrust upwards in defiance, "that this was the one and only place among all those locations that you were expressly forbidden to come back to. I suppose if she was a less direct sort of person she'd realize you couldn't resist the temptation, but my guess is that if and when the SFS does start retracing those locations, this will be the last place they'll look precisely because they wouldn't think you'd be slime enough to betray their trust."

That did it. Anders knew it. Despite the circle of watching adults, Dad actually took a step toward Anders, his hand raised to wallop him as he hadn't done since Anders was old enough to understand words. Something was shattering in Dad, breaking the shell of civilization.

Behind Dad, Virgil was taking cautious steps forward, obviously prepared to intervene. Anders shook his head to stop Virgil. After all, wasn't he doing this especially for him and Kesia?

"Dad," Anders said, fumbling for words that would slow his father before he did something foolish, but at the same time reluctant to relinquish his position. "Dad... I'm sorry, but..."

"Anders, I've put up with enough of your insubordination!"

Dr. Whittaker's hand continued inexorably toward Anders. Was it really moving in slow motion? Anders watched, horrified, knowing exactly how that meaty fist would feel, especially with all the extra force of Sphinx's gravity behind it.

That last realization awoke Anders' sense of self-preservation. He dropped his hand to his counter-grav unit, switching up the power just long enough so that he could dodge out of the way. Dr. Whittaker's hand swept through open air, the violence of the gesture enough to cause him to stumble and fall forward. Anders started running, his feet still unnaturally light.

Dr. Whittaker struggled to his feet, rage fading into confusion. "Anders... I... Anders, come back here!"

But Anders was already gone.

✧   ✧   ✧

Stephanie—and Jessica, who was sleeping in her room—were awakened slightly before dawn by Stephanie's dad. Richard Harrington looked grim.

"Steph, get up and moving. The search has been called off, but you're still needed—more than ever, in fact."

"What? Called off?"

"You'll get briefing from the SFS with more details than I have," he said, giving her a quick hug then hurrying for the door. "A lightning strike last night in the foothills north of here set off what's rapidly becoming a raging fire. I'm going to wake up Karl. Your mom set out food before she left to go save some experimental plants that could be threatened if the fire moves west. I'm off to my clinic in town. They're bringing the injured to me there since Twin Forks is likely to remain a safe point."

"Right, Dad. Thanks!"

Stephanie had rolled out of bed and was now pulling on her clothes. Jessica was doing the same. Faster than Stephanie would have thought possible, they were dressed and downstairs.

Karl joined them a moment later.

"Grab that stuff," he said, pointing to the array of protein bars and fruit Marjorie Harrington had set out. "I'll get the car. Time enough to eat once we're moving."

Stephanie, Karl, and Jessica arrived at the SFS regional headquarters in Twin Forks and hurried inside. Even though the fire was hundreds of kilometers distant, the smoke overhead was thick enough that the light of the rising sun was dampened into an artificial twilight. A faint, not completely unpleasant scent of burning wood tinged the air.

Inside the station, they saw that the largest meeting room had been transformed into command central for those working the fire. There they found Frank Lethbridge in charge of immediate operations.

Although he had cleaned up some, the ranger had evidently already been out at the fire. Grime clung beneath his fingernails and had settled into the creases of his face. He smelled strongly of smoke. When they came in, he was just finishing talking to a woman in an SFS uniform—Assistant Ranger Geraldine something or other. Stephanie had met her a few times, but didn't know her well.

"Go and triage that latest group of volunteers," Lethbridge was saying. "Remember, even those who can't be cleared to go out to the fire itself can help. We're going to need pilots to shuttle people back and forth from the various fire areas. We're going to need people to man relief stations in the safety zones. Oh! And someone needs to take a van to the warehouse and bring out more of those emergency kits—the ones with a suit, shelter, and a Pulaski. Have them bring some bladder bags and drip torches, too, but be careful who gets those—especially the torches. Oh! If you find anyone with experience flying heavier vehicles, send them to Smitty. He's coordinating the water drops."

Geraldine hurried out, giving the three young people a quick, tight nod as she passed.

As was so often the case in times of crisis, momentarily, the room was empty.

Frank Lethbridge greeted them with a weary nod. "Thanks for coming so quickly. I've got a job picked out for you already."

He indicated a holomap. "Here's the head of the fire. It's moving northwest, picking up speed as the winds rise. As you can see, although the lightning strike hit within a Forestry Service district, if it continues in that direction, it's going to threaten Hayestown and the Painter settlement, as well as several smaller holdings. We're hoping to use branches of the Weeping River as an anchor point from which to build a fire line.

"What I want you to do is go south. We've had a report that there was a second lightning strike down that way. The level of heat and smoke from the main fire is intense enough that it's reducing our ability to tell how this secondary fire is spreading. However, we do have reports the wind is shifting from the original northwestern push, acquiring a southern dimension."

Stephanie frowned. "You didn't call us out at dawn just to put us away from where we're needed, did you? If that's the way it is, I'd like permission to go back to looking for the missing xenoanthropological crew."

She knew she was being rude, but the food her mom had put out seemed to have filled her belly without giving her any strength. Worry washed through her like waves against a cliff, battering her normal composure to sand.

Lethbridge shook his head. "Stephanie, this is not make-work. You and Karl have shown yourselves capable both of being methodical and taking initiative when needed. Right now, we have ample strong backs. What we need are people who can take a look at forest conditions and decide how serious the situation is. Usually, I'd delegate a couple of rangers, but right now, with the main fire encroaching on so many human habitations, we're getting lots of volunteers and we need the rangers to brief and coordinate them."

Karl cut in. "And that's one job we can't do. No one would take us seriously. Right, Frank? I mean, Ranger Lethbridge..."

"Right," Lethbridge said. "But we do take you seriously. Can you handle this?" He gave a tired grin. "And 'Frank's' okay as long as it's just us..."

Stephanie nodded slowly. "But the xenoanthropologists... Yesterday their being missing was a major crisis with not only personal but political ramifications. Today they're just being forgotten?"

Frank glanced at the hologram of the fire. Updated from satellite feed, it was a living map. For now, the fire showed as clouds of thick white and gray smoke, an angry red glow beneath. From her training, Stephanie knew how quickly that red might climb to the treetops. If the wind caught it, then what was already a wildfire would mutate into something far worse—a crown fire, spreading from treetop to treetop, capable of leaping both human-made control lines and natural barriers such as rivers.

Whatever Frank saw in that image, apparently it reassured him that he could spend a little more time explaining the situation to the probationary rangers and their friend.

"You're not the only ones who are worried. We are, too. Last night, Chief Ranger Shelton had the spouses of two of the missing people in his office demanding a full-scale search be mounted. The woman was weeping and looking sick. The man was threatening lawsuits. Only Dr. Hobbard's powers of persuasion are keeping them from taking the story to the newsies."

Frank pressed his eyes closed, and Stephanie guessed that he'd been present for the unpleasant scene.

"By then, however, we knew the fire which had been reported that afternoon was turning nasty, so Chief Ranger Shelton decided that the search for the xenoanthropologists must be given lower priority. If Dr. Whittaker and his team are still alive—and I sincerely hope they are—the area where they went down is quite distant from that threatened by the fire. Basically, they're safer wherever they are than we are right here. Right now many square kilometers of forest are threatened. That's bad enough, but if the fire gets any further out of control, then hundreds of humans' lives are at risk. When you weigh that against seven people, it's a pretty cold equation."

He paused and indicated the fire. "Are you going to follow orders, Probationary Ranger Harrington, or would you like to be released from duty?"

Heart beating strongly in her ears, Stephanie struggled against the impulse to pull out her treasured badge and throw it on the table. But that grand gesture would be far from grand. It would be a fit of temper, worthy of a child, not of a young woman who wanted to live up to the trust that badge—an emblem of a post Chief Ranger Shelton had created for her and Karl—implied.

Stephanie gave a smile that she hoped would show nothing of her inner turmoil and said. "That southern fire needs checking out. Can we have a kit for Jessica, too?"

Frank Lethbridge gave her a lopsided grin, one that revealed for the first time how much he had dreaded that Stephanie would elect to follow the prompts of her own considerable will.

"Absolutely. Report in as you find how the southern fire is spreading. You'll have access to a version of the data here, so you'll be able to see when we need updating. Otherwise, consider yourselves free agents. As I said, what we need is your capacity for taking initiative."

When they collected a kit for Jessica, they were also issued bladder bags already loaded with a mixture of fire-retardant chemicals and water.

"I'm giving you," Geraldine said, "a pair of drip torches. You know how to use the torch?"

Karl nodded. "We've had training."

"Right. Just...be *careful* if you have to use them, okay?"

"We will." Karl flashed a grin. "We have no desire to have the next big one called the Zivonik/Harrington fire."

When they were back in the air car, Stephanie suggested they get into their fire-suits as they drove.

"If we need them," she said, "it's going to be when we don't want to waste time getting into them."

Karl immediately set the auto-pilot—they were in open space, speeding over the green canopy of a forest that did not yet know its danger—and pulled his suit on over his clothes. As Stephanie did the same, she glanced to the backseat to see if Jessica needed help. The other girl was doing fine, but Stephanie found herself feeling just a tiny bit jealous of the interesting way Jessica's fire-suit emphasized her curvaceous figure.

On me, she thought, *the darn thing just covers over what little curve I've got!*

Lionheart bleeked in what Stephanie was certain was amusement.

Jessica looked up from where she had been fastening the ankle tabs on her suit. "What will we do with Lionheart if we need to go out?"

Stephanie stroked the treecat's thick gray fur along his back, trying to hide her concern.

"I'll try to convince him to stay in the air car, but the decision is going to be his. He's not a pet or a child. He's a person—a grown-up person. If I'm going to respect that, I'm going to need to allow him to make his own choices."

"But what if he gets burned? We have these suits and goggles and respirators, but what about him?"

"Lionheart's pretty smart about avoiding danger," Stephanie said. "When Karl and I did our training classes, one of the things we learned to do was use a fire shelter."

She held up a package not much larger than a folded man's shirt. "Have you ever seen one of these?"

"No, I haven't. How could something that small be a shelter?"

"It's made of light thermwall material, so it folds down pretty tight. Like our fire-suits, the material is fire-resistant and protects against radiant heat. Okay, imagine the following situation. We're out there taking a look at a tongue of a fire, judging how great a risk it offers."

"Right."

"The wind shifts—winds do that a lot during fires because the heat of the fire itself creates wind—suddenly, though you'd been standing ten meters from the fire, you realize a tongue of fire too wide for you to safely make it through, even in your suit, has cut you off from a safe point. Worse, you can see the flames are coming toward you. You rip open this packet and pull this tab.

It opens up into a small tent. You crawl inside and seal it shut. The flames race over you, leaving you maybe a bit hotter, but unburnt. When the flames have passed, you come out and get to safety."

"But what if the flames don't pass?" Jessica asked. "Do I just sit in there and cook?"

Karl chuckled. "Unless you set your tent up on top of a pile of brush or a tree trunk or in a grove of trees or something, the flames will pass. No matter how powerful a fire may seem when you look at something like the holomap Ranger Lethbridge had, fires need at least four conditions or they can't exist. Steph?"

Dutifully, Stephanie recited: "Oxygen, fuel, heat, and a self-sustained chemical reaction. Eliminate any of these and the fire will die. That's called the 'fire tetrahedron.' An easier version to remember is the 'fire triangle'—oxygen, fuel, and heat."

"So in that lovely little story you told," Jessica said, "I've had the brains not to put my tent right in the middle of a heap of fuel. Oxygen can't really be eliminated out in the open and there would be plenty of heat, but once the fire burns up the fuel, then it can't stay there. Right?"

"You've got it," Stephanie said. "Moreover, as your teammates, we'd be doing what we could to help. The bladder bags contain water mixed with various fire-suppressant chemicals. Water eliminates heat as well. We'd spray it in the area around your shelter."

"So these bladder bags are basically like the fire extinguisher we have in the kitchen at home?"

"Pretty much, but the sprayer has a lot more range and the chemicals have been tailored to deal with a fire that will have unlimited oxygen, unlike a structure fire, where the structure itself can dampen the fire for a time. They're also equipped to be quickly refilled, unlike your home extinguisher, which is pretty much a one-use item."

Jessica nodded. "You started this because I asked about how Lionheart would deal with a fire. Did you teach him how to use a fire shelter?"

"We did," Stephanie said. "It wasn't easy, because he has a treecat's ingrained caution regarding fire, but he's smart. Once he saw the demonstration a few times, I think he figured out how useful such shelters could be."

"That reminds me," Jessica said. "I wanted to ask about the last piece of equipment you were given, that drip torch. It sounded to me like the ranger was actually suggesting you might need to *start* a fire. That sounds crazy."

"It does," Stephanie agreed, "but using fire to fight fire is an old technique and one that still has its place. Remember how I said that 'fuel' is one of the key elements in creating a fire-ready condition?"

"Yes."

"Well, if you eliminate fuel, you can eliminate one of the directions in which the fire can spread. Sometimes you can do that by soaking the fuel in advance of the fire. Sometimes firebreaks are built—either with tools or, if there's time, using machinery. You cut away the trees, limbs, and snags, leaving nothing but bare dirt. When fire gets to the break it's stopped. If the fire isn't too fierce, sometimes even a line made with the side of a boot—as long as it clears the area down to bare dirt or rock—can create a large enough break."

Karl took over. "But there are times when it's faster to burn the fuels up in advance of the fire. That works well with 'light' fuels like grass, leaves, pine needles, and dry slash. You make certain you have a fire line around them, then burn out the middle. When the main fire arrives, it finds bare earth where a meadow full of yummy dried grass would have been."

Jessica shuddered. "It sounds horrible, transforming a meadow into a burnt waste."

"The fire would have done it anyhow," Stephanie said, "and this way the forest on the other side is protected."

"Mostly, these days," Karl said, "fire is used for clearing a safe zone. That's what that Franchitti idiot said he was doing when he started the fire a few weeks ago."

He glanced at the navigation screen and made a few adjustments.

"We're closing in on the southern side of the fire. I'm going to bring us down beneath the canopy now. Time to stop talking and start watching."

Stephanie nodded and turned her attention to the window. Lionheart climbed into her lap, equally intent.

Yet even as Stephanie turned her attention to charting the spread of a tongue of the secondary fire, a sense that she was partaking in a deep betrayal filled her. She shouldn't be here. She should be out there, searching for someone. For one someone. For Anders.

There were times when being smart enough to know where duty lay distinctly sucked.

CLIMBS QUICKLY SAT IN DEATH FANG'S BANE'S LAP and watched with horrified fascination as fire devoured trees only a few body lengths away. He could sense that the three two-legs who rode in the vehicle with him were alert and watchful. Their certainty that they were all out of reach of the fire, that they could escape if the fire began to rage, made it possible for him to keep from panicking, although every bone in his body tingled with the urge to get away.

The People did use fire, but rather than that making them careless, certain they could control its various moods, they were extremely careful. From the time they could scrabble about, kittens were taught that when a spark landed in their fur the worst thing they could do was panic and run. That created the wind that fed the fire. Instead, they should find a patch of bare earth and roll on it, smothering the fire before it could spread. Fortunately, the natural oils in a living Person's coat meant a spark was more likely to smoulder, giving time for such measures.

But no amount of rolling would smother the flames that now raged so close at hand. Climbs Quickly mused that he was much more tense than on the day when they had rescued Left-Striped and Right-Striped. Doubtless that was because on that day something had needed to be done, leaving no room for apprehension or fear.

Perhaps it was thoughts of that day that caused Climbs Quickly to send his thoughts roving. He had no idea where they were in relation to anywhere else, for the manner in which the air car sped over the treetops robbed him of his usual tracking abilities. He didn't think he was anywhere near where his own Bright Water Clan denned. Not only was there no hint of Sings Truly's mind-voice, but he thought that Death Fang's Bane—who had taken his clan as her own—would be more troubled.

Even more troubled, he amended. Ever since she had awoken that morning, his two-leg had been nothing but a mounting bundle of conflicting emotional impulses. On the surface, she was the calm and rational person he had come to love and trust, but beneath that lay an emotional storm at least as hot and raging as the forest fire—but he hoped less destructive.

All his life, Climbs Quickly had been told he possessed a very strong mind-voice. After he bonded with Death Fang's Bane, that voice had become even stronger. Now, as he cast his thoughts through the surrounding area, seeking any who might be in distress, he came upon far more than he had sought. This time the voices were not calling, but rather were "overheard" as they spoke loudly to each other.

<Move quickly! Scouts report that the fire approaches.>
<Get those kittens away from there!>
<Help the aged one.>

<No!> A sense of violent protest. <Nothing will be lost if my bones go to earth a season before their time. Help Wide Tail instead.>

This and more, for the People's language was not restricted to units of communication as Climbs Quickly was coming to suspect the mouth noises of the two-legs were. Wordless images were his to comprehend. He saw a clan of the People, new, he guessed, to this dwelling area, gathering themselves for flight, yet knowing that they might not be swift enough to escape the encroaching flames.

He saw the reports of their scouts and from these pieced together the awareness that the greater fire had been thought to be no real threat since a branch of the much larger river provided a natural barrier.

Therefore, although the clan had been making preparations to move out if danger threatened, there had been no immediate urgency.

Having only been in this new location a short time, this clan had not yet had an opportunity to check the full length of the branch of the river they now trusted to keep them safe from the fire, nor had they considered how the picketwood they had used to cross the stream would also carry fire.

Climbs Quickly shook his head slightly, as if the motion would help organize all this information. He could see what the scouts had seen and knew the danger these People were in. He also realized he knew what clan this must be. This must be the Damp Ground Clan, the same clan for which Right-Striped and Left-Striped had been scouting when that other fire had caught up to them. He reached for his friends' mind-glows, but did not find them.

Were they then dead or were they merely out of reach of even his powerful mind-voice? As young scouts, well-seasoned in the dangers of fire, they might have been chosen for some particularly dangerous mission.

All of this had come to Climbs Quickly in a few breaths. Now he tried to think how best to alert Death Fang's Bane. He had seen the air car loaded with what he knew were devices for fighting fire. They might be enough to slow this new blaze so that the Damp Ground Clan could make their escape.

He must guide them to the endangered clan. He only hoped he was up to the challenge... and that they would arrive in time.

◇   ◇   ◇

Stephanie focused hard on tracking the spreading western tongue of the South Fire against the SFS map, because if she didn't, her mind wandered and she found herself wondering just what had happened to Anders. Where could the xenoanthropologists have gotten to? She didn't like to consider the possibility that—as in the case of Tennessee Bolgeo—once again the SFS and Dr. Hobbard had been fooled into accepting fakes.

There was only one problem with that theory: Lionheart. The treecat had never liked "Doctor" Bolgeo, even when he was at his most charming. His reaction to Dr. Whittaker's group had been calm and accepting. He'd seemed to like Anders during the time they'd spent together. He hadn't bristled at Dr. Whittaker or any of his crew.

Stephanie hadn't realized how much she had come to trust the treecat's judgement until this moment. Now she'd have given almost anything to remember some incident of Lionheart demonstrating anger or disapproval, but there was nothing, and that meant...

In her lap, Lionheart suddenly stiffened, shifting from his comfortable sitting position onto his hindmost pair of legs. Swiveling his flexible torso, he turned so he could meet her eyes with his own. Assured that he had her attention, he very carefully pointed along the line of the fire.

"Bleek," he said, then more urgently, "Bleek!"

"Lionheart seems to be suggesting we move along the edge of the fire. Since that's what we're doing already, maybe he wants us to go faster."

Jessica leaned forward from the backseat, clearly fascinated. "Is this what he did when you rescued those treecats?"

Karl sped up, nodded. "Pretty much, but that time he wanted us to change course. I wonder what he wants this time?"

Lionheart had turned and was watching intently out the air car's front window, his hand-feet braced against the dashboard.

Stephanie shrugged. "I have no idea, but especially after last time, I figure we'd be idiots not to take him seriously."

Her uni-link signaled an incoming call. Although she was reluctant to take even a little of her attention from Lionheart and the call wasn't from her parents—they had their own unique chimes—she glanced at the readout.

"Chet Pontier!" she said, surprised, recognizing the name of one of the hang-gliding club members. "What could he want?"

"Maybe he and Christine had a fight and he wants to ask you out," Jessica said impishly. "Go on, answer it!"

Blushing and looking sideways at Karl, though she had no idea why, Stephanie took the call.

"Stephanie here."

Chet's holo appeared floating above the tiny screen. "Hi, Steph. Listen, I don't know if you've been listening to the reports, but the fire up north has gotten bad enough that they've expanded the call for volunteers. Christine and

I qualify for the age cut-off, easily, and Toby wants to try. They said fifteen and up, and he's just a few months shy. We wondered if there was anywhere in particular you thought we should go so we don't get stuck pouring punch somewhere."

Stephanie considered. "They've posted more than one place where you can report?"

"Yeah, they're handing out kits in downtown Twin Forks, even."

"Don't waste time going to Forestry Service head-quarters," Stephanie said. "When we were there really early this morning, they were already swamped. You'd probably do better at the Twin Forks general recruitment post. They'd be more likely to overlook Toby's age, too."

"Thanks." The tiny holo generated by Stephanie's uni-com didn't show much detail, but she could see Chet looked a little sheepish... Or was that embarrassed?

"We all admired what you and Karl did during the last fire," Chet said, "so, well, we wanted to ask your advice. Maybe we'll see you on the fire lines."

Stephanie wanted to start reminding Chet that this was no time for heroics, but Lionheart was shifting nervously in her lap. She settled for "Good luck. Be careful!" and commed off.

At their greater speed, they had probably missed some smaller details of the fire, but now they had arrived at the leading edge of this particular tongue. It wasn't advancing very fast. The dominant wind was pushing it more to the west, conflicting with the earlier southern wind.

Stephanie was not particularly surprised to see Lionheart now pointing for them to turn west, to go past this edge of the fire and into a zone that was, as yet, unburned. The key phrase here was "as yet." If the wind whipped up, that area would certainly be more dangerous than their current location.

"Lionheart wants us to go toward that island," Stephanie said. "From the SFS map, that region should be mostly safe, at least for now. The Makara River will provide a natural firebreak."

"I can take the air car up if we run into trouble," Karl said, changing their direction, but giving the fire a wide berth. "We've got to try something. Lionheart is really upset."

"Let's go in a ways," Jessica urged. "Like you said, we can always pull up. The fire here is mostly burning the lower reaches. It hasn't gone up into the crown like it has in the northern fire."

Lionheart relaxed slightly after Karl made the turn, but he did not settle back into Stephanie's lap. Instead, he continued to focus forward, suggesting occasional course corrections with motions of his remaining true hand. Eventually, he directed them to cross the southern branch of the Makara River to the island.

Stephanie scanned the area below and saw something that filled her with dismay.

"Damn! Look down near the eastern tip of the island. See where the picketwood crosses from the mainland to the island?"

"You mean where the river branch gets narrow?" Jessica said.

"That's it." Stephanie said a word she wasn't supposed to use six times. "Given the wind direction, the fire's going to hit right there. The picketwood will be as good a bridge for fire as it is for any of the local wildlife."

"One of the weaknesses of picketwood," Karl agreed. "Your mom's research shows it can seal off diseased sections within itself but it can't do anything about fire. I wish it could create natural firebreaks that way, too, instead of actually helping the flames spread."

None of them felt any doubt that the fire would reach

this point. Although they were farther from the actively burning areas, the air was thick with smoke. Karl was relying heavily on the air car's navigation systems to help him avoid the trees. It was almost maddening to see him looking at the heads-up display, not through the windshield, as he steered.

Stephanie leaned forward as if somehow that would help her see more clearly. She might have felt foolish but for the awareness that Jessica was doing the same thing.

Occasionally, they saw shadowy forms moving through the smoke. Most were indistinct, but once or twice Stephanie could clearly make out one of the mid-sized herbivores the colonists lumped together under the name "near-deer." Another time, more heartbreakingly, she saw a pair of near-otters pushing along. Bodies well-adapted to water struggled on land as they strove to reach the Makara River.

"They don't think this area's going to stay safe much longer," Jessica commented, her voice tight and choked. "I wish we could give them a ride."

"They'd just panic," Karl said, but he also sounded miserable.

When Lionheart "bleeked" loudly and pointed, at first Stephanie thought he was indicating another near-otter, which, for some reason, had climbed up into a tree.

No, she realized. *That's not a near-otter.*

"A treecat," she gasped aloud, gesturing in unconscious imitation of Lionheart. As Jessica and Karl turned to look, forms within the smoke moved. They saw clearly furry masses staring down at them. "No! It's not one treecat. There are at least four of them. They must be part of a clan, trying to escape the fire."

Karl set the air car to hover they could assess the situation. "Steph, a treecat clan is too large to fit in this car, even if we got out and walked. We can't save a whole clan."

"Yes, we can," Stephanie said defiantly. "The first step is to slow the fire."

✧   ✧   ✧

Anders was in mid-flight when he heard Dr. Calida say, "Does anyone else smell smoke?"

There was something in her voice that made Anders stop in mid-step and edge his way back into the company. His dad was standing open-mouthed, staring at his own hand as if he couldn't believe what he had been about to do. Everyone else had frozen in place, then Dacey turned to look at the little field stove on which she had been doing all of their cooking.

"It's not from here," she said, sniffing the air, "but I think you're right, Calli. I do smell smoke—wood smoke."

Anders sniffed and caught the distinct scent of burning wood. At first his heart leapt. Maybe someone was coming to the rescue! Then reality struck. No rescuers would be burning anything, not in this dry season. This had to have another source.

A quick check around their arboreal camp showed that none of their equipment was the source of the odor. Anders volunteered to climb up to where he could see above the immediate forest canopy. The rapidity with which everyone agreed that this would be a good idea was significant.

We need to forget what Dad almost did, Anders thought as he puffed his way aloft. *For now . . . But I'm not sure I'll ever forget . . . or forgive.*

Without the long "tail" of his flagpole pulling him down, the climb went more easily, even with his counter-grav unit reset to save power. Anders wondered if he was finally getting used to the pull of the extra gravity—or at least was developing reflexes to compensate. He thought of Karl Zivonik's broad shoulders and heavier build, how muscular and well-developed he was, especially for a young man of his age.

I wonder, if I stayed here, would I get like that, or do you have to grow up in this sort of environment?

Anders knew he was thinking like that to quiet the latent shaking in his muscles, his fear that when he went back down his dad would go after him again. Instead, he concentrated on finding and testing each hand- and foothold, all too aware of the price he'd pay if he fell. At last he was up where he could poke his head above the leafy boughs. What he saw was poor reward for his labors. Even as cooler breezes caressed his face, drying the accumulated sweat, he saw in the distance a pillar of white and gray smoke billowing upwards to the east.

At first, the smoke looked self-contained and quite small. Then Anders' perspective adjusted and he realized that the plumes of smoke were enormous. Beneath them, he glimpsed a reddish-orange glow. Belatedly, Anders recalled that he'd been sent aloft with a pair of high-powered binoculars. With these, he was able to pick out more detail. He realized that this fire was only one of two—a much larger one was burning to the north.

Although Anders was aware of voices shouting up at him from below, he did not reply. He was too high up to shout with anything like clarity and he certainly wasn't making this climb again. Dismissing the northern fire—which, despite its size, posed no threat to their group—he focused again on the one to the east.

His initial impression had been that the plumes of smoke were going straight up, but now he realized that this had been an illusion created by their vast size and his own position relative to them. As he studied them more carefully, he was able to guess at wind direction.

He swallowed hard. There was no doubt about it. Although the main body of the fire was still a good distance away, the conflagration could eventually head in their direction. The main push of wind was from the south, but a secondary current was slowly shoving the fire west.

"I'm coming down," Anders called. "Wait a minute."

When he reached the location of their camp, he reported what he'd seen, ending, "I think we're safe for now, but we should get ready to evacuate."

As he fully expected, his announcement caused considerable debate. Virgil was ordered up the tree to take a look at the fire himself, since Dr. Whittaker felt "we cannot plan solely on data supplied by a boy my son's age." Anders guessed that maybe he deserved that, since he really hadn't been able to evaluate distances or provide any idea how rapidly the front of the fire might be progressing in their direction—but in light of their recent conflict the words stung.

Virgil's scouting expedition didn't provide much more information, but he did second Anders' recommendation that they should prepare to evacuate if necessary.

"If necessary" was said with an uneasy glance toward the comatose form of Langston Nez. This morning the sick man had seemed a little . . . Anders wasn't sure if "better" or "stronger" was the right word, but both Dacey and Kesia agreed that Langston was swallowing more readily and that his bladder was beginning to function. Kesia cheerfully admitted to having rigged a sort of diaper for him from a couple other items out of her supply of clothing.

However, swallowing and peeing did not translate into "up and ready to go." Therefore, any plans for evacuation had to include how they would move Langston—plans that would doubtless mean exhausting more of their nearly depleted stock of power packs for the counter-grav units.

Making matters worse was the fact that Dr. Whittaker was reluctant to leave behind any of his precious artifacts.

Never mind that Dr. Calida had pointed out none too gently that treecats were hardly an endangered species and that doubtless other such items could be gathered in the future. Dr. Whittaker's attachment to these bits of stone and fragments of basketry ranged on the fanatical.

"Don't you understand?" he urged, cupping a particularly fine flint point in the palm of one broad hand. "As the SFS actions following the Ubel disaster demonstrate, they are perfectly willing to contaminate treecat culture with material from our own. These represent uncontaminated specimens—gathered without the treecats' knowledge. The history of anthropology is full of situations where a people under examination told the anthropologists what they wanted to hear and so distorted and contaminated the study sample."

"Bradford," Dr. Calida said, speaking so gently that Anders knew she distrusted his father's mental stability, "I don't think the situations are comparable. The treecats are not going to invent technologies simply because they think you might like to study them. Even if they do, well, I would think that level of adaptability would be proof of their intelligence that no one could doubt."

"Yeah," quipped Kesia. "If one of those furry little critters showed up right now with a heap of packs for the counter-grav units, I'd be thrilled, even if the packs were made from leaves and berries."

"As long as they worked," Virgil agreed with a grin, then swallowed hard when he saw Dr. Whittaker glowering at him. "What I mean is we wouldn't want a cargo cult situation, where the locals were making facsimiles of what was then high-tech equipment like airplanes, in an attempt to bring the benefits of that technology to them."

His answer seemed to satisfy Dr. Whittaker.

"Non-functioning imitation is an interesting possibility," he said. "There has been some evidence that treecats are developing agriculture. Dr. Hobbard has written a report indicating that this development may post-date human arrival on Sphinx—that is, that the treecats have learned from observation."

"Well," Kesia said, her tone almost sassy, "I don't think they're likely to learn flintknapping from any human on Sphinx, so I guess we can leave the spear points behind. I, for one, am not shlepping rocks with everything weighing at least fifteen percent more."

Her open mutiny so stunned Dr. Whittaker that Anders was able to get a word in.

"We can't get far, not carrying Langston. I suggest we move back into the bog where there's water. True, there isn't a lot, but fire and water don't mix."

"Into the bog?" Dr. Whittaker scoffed. "So we can sink along with the van?"

"While Anders and I have been foraging," Dr. Calida said, "we've located some stable areas—islands, you might say. There's at least one that's large enough to hold all of us."

Everyone fell silent as they contemplated this option, then Dacey spoke up.

"There's something else we need to consider," she said. "Smoke. Even if the fire doesn't reach us, eventually smoke will. Langston is having trouble breathing already. He's not going to handle poor air quality well at all, even if we rig him some sort of filter."

"Smoke rises," Anders mused aloud, "so our tree house will be a weak point then. If we move out into the bog, we'd be at ground level, the fire might go around us, and yet we wouldn't have to move anything—Langston or Dad's artifacts—more than a hundred meters or so."

Virgil nodded. "I like that. You and I are the only ones who have actually seen the fire. I'll admit, I'm just not comfortable sitting here waiting up in a tree and hoping the fire doesn't come this way."

Dr. Whittaker nodded. His hand wrapped around the piece of worked flint he held so protectively.

"Very well. I don't much like the idea of settling on ground that could give under us at any minute, but hopefully we won't be out there for very long. Maybe the SFS will finally get its act together and do its job."

Anders turned away, swallowing a sigh. The SFS was doing its job. He didn't doubt for a minute they were out risking their lives, fighting that raging crown fire to the north. He also didn't doubt that they didn't have time to worry about seven missing people when the lives of so many others were at stake.

❖   ❖   ❖

"Slow the fire?" Karl said. "We don't have the equipment to put out a forest fire."

"Slow," Stephanie repeated. "Not stop."

Jessica cut in. "Stephanie, don't you think we'd do a lot better calling this in to the SFS?"

Stephanie shook her head angrily. "I don't. Remember what they said when I asked about keeping up the search for Anders and his group? They're stretched too thin already. The SFS is a great organization, but Jess, look at the map. You've been following the updates. The northern fire is now officially a crown fire. Every time they think they have it blocked, some bit skips ahead of the fire line. Hayestown and the Painter settlement are seriously threatened. How do you think the residents of those areas would react if the SFS suddenly pulled out a team saying, 'Sorry. We've got to go rescue a bunch of 'cats'?"

Jessica pushed her lips together in a tight line. "I get it. But do you think just the three of us can do anything?"

"Yes," Stephanie said. "And it doesn't have to be just us three. Karl, we're going to need to figure out where the fire is in relation to the treecat colony. Can you move us away from here?"

Karl nodded, but as he started the air car moving, Lionheart bleeked loudly and pounded at the window with his hands.

When Stephanie—who had been about to make a call on her uni-link—looked down at him, Lionheart very gently moved his paw to press the latch that operated the door. Ever since the treecat had learned how to open them, they'd routinely kept the doors locked from the master control. Stephanie frowned. She didn't want him to go out there, but . . .

"Karl," she said, "unlock the door so Lionheart can get out. I think he wants to get closer to those treecats. Maybe he can tell them that we're going to do our best to help and not to be afraid."

Karl bit his lip. "Steph, I've been checking and the fire has definitely crossed east of us. He's not going to be safe out there."

Stephanie felt her heart twist, as if someone had taken it in two hands and wrung it. Then she looked at Lionheart.

"It's dangerous out there," she said. "Are you sure?"

Lionheart bleeked and touched the door latch again.

"Let him go out," Stephanie said. "He's a person and deserves that chance to make his own decisions . . ."

Tears welled up in her eyes as she opened the door so the treecat—*her* treecat, no matter what she said to others, *her* best friend—could go out. Air thick with smoke set them all coughing. Lionheart sneezed.

"Be careful," Stephanie said. "Please, be careful."

The treecat nodded once, as if he understood every word. Then he stood up and made the "wait" gesture.

"He wants us to wait," Stephanie said. "So he's not going to run off."

Relief washed over her as Lionheart raced to where the 'cats up in the branches were watching uneasily.

Behind her, Stephanie thought she heard Jessica sniffle as if suppressing a sob.

It's a good thing I can code in without seeing the pad, Stephanie thought miserably as she finished pulling the contact information from her uni-link.

"Chet," she said. "Where are you all?"

"We've just gotten our gear," he said, "and we're heading toward my truck to go to the fire line. Christine and I are going out to help, but Toby's been told he has to stay back in a safe zone and pour drinks."

"Creeps," came Toby's voice from the background.

"Listen," Stephanie said. "I've got an offer for you. It's a heck of a lot more dangerous, though, so I want you to think carefully."

"Go ahead," Chet said. Stephanie had the impression he was angling his uni-link so Christine and Toby could hear.

"We've just discovered—as in like five minutes ago—a clan of treecats on the move from the southern fire. We're going to try to help them get out, 'cause from what I'm seeing here, I don't think they can move fast enough on their own. Would you come and help? Bring the gear you were issued, especially any bladder bags and shelters. Were you given fire-suits?"

"All of us," Chet said, "but Toby only got the suit, none of the other stuff."

"Still, that's enough to work with," Stephanie said. "Can you come—and can you sort of 'forget in the excitement' that you didn't tell anyone of your change in assignment?"

Chet's expression showed that he was aware Stephanie was acting without orders.

"Are you sure about this?" he asked.

"I am," Stephanie said. She thought about a night three years ago when she had ventured out into a thunderstorm, knowing her parents would not quite approve.

"Sometimes it's better not to ask; that way, no one told you that you couldn't do it."

There was a murmur of voices, then Chet was back on. "We're coming. Christine insists on leaving a delayed message for her folks, but they won't get it unless she isn't back by midnight tonight to deactivate it. That's okay?"

"Fine," Stephanie agreed. "One way or another, this is going to be over long before nightfall."

❖   ❖   ❖

The smoke was thick, even near the ground, but it was choking when Climbs Quickly scampered up the trunk of the tree to join the People who huddled there.

They were younglings, he saw, not kittens, but not much older than a full season's turning. Knowing how his own Bright Water Clan dealt with such evacuations, he guessed that these had been sent out ahead of the main body of their clan—considered too young to help with evacuating the slower ones, young enough that they might be a danger to themselves as well as to others.

Certainly their behavior showed that assessment had been perfectly accurate. Looking apprehensively over at the air car, they stayed huddled in the choking smoke, blinking green eyes at him as if he were a death fang or snow hunter.

<Get down closer to the ground,> Climbs Quickly ordered. *<The air is less smoky. What are you doing up there anyhow? Surely your parents taught you better.>*

He knew the edge in his mind-voice was unkind, but the tension and worry in Death Fang's Bane's mind-glow didn't help. Three of the younglings obeyed, but the fourth—a dainty female who carried her tail as if she was much prized by all around her—blinked her large eyes at him.

<You are Climbs Quickly,> she said, beginning her

descent from the tree only after making clear that she was doing it because she wanted to, not because he had given any sort of order. <*My father says you are a disgrace.*>

<*Little Witness!*> One of the males spoke up, embarrassment shading his voice. <*Our mother says Climbs Quickly is a hero. And you have no manners.*>

Little Witness, for so this sassy female must be called, only flirted her tail in reply and scampered along. Her name explained much. It was likely that—like Climbs Quickly's own sister, Sings Truly—Little Witness already showed promise of a strong mind-voice, perhaps even of being a memory singer some day. In some clans, especially those where a memory singer valued herself very highly, those with promise gave themselves airs.

And, strong-voiced or not, in any case, Little Witness was a very cute youngling and evidently knew it.

<*I am Springer,*> the young male introduced himself shyly. <*We went up the tree only when we heard that flying thing coming. It felt like a person, but not like a person. We didn't know what to do.*>

Climbs Quickly stroked his whiskers. <*Are you far ahead of the rest of your clan?*>

Springer's reply was troubled. <*Not very. Most of the clan has not yet left where we were denning. The fire caught us unawares. The elders and the kittens cannot move quickly. I wanted to stay and help, but we were told we would only slow them further. We came this way to see if our net-wood bridge across the river is still intact.*>

<*I fear it is not,*> Climbs Quickly said. <*From what we saw, the fire is using it now.*>

<*Then what will our clan do?*> Springer asked. <*The fire may eat all this island.*>

<*I will hurry to them,*> Climbs Quickly assured Springer, <*and do what I can to help. My two-legs will also help,*>

*be sure of it. Your clan may yet be saved. Turn around
and hurry to rejoin them. Go!>*

He would have liked to try and convince them to get
into the car, but he knew that Little Witness, at least,
would have been stubborn, and time was not to be wasted.
From images he had gleaned from Springer, they were
not far from the clan's central nesting place.

Turning from the four younglings, Climbs Quickly
bunched his muscles and ran as rapidly as he could back
to the air car. Inside, the air was sweet and clear, but
even as he filled his lungs with it, he began pointing—this
time in the direction where the Damp Ground Clan was
battling against time and encroaching fire.

12

WITH LIONHEART TO GUIDE THEM, THEY FOUND THE endangered clan far more quickly than they would have otherwise. Treecats and their dwellings blended very well into their surroundings.

Stephanie had visited Lionheart at "home" and knew what to look for. Treecats didn't impact their environment as much as humans did, but they did create sleeping platforms and places where they could store food.

Examining the section of picketwood to which Lionheart had brought them, Stephanie thought that at any other time this would be a very nice place for treecats to live. A stream originating from some inland source—probably a freshwater spring—created the eastern border, while in the near distance the southern fork of the Makara River ran to the south. To the north, she could glimpse a large meadow thick with waist-high grass. The picketwood grove itself looked strong and healthy. Now, however, with smoke wreathing through the tree limbs, cutting off the daylight so that the lurid glow of the approaching fire seemed like dull, angry sunlight peering out sideways, the area was ugly and unsettling.

It was also a scene of chaos—chaos, Stephanie realized, that had been triggered by their own arrival.

Lionheart bleeked authoritatively and tapped the door with one hand. This time Stephanie opened the door for him without hesitation. If he didn't calm the 'cats, their arrival would do more harm than good.

"We'll wait here," Stephanie said. "Go on."

Whatever Lionheart said to the gathered treecats, it was not accepted with universal approval. Several of the males hissed and spat. They didn't quite arch their backs as Terran cats might do—their long, six-limbed torsos were shaped differently—but the attitude was much the same.

Whatever Lionheart "said" in return did not immediately defuse the situation. From the backseat, Jessica muttered in a mock "hick" accent, obviously speaking for the resident treecats.

"Go away. We don't need your type here, stranger. We're doing fine, just fine, on our own."

Despite the tension of the situation, Stephanie giggled. Karl quirked one corner of his mouth in a half-smile, but when he spoke his voice was tight.

"The fire crossed to this island along the picketwood to the east. As of yet, the wind hasn't carried it to the crown, but when it does, it's going to be too late for these guys, even if they run all out."

Stephanie nodded. "So let's do what we can to slow the fire's approach and keep it from climbing into the crown. That little stream's too narrow to do more than slow the fire, but it does give us a source of water. It's also a logical place to start a fire line."

"Agreed," Karl said. "Let's leave the car back west of the stream. It's just a passenger vehicle—and a light one at that. We can't use it to take down trees. I'm going to set my uni-link to send automatic updates to the SFS."

"Won't they notice we've stopped?"

Karl grinned. "Well, I'm not being precisely dishonest, but I'm programming to send messages that will show us checking out the extent of this particular tongue. I'm guessing that unless we flag something 'urgent,' our data is going into a computerized mapping program. They don't have enough humans to process data by hand."

"It's not precisely dishonest," Stephanie agreed. "Let's get going."

As she and Karl laid their plans, Stephanie had been peripherally aware of Jessica speaking in the backseat. Now the other girl interjected herself into the conversation.

"I called Chet and updated him on our location. A bit of good news. Since he knew he might get assigned to shuttle service, he's piloting one of his family's older 'trucks. It won't be strong enough to take out trees either, but if we can convince the treecats to trust us, we're going to be able to move a bunch all at once."

"Diplomacy," Stephanie said, getting out of the car and casting a worried glance over where Lionheart was now exchanging hisses and snarls with a couple of husky 'cats, "is going to be Lionheart's job."

And let's hope, she thought as she unloaded her gear from the back to the air car, *he can manage it without resorting to violence.*

Unlike most humans, Stephanie Harrington knew all too well how dangerous treecats could be. She'd been in pretty bad shape when the furry mass of Lionheart's clan had swarmed down from the treetops to take on the hexapuma that had attacked them both—drawn, she now suspected, by the scent of her blood from when she'd crashed her hang glider. However, she'd seen the aftermath, heard Frank and Ainsley talk about how badly shredded the corpse had been.

If this group decided to go after Lionheart, he wouldn't have a chance—not one against many, not crippled as he was. She had her handgun with her, but could she shoot at a bunch of treecats, even to save Lionheart? She didn't know and she really hoped she wouldn't need to find out.

Leaving that train of thought behind, Stephanie slung the bladder bag over her shoulders, wearing it like a backpack over her fire-suit.

Such devices had been in use since the earliest days of mechanized firefighting, but this model had a great advantage over its predecessors. When those were empty, that was it, but this one contained a powerful miniature pump and a supply of tablets to recharge the chemical supply. All one needed to do was drop a feeder hose into a source of water and the pack would refill, feeding in the necessary chemicals. Once her own pack was on, Stephanie turned to help Jessica adjust hers.

"Remember what we told you about the fire triangle?" Stephanie asked Jessica.

Jessica nodded, moving next to Stephanie as she hurried toward the stream.

"Yes. Fires need heat, oxygen, and fuel or they can't keep going."

"Right," Stephanie hefted her Pulaski. "That's where this comes in.

"You help your mom with her garden, so use the skills you already have." They were down by the stream now, and Stephanie demonstrated. "Trim away all these little shrubs and suckers. That's what the fire will use first as fuel. If you come across something too thick, activate the vibroblade. Then use the hoe to pull the slash back a few meters. Clear away leaf matter, too. When you're done with an area—say a couple of meters wide, activate the bladder bag and soak the ground. Soak the tree trunks for a couple of meters up their length."

Jessica immediately fell to work. Her technique wasn't SFS-approved, but it was good enough—and fast.

"I get what we're doing," she said, the radio in her suit carrying her voice in short bursts. "First we eliminate the fuel, then we soak the area so it's cooler."

"Right," Stephanie said, from where she was working a few meters upstream. "The chemicals we're mixing in also help keep the fire from processing fuel. If we get a chance, we'll clear both sides of the stream, but one is enough for now."

"But what about the tree trunks?" Jessica asked. "Aren't they fuel?"

Karl's voice joined the conversation. "This stuff we're cutting away is what's called 'light fuel.' It burns fast. Tree trunks are 'heavy fuel.' It takes the fire more time to get a hold of them. Sure, when they do, it's a real pain, but if we can stop them from catching..."

"Like when you're trying to get a fire started when you're primitive camping or something," Jessica said. "You can't just put a match to a log and expect it to catch. You need tinder, then twigs..."

They worked together in easy cooperation. If it hadn't been for the fire they could see burning closer with every minute, Stephanie thought they might even have enjoyed themselves. She'd connected her uni-link to the suit's com system. Just as she was finishing trimming down a stand of saplings, Chet's voice came into her ears.

"We're close," he said. "We've got a visual on Karl's car. Should we land next to it?"

"Do it," Stephanie said. "Are you suited up?"

"All of us," Chet reassured her.

"I'll meet you and show you where to go. Listen, the treecats are really edgy. I don't know if Lionheart's convinced them we're on their side or not, but it's best if you don't go near them."

"Got ya," Chet said. "We're coming in."

Stephanie knew Karl and Jessica had heard Chet's call, so, bending to grab a bunch of the saplings and haul them back out of the cleared zone, she hurried off to meet the new arrivals.

Looking ahead of her, she saw Lionheart and the tree-cats, apparently unchanged from before. Or were they?

The thrum of the approaching truck made everyone look up. Stephanie, fearing that what looked like a delicate situation was about to become unbalanced, hastened to meet it.

Lionheart, she thought, *I wish I could ask you what's going on . . .*

✧   ✧   ✧

<Go away,> said a big male who had introduced himself as Nose Biter, including with the name a short but very vivid image of how he had earned the title.

Climbs Quickly had no doubt that out there was one snow hunter who—no matter that it had been quite young at the time—would never ever go near one of the People again, much less make the mistake of thinking one might serve nicely as the main course for lunch.

However, admirable as Nose Biter's ferocity was in defense of self and kin, it was misdirected and just plain stupid now.

<We are here to help,> Climbs Quickly said. *<Is this not the Damp Ground Clan?>*

<We are,> growled Nose Biter.

<Then,> Climbs Quickly said, not hiding his confusion, *<why are you so hostile? Surely Right-Striped and Left-Striped told how my two-leg and her friend saved them from the burning green-needle tree. Where are they? Have they been sent away like the younglings I met—Springer, Little Witness, and their litter mates?>*

<*They have not,*> came the reply, underscored with a hiss and a snarl. <*Although they should have been. No. The twins have been sent forth to scout the route back to our former nesting place, checking if the way is open. They were eager to redeem themselves for their earlier foolishness.*>

Climbs Quickly thought that if the smoke didn't make smelling anything else impossible, that this Nose Biter would smell very much like Broken Tooth, a senior elder of his own Bright Water Clan and an individual so hidebound that one needed to jump up and down on his head to make him see reasons for change.

Yet, to be fair, more of the People were like Broken Tooth and Nose Biter than were like himself or Swift Striker or even his own sister, Sings Truly. They were capable, but change was not viewed as particularly good or even something to be sought. This was why the People had avoided the two-legs, although they had known of them from the moment the first of their shiny eggs had broken the sky and left the world forever transformed.

Indeed, had Climbs Quickly not been discovered—let himself be discovered—as some still hissed, the People still might be trying to hide from the inevitable. Two-legs had not landed like some strange migrating bird only to flap off and leave nothing but a bright feather and a tale for the memory singers to relate on a dull winter's afternoon. The two-legs were here to stay—and were spreading like fan ears after a rain shower.

Two of Nose Biter's confederates—possibly litter mates, for they shared a similar heavy build—had lumbered forward to flank him, standing between Climbs Quickly and the frightened members of the Damp Ground Clan.

Behind him, Climbs Quickly was aware that Death Fang's Bane, Shadowed Sunlight, and Windswept had gotten out of the car and were taking equipment from the back. Death Fang's Bane was talking in a low voice to Windswept. He felt her mind-glow, calm and steady, brighter somehow than the devouring fire. He also sensed her trust that he could handle these idiotic members of the Damp Ground Clan.

Climbs Quickly projected his mind-voice to address all who cared to listen.

<We are here to help. This fire is larger than you might realize. It was born when lightning touched in the mountains to the east, but now the winds carry it here. Two-legs are attempting to stop the fire—I do not ask you to believe me—if you live, you may speak to others who surely have witnessed their actions. My two-leg and those others—and myself—came to see how the fire was progressing. I heard the unguarded speech of some who 'shouted' and brought us here. Now that we are here, we will not 'go away.' At the least, we will make time for your clan to flee. And I suggest you do so quickly—and hope the fire does not chase you so far that your only hope is to take your chances with the river.>

There was noise from back near the narrow freshwater stream. Climbs Quickly glanced back to see that Death Fang's Bane and her friends were using their tools to make a barrier near the stream, obviously hoping to slow the fire's approach.

<Are they trying to stop the fire?> asked a new voice. This belonged to another male, one who offered no name but did send the sense that he was kin to the twins.

<Yes. They are clearing away the dangerous brush.> Climbs Quickly decided a little sarcasm was not out of line. <A precaution that doubtless this clan meant to take when it was not more pleasant to gather late summer nuts.>

A general flush of embarrassed thought let him know that his guess had been close to what had happened— that there had been those members of the clan who had argued that with fire weather in the air, some needed to protect this new nesting place. Doubtless, after living over such a wet area as he glimpsed in their mental images of their former home, they had forgotten how dangerous scrub growth could be.

<Why then, if clearing the brush is all they do,> retorted Nose Biter, hostility in every note, <do they also scent mark where they are? See how they pee all over the cleared ground? Disgusting behavior! They mark their territory as does a death fang in heat.>

Climbs Quickly whooped aloud, nearly choking on the smoke as he laughed.

<They do not scent mark. Those are tools for carrying water, as we use gourds and lined baskets. They seek to make the earth too wet for the fire. Like us, they know the two are not friends.>

In the far distance, he heard the sound of an approaching air-vehicle. Doubtless Death Fang's Bane had enlisted help. Although the two-legs did not have mind-speech, he had learned they used tools to throw their mouth noises over vast distances.

Already some of the members of the Damp Ground Clan were edging away, panic bright in the air. Climbs Quickly caught fragmented images as they murmured among themselves. The tale of Speaks Falsely and how he had stolen away many of the People and kept them in bondage had come to this place. Apparently, several members of this clan feared that all two-legs were the same.

Death Fang's Bane was trotting up from the side of the stream, hurrying to meet the approaching vehicle. Climbs Quickly knew he only had a few breaths before the most panicked fled—and in fleeing might drive themselves into the very danger he had come here in the hope of avoiding.

<More helpers,> he said. <Two-legs know that it takes many hands to slow a fire. Will you take advantage of

*the time they give you or will you act like kittens who
tremble when a death wing's shadow covers the moon?>*

Three other two-legs spilled out of the vehicle almost
before it had landed. Climbs Quickly recognized them as
members of the hang-gliding club. He was pleased and
let the other People feel his pleasure, sending them an
image of how these younglings caught the wind, master-
ing it as did birds.

Did that image tempt fate? Climbs Quickly wasn't certain
he believed such things, but it was at that very moment that
the wind itself took a hand in the battle of wills.

The border Death Fang's Bane and her friends had
been making to hold back the approaching fire paral-
leled one edge of the net-wood grove which the Damp
Ground Clan had adopted as their new home. Another
edge was a wide meadow, thick with the high summer
grasses, seasoned to golden brown with the coming of
cooler nights and the reduced water in these dry days.

Climbs Quickly felt no doubt that this meadow was one
reason the Damp Ground Clan had chosen this particular
section of net-wood. Not only would the thick grass make
excellent lining for winter nests, but the stubble fields would
attract foraging burrow-runners and other little ground
dwellers, making for better hunting. Lastly, the open area
on this flank would be easy to watch over in the cold times,
when hunger drove the great predators to take risks.

Already the edge of the meadow showed evidence of the
beginning of the harvest, but although the People did eat
some plants, their teeth were not well-adapted to cutting.
Most such harvesting needed to be done with sharp-edged
stones, a slow and wearisome labor. The border that had
been cut was only about a body's length—and that without
the tail—not enough to stop fire.

And at that moment, upstream from where the two-
legs worked so intently hacking away at the shrubs and

branches and spreading their "pee," a gust of wind hurled across the stream a branchlet live with sparks and blew those sparks into flame. The flaming branch landed in a patch of dry grass at the far side of the meadow as gently as if it had been placed there and, like an exotic flower blooming, burst into flame.

Death Fang's Bane shouted something, then began running directly toward where the meadow fire now raged.

✧   ✧   ✧

While Anders and Dr. Calida went to mark a path to a stable island in the bog, Virgil and Kesia started lowering crucial equipment to the ground so it could be transferred to their new camp. Dacey Emberly prepared Langston Nez to be moved, easing him limb by limb onto a stretcher and tying him into place.

Only Dr. Whittaker continued to place his own priorities first. When Anders gently suggested that perhaps bedding was more important than artifacts, Dr. Whittaker shook his head with pity. He, for one, seemed to have forgotten how close he had come to hitting Anders. Anders wondered if he was going crazy.

"My boy," Dad said kindly, "aren't you the one who has been reassuring us that we're going to be rescued any moment?"

Anders hadn't, but he really didn't think this was the time to mention that. He climbed over to where he could check the knots that held Langston's stretcher—they were very firm, if somewhat elaborate, a heritage of what Dacey called her "macrame phase." Then, with both Dacey and Virgil's help, he began easing the stretcher toward the ground.

As Anders strained every muscle, he was aware of his father's chattering, apparently completely unconcerned about a man who had been his closest assistant.

"Remember what we talked about on the trip here? It has already been conclusively shown that the treecats use tools. That hasn't been enough to prove to the narrow-minded plutocrats who have such influence here in the Star Kingdom that treecats are intelligent. What will convince them conclusively is proof that the treecats also practice art and possess philosophy and religion."

As he spoke, Dr. Whittaker waved the broken pieces of a gourd scoop that had been one of his most recent finds. Although purely functional, it was etched around the edges with what were clearly images of the long, splayed picketwood leaves, fanning out realistically from a bough that began at the lower bowl of the scoop.

Anders thought the "art" wasn't much more than what he'd done as a small child, but he had to agree that it clearly was meant to be representational, not random scratchings.

Langston was a few feet from the ground now. Kesia was raising her arms to steady the stretcher and guide it level.

"What's wonderful about this piece," Dr. Whittaker went on, wrapping it in what Anders recognized as his own spare shirt, "is that no one can argue that it was done under human influence. That makes it seminal."

Langston was down now. Anders rolled his shoulders and began the slow climb down so he could help carry the stretcher.

"Anders!" Dr. Whittaker snapped. "Couldn't you at a least help a little? Surely you could carry one of these bundles down. No need to go empty-handed."

"Sorry, Dad," Anders said without pausing. "If you'd been up and down these ladders as many times as I have, you'd know I need both hands."

He got to the bottom and trudged over to join Kesia. She spoke very softly. "Don't think too hard of your

dad. He's suffering from what psychologists call 'displacement.' My grandmother went through something like it
when my granddad died in an unexpected wreck. She
couldn't deal with the idea that something so horrible
could come out of nowhere. Suddenly the health of her
pet fur-button became the most important thing to her.
Dr. Whittaker will probably snap out of this, uh, obsessive behavior when we're back at base. Right now, he's
trying to convince himself that something good will
come out of this."

Anders bent to pick up the top of the stretcher, flex-
ing from the knees as he raised it. His words, when he
spoke, were gasped out around the effort.

"Maybe, but I'd like him a whole lot better if he'd just
admitted he f..." He hesitated out of respect for Kesia,
not that he hadn't heard her use worse.

"That this is mostly his fault?" Kesia grunted as she
picked up the other edge of the stretcher. "That he has
behaved unconscionably? Believe me. He's not going to
be allowed to forget it."

Anders wondered if this was a prediction or a threat—
maybe a bit of both. For a moment gladness coursed
through him. Then he realized what it would mean.
If Dr. Whittaker was disgraced, then he'd lose the
project. Anders hated the idea of Dr. Whittaker losing
the project. That would mean leaving Sphinx and the
treecats—and Stephanie, who was becoming a friend,
and Karl and Jessica...

Worse, this would be the second time off-planet
scientists—not that Tennessee Bolgeo had really been a
scientist, but Anders had heard more than one person
refer to him as "Dr. Bolgeo"—would have fallen short
of the Star Kingdom's high expectations. What would
that mean for the treecats? At the very least, a delay in
having their status as sentient creatures verified.

Anders and Kesia were alone now—except for the unconscious Langston Nez—and as they picked their way slowly along the trail he and Dr. Calida had marked, Anders spoke softly.

"Kesia, I know my dad has been a blackhole, but... You do realize that if this all blows up, the project is doomed. Dr. Calida is a xenobiologist with an interest in anthropology, but she couldn't take over. You and Virgil are depending on the research you'll do on this expedition to finish your degree work... And Langston..."

There was a long pause from where Kesia carried the back end of the stretcher, then she said, "You're not saying we should defend Dr. Whittaker?"

"I'm saying," Anders said, "that he's behaved like a self-centered jerk—but like you said, that's this 'displacement' thing. Not for one minute has he forgotten the treecats."

"No. Just the humans."

"Still, think about it?"

"I will."

If hauling all the gear to shore from where the van had sunk had been bad, hauling it back was three times worse. Yes, there was less—they'd given their last power pack to Dacey and they were pretty much out of their own food—but they were much more weary.

The odor of smoke hadn't become stronger, or maybe their noses had just accepted it as part of the background. Maybe the fire was even being gotten under control. Anders didn't think he had the energy to climb above the canopy again, at least not until he'd had something to eat and maybe a nap.

He picked up a pair of high-powered binoculars and scanned the tree line, trying to see if he could glimpse his flag. Motion lower down in the tree caught his eye.

He saw them only for a moment, clearly defined against

the leafy background: two treecats, gray-and-cream males. It seemed to Anders that their gazes met his own across the distance—although that was impossible. Then they were gone.

For a moment, Anders thought about mentioning what he had seen to the others, then he stopped. What good would that do? His dad might call him a liar or, worse, insist they go back and see if the treecats were still there.

Anders' legs ached; so did his neck and shoulders and back. In the end, lying back on a blanket and resting, even with the extra gravity pressing down on him, was all he wanted.

Closing his eyes, Anders didn't so much drift off to sleep as plunge off a cliff into purest exhaustion.

❖   ❖   ❖

Relieved and delighted as she was when Chet, Christine, and Toby arrived, Stephanie knew they were fighting a losing battle. Sensations of uncertainty and guilt surged through her. If they hadn't meddled, would the treecats have managed matters on their own? Had the presence of humans disrupted their usual behavior patterns?

She remembered how many years ago on Meyerdahl she'd brought home what she thought was an abandoned baby squirrelette, how her father had taken it from her, concern drawing lines on his face.

"Steph, never move a baby animal. Likely its parents are close by, ready to help. This little one . . ."

He didn't say more, but Stephanie could tell from his expression that he was concerned that her actions had doomed the little creature. It would have been doomed, too, except that her father was a vet and had happened to be home. The experience had cured her from "adopting" wild pets forever. When they'd left Meyerdahl, she'd found homes for those pets she did have, knowing it would be cruel to transport them to an alien planet just because she loved them.

Was this the incident of the squirrelette all over again? Had she condemned these treecats through her arrogance?

Stephanie hacked violently through the base of a shrub, not even bothering to turn on the vibroblade edge. Realizing she was wasting energy she could spend more productively, that she was letting her temper—that wild and dancing flame that ate into her as the fire now consumed the shrubs on the other side of the stream—rule her, Stephanie wished for Lionheart's soothing presence.

Glancing over at him, she remembered that *he* was the one who had guided them here, so clearly he had thought they could do some good. She was turning back to the next section of her patch, when she saw a windblown branch come sailing across the stream and land in the midst of the farther edge of the grass-filled meadow.

"Karl!" she yelled. "Fire line's been broken. I'm going in."

Grasping her Pulaski firmly in one fist, Stephanie galloped beneath the picketwood trees, in the direction of the burning segment of the meadow. Her bladder bag had long emptied its original load, but she'd had the siphon in the stream, so she had some water with her. Even so, playful tongues of wind were spreading the fire through the dry meadow grass faster than she could reach it.

"Steph," Karl called, his voice reaching her through her fire-suit's radio, "we're not going to be able to put that out. Do you have your drip-torch?"

"Yes."

"I think we have enough room to start a counter-fire. It's risky, we've got to try. If that fire takes the meadow, it's going to reach the trees and then..."

He trailed off, perhaps remembering that his words were audible to anyone on their channel. She knew what he had been about to say. If those flirtatious winds pushed the fire in the direction of the tree line, there would be no saving the treecats. There might be no saving themselves, either.

Within a few steps, Stephanie reached the edge of the meadow. One corner of her mind noticed that a few meters of the tall grass had already been cut down to a few millimeters' height. That might slow the fire if the wind was not driving it, but not enough to count on—especially since the grass had only been clipped, not raked down to bare earth.

When she dashed out into the taller grass, she cursed her lack of height. The grass came up to her neck in places, making progress difficult, but she could hear the whoosh of the fire as it licked at the dry stalks, and knew the direction in which she must go.

Karl's voice again. "Steph, we're deep enough in. If we go much closer, we're going to just join up with this fire. Ready?"

She glanced over, saw Karl standing about three meters to her right.

"Ready. I'm starting now!"

Essentially, the drip torch was nothing more than a tube holding very flammable liquid with a quick-lighter set at the tip. Stephanie pressed the tab that caused the tube to elongate outwards so that she wouldn't be starting the fire at her own feet. Carefully, pretending this was nothing more than a training exercise, she drew a neat line with the liquid, then set it alight.

Fuel, heat, oxygen, she thought, fanning the flames so they'd burn away from her, back toward the already existing fire, not toward the trees. When her backfire was burning well, she traded the drip torch for her Pulaski. Turning it hoe side down, she started raking back the grass on her side of the new blaze so that even if the wind decided to take part, the flames would only find bare earth.

Over to her right, Karl had also started drawing a new fire line. Then, to her left, Stephanie became aware someone else—shorter even than her—was tearing away at the grass.

"To—" she started to say, but this person was smaller even than Toby. In fact, this person wasn't even human. It was a treecat, a very large treecat. The same treecat, she somehow felt certain, who had confronted Lionheart upon their arrival. To his left another cat was digging away at the grass, exposing the bare, unburnable earth.

Wow! Stephanie thought. *I wish Dr. Whittaker and Dr. Hobbard were here. They'd love this.*

She swallowed a laugh. She supposed the opponents of treecat intelligence could still claim that constructive firefighting wasn't an indication of constructive thought. They'd say that what treecats were doing was a matter of instinct or imitation or that anyone who thought running towards a fire, rather than in the opposite direction, was an indication of intelligence needed their heads checked.

Time vanished into motion as Stephanie concentrated on building a barrier against the fire. Occasionally, one of the human members of her team would ask a question, but common sense and initiative were the order of the day.

Over across the stream to the east, the fire was spreading.

We're not going to be able to stay here much longer, Stephanie thought. *I hope Lionheart convinces the treecats to let us get them out of here.*

She glanced over to where Jessica, Toby, Christine, and Chad, assisted by a few treecats, had done a good job clearing their side of the stream. Stephanie knew all too well that all it would take was another stray branch or windblown bundle of leaves and that hard-won fire line would be broken.

Already the drought-dry leaves in some trees were

catching fire. One dead near-pine went up in a blaze of isolated glory.

Candling, Stephanie remembered. *That's what they called that effect in class. Weirdly pretty...*

She was turning back to her work when the flames coursing up the near-pine flared and burned scorchingly hot, probably as they consumed a pocket of resinous material. With a loud cracking noise, the tree trunk exploded, showering sparks. Then the entire burning mass tumbled down, directly toward Jessica.

A shrill scream cut through Stephanie's earphones, followed by a mass of confused chatter, chatter in which Jessica's voice was conspicuously absent.

CLIMBS QUICKLY WAS PLEASED WHEN NOSE BITER AND his clanmates had the good sense to join the effort to stop the grass fire. After all, if the fire spread, the question of whether the People accepted the two-legs' aid or ran for what safety they could find on a burning island would be moot. Fire that had grown fat on dried grass and fragile shrubbery would be well-prepared to gorge upon the leaves beneath the spreading branches of the net-wood grove.

As much as he longed to be close to Death Fang's Bane, Climbs Quickly did not join those fighting the fire, but turned his attention to those of the Damp Ground Clan who trembled between a desire to flee on their own six legs and to accept the offered help. Among those who now balanced on the brink of decision were several mothers with kittens of various sizes huddling near them. These would be the most vulnerable in a traditional flight, and he turned his attention to them.

<*I swear,*> he said, <*Death Fang's Bane has often visited our clan and shown only the greatest care and respect. She is a youngling, of course, and delights in games with the kittens...*>

Here he shared an image of his two-leg, her arms extended in a wide loop as she used one of her devices—the one that seemed at times to almost let her fly—to give a hooting and squeaking armload of very small kittens a ride from branches to duff, the entire giggling mass landing as lightly as did a flower-wing on a leaf.

The Damp Ground Clan kittens were captivated, for a moment forgetting their fear of both fire and strange creatures. Climbs Quickly felt fringes of "Me, too! Me, too!" from their mind-voices. He wished he had time to pull Death Fang's Bane from her labors so she could enchant them with the warmth of her mind-glow, but there was no time.

Less time, indeed, than he had estimated. At that moment, the breeze became suffused with the odor of burning near-pine sap—doubtless one of those pockets that collected in a dead tree and were considered treasures by any treecat who excavated them, since, if carefully warmed, the sap could line a basket so that it would carry water.

The odor was followed by an ear-foldingly loud explosion as the heat-suffused sap caught fire all at once and exploded. The top of the tree vanished into sparks and flaming bits that eddied toward the ground like shooting stars. The trunk of the tree tottered and crashed down toward the stream.

Climbs Quickly knew his was not the only mind that shouted warning, but as swift as were sight and thought, in this case the falling tree was swifter. Slender as the dead near-pine had seemed when among the company of its fellows, the fiery mass that plummeted downwards was vast and terrible, trailing flaming branches that snagged and broke against the tangled trees on either side of the stream.

Two-legs and six-legs alike scattered away from the falling menace, but two were unable to escape—Windswept and one of the People. Even as they vanished beneath the flaming mass, Climbs Quickly knew the lost member of the Damp Ground Clan in the flashes of frantic memory spread by the panicked members of his clan.

Dirt Grubber was his name. He was a patient soul, older than Climbs Quickly by five rings on his tail, never mated, yet a valued member of his clan, first as a young scout, later shifting his attention from game animals to the plants the People valued. He had been among the few in this conservative clan who had not thought avoidance of the two-legs was the wisest course. Indeed, he had a fascination with their growing places, and had pestered the memory singers for images.

All this in a second, all this as Climbs Quickly bunched his limbs and began to run in the direction of the burning tree. He had felt Death Fang's Bane's first flash of shock and horror. He knew that his two-leg would not accept that her friend was lost until she held the burned body in her arms. Surging through Death Fang's Bane's mind-glow was determination that muted a budding grief. She was not one to wail mindlessly when something might yet be done.

Nor, he saw, were her friends. Running back from where they had made their escape, they raced in the direction of the burning tree. The older two wielded their cutting/hauling tools with grim efficiency, clearing away the outer layer of burning material. The younger boy stood waist-deep in the stream, playing water through one of the peeing bags so that it soaked the nearby area, keeping the flames from spreading.

Shadowed Sunlight, his mind-glow a turmoil within which the darkness threatened to overwhelm the sun, apparently thought this a wise move, for as soon as he was close enough, he began to do the same from the other side. Meanwhile, those of the People who had been helping build the fire line went from point to point, scraping dirt over those sparks or bits of flaming material that escaped the two-legs' attention. Through the sharp, permeating scent of burning green-needle, Climbs Quickly could smell the scent of singed fur and blistered flesh.

His own skin burned in a few spots, but it took more than sparks to set the fur of a living Person alight. He hastened to join Death Fang's Bane where she, with typical determination, was trusting to the extra skin she had donned to protect her from the worst of the flames as she pushed in to where she could get a hold on the burning tree itself.

Climbs Quickly had long known that Death Fang's Bane was stronger even than two-legs much larger than herself. These wore devices that helped them to move about with ease and he had seen how without them they were slowed. Some—like Shadowed Sunlight—often managed without such aides, but when he did the extra effort was obvious. Such was not the case with Death Fang's Bane. She was strong enough to move as gracefully as a Person under her own power. However, she was a two-leg and like all such did not often go far without tools.

Now, reaching the burning trunk of the green-needle, she yelled something. All Climbs Quickly could understand was the word "Karl," but her meaning soon became clear. The young male turned the force of his pee-bag's flow to soak the section of the tree nearest to Death Fang's Bane. As he did so, she took off the making-lighter thing and strapped it to the tree trunk, protecting it with a wrap made from one of the fire-shelter bags she carried.

When this was in place, Death Fang's Bane shoved with all her might to raise the tree trunk so that any trapped beneath it—living or dead—might be freed. Shadowed Sunlight, seeing her intention, moved to help her, his greater height and broad, muscular shoulders a tremendous asset in this labor, the fierce darkness in his mind-glow seeming to give him extra strength.

When Shadowed Sunlight had raised the tree trunk higher than she could reach, Death Fang's Bane trusted her burden solely to the young male. Then, partly in the water, partly out, she thrust herself deeper in and began feeling around for those who had been trapped.

Here, at last, was a task with which Climbs Quickly could help. He had been sorting through the confused flood of mind-voices, seeking two that—if they still existed at all—would be faint and weak. Once or twice there had been traces. Following these as he might have scented after a bark-chewer when hunting, he waded into the stream and joined his two-leg in her search.

Almost as one, their hands found the slick fabric of Windswept's suit. As one, they pulled with all their combined strength, seeking to dislodge the limp and inert burden. One hand tight on the fabric, Death Fang's Bane hacked with her fast-biting knife to break loose the twigs and branchlets that had caught on Windswept's clothing. Climbs Quickly might lack a true-hand, but he still had five good limbs. With the upper three he gripped Windswept's clothing, kicking hard with his true-feet braced against the near-pine trunk.

He wondered at the difficulty they were having getting Windswept free. True, this youngling was more curved and bumped than his own Death Fang's Bane. True, the tree had fallen on her, so it was to be assumed that even the tough material of her clothing had been pierced and snagged, but still her shape seemed all wrong, resisting extraction.

At last, though, the two of them forced the mass free from beneath the green-needle, dragging it into the smoky air.

Climbs Quickly had been peripherally aware that the smell of close-by burning had become that of sodden wood, but he had been so tightly focused on his task, on trying to touch and hold the mind-glows of the captive two, that he had lost any sense of his surroundings. Now he emerged to find that two of the young fliers were playing streams of water over the fallen green-needle. Enough water saturated the air that, had he not known otherwise, he would have thought he was emerging into rain.

When they were free, Shadowed Sunlight dropped the smouldering tree and came to help move the injured girl. Climbs Quickly was glad, for apparently Windswept had possessed the good sense to jump into the stream when she realized she could not escape the falling tree, taking the risk of being drowned rather than accepting the certainty of being burned. She was sodden, heavy with water.

Climbs Quickly wondered fleetingly why Windswept—like Death Fang's Bane—had not trusted to her suit. Was it because she had less experience? Had she given in to fear?

He was turning to go seek after Dirt Grubber, when a cry from Death Fang's Bane made him realize why Windswept had been so difficult to move. As Shadowed Sunlight helped Death Fang's Bane to lift Windswept, the oddness in her shape was explained. At tremendous risk to herself, Windswept had torn open the front of her suit so that Dirt Grubber could be protected inside from the fire, held in her arms above the water.

But had her sacrifice been sufficient?

Once Shadowed Sunlight had helped move the injured pair clear of fire and water, Death Fang's Bane ripped open Windswept's suit. Its shredded fabric made amply clear that it could no longer provide any effective protection.

Soon, Windswept lay limp on the muddy earth near the stream, her arms curled protectively around the sodden Person she had rescued.

Death Fang's Bane began poking and prodding the two in a manner that reminded Climbs Quickly of her father's working over the injured. Raising her head, she made mouth noises in which Climbs Quickly recognized her name for him.

"Lionheart . . . Jessica . . . Lionheart!"

Climbs Quickly understood what his two-leg wanted to know only because he desired the same. He was sure Windswept and Dirt Grubber were alive, but that did not mean they had not been injured beyond recovery—or damaged beyond the ability to think. He placed his hands on the quiet pair, probing to see if sense lay beneath life. When he had learned what he could, he met Death Fang's Bane's anxious gaze and nodded, flooding their link with reassurance that the two lived.

As he did so, he felt again the frustration that he could not tell her more.

Climbs Quickly wished he could tell Death Fang's Bane that he sensed both Windswept's and Dirt Grubber's mind-glows, faint but present, aware though encased in bodies too weak to communicate. He wished with all his heart that he could tell Death Fang's Bane the other thing he felt—something he was certain that no one in the Damp Ground Clan had yet sensed. These two mind-glows were intertwined. Somehow, on the edge of death, caught beneath fire and within water, these two strangers had found in each other a reason beyond reason to fight for life.

"Bleek," he said, and nodded vigorously. "Bleek! Bleek!"

Then he turned and indicated with gestures that the time for retreat had come. Would the Damp Ground Clan understand the battle was lost?

As Climbs Quickly ran in the direction of the air cars, what he saw made his heart suffuse with a strange joy. Every member of the Damp Ground Clan who had not been able to join in fighting the fire—the females with kittens, the elders, the crippled—now waited in the bed of the truck.

As the two-legs approached—Shadowed Sunlight and the larger boy carrying Windswept, the tall girl holding the battered Dirt Grubber cradled in her arms—every single one of those gathered clan members held out their arms, offering without words to hold and succor the wounded, mutely expressing that they trusted the two-legs would carry them away to safety.

✦   ✦   ✦

Knowing from experience how soothing treecats could be, Stephanie accepted the invitation that the injured two ride in the back of the air-truck. She climbed in first, directing Chet and Karl to place Jessica's head in her lap. The treecats—among whom were doubtless relatives of the 'cat Jessica had rescued—took charge of their clanmate. As the males spilled in to join the females, young, and infirm, the back of the truck became quite crowded.

"Where are we going from here?" Chet asked as he headed for the pilot's seat of the truck. "I mean, the treecats seem to have accepted our offer of a ride, but where do we take them?"

"Out of here first," Karl said practically, from his own vehicle. "The main body of the fire is spreading from the southeast. So we head west. Steph, you let me know if the treecats get agitated or something, okay?"

"Okay," Stephanie said somewhat absently.

Toby had brought her the enhanced first-aid kit from Karl's car before going to join him. Christine was riding with Chet. Now, Stephanie focused on trying to figure out what was wrong with Jessica. The other girl was breathing raggedly, doubtless because in opening her suit to hold the treecat, she had inhaled a lot of smoke. She was also soaked, so she might have breathed in water as well.

Stephanie placed her hand against Jessica's bare skin and was shocked to feel how cold it was.

"Okay," she muttered. "Hypothermia. Being surrounded by treecats should warm her up . . . Let me see what I can do for her breathing."

The med-kit contained a compact oxygen mask—Richard Harrington's addition after the rescue of Right-Striped and Left-Striped. He'd insisted that if Stephanie and Karl were going to be out in fire territory, they needed to be prepared for the worst.

"You might not need it," he'd said when Stephanie had protested that she and Karl weren't such zips as to forget to use their respirators. "But someone else might not be that lucky."

Stephanie fitted the mask into place and set the pressure low, watching carefully to see if Jessica started coughing. That would indicate water in the lungs. However, after a few breaths, Jessica seemed more relaxed. Her eyelashes fluttered slightly.

"Take it easy," Stephanie murmured, wondering if the thrumming of the surrounding treecats meant much the same thing. "You're safe now. So's the 'cat. We're getting away from the fire as fast as we can."

Too fast, so it seemed. Stephanie heard Lionheart "bleek" for her attention, and looked up. The treecats clustered in the back of Chet's truck were stirring uneasily. A few were looking over the side, as if contemplating jumping.

"Slow down, Chet," Stephanie said through her uni-link. "Seems that all treecats aren't addicted to speed like Lionheart. I think some of your passengers are getting motion sick."

Chet slowed down immediately. "How about elevation?"

"That doesn't seem to bother them as much," Stephanie said, "maybe because they live up in trees. Still, I think we'd better stay under the canopy."

Christine's voice cut in. "We're not going to be able to cover much distance if we stay low and slow."

"As long as we stay ahead of the fire," Stephanie said, "and get out of the worst of the smoke, we're doing good."

She listened to the feed over her uni-link. The SFS reported that containment of the northern fire was far from achieved, but that the fire had been diverted from Hayestown. Water drops had succeeded in downgrading the fire in some areas from crown level to surface level. A few teams were now being diverted to where the southern fire still raged in the mountains. However, the battle on either front was far from won. A call had gone out for volunteers to spell those who had been on duty since before dawn.

"What time is it?" Christine said, then answered her own question. "I can't believe it's only a few hours past noon. I wonder if we've been missed?"

"Check your uni-link," Chet said practically. "If you don't find a stream of messages from your mother, you haven't."

"No messages. I guess if anyone has missed us, they think we've been diverted to another area."

Toby chuckled. "As we have been. We're on the probationary rangers' team. Hey, Steph and Karl, do you think we could qualify?"

Karl's reply was very dry. "Either you'll qualify or Steph and I are going to be out of a job. SFS isn't a military organization, but we've bent the rules. I'm guessing that the only reason someone isn't worrying about what we're up to is they have a lot more to worry about."

"Out of sight, out of mind," Stephanie agreed. "Though

the automatic messages you arranged to send were a good idea, Karl."

"Thanks. How's Jessica?"

"Coming around. She seems to be breathing easier. Since we're out of the worst of the smoke, I'm going to work the mask off."

"How about the treecat?" Toby asked.

"I think he's all right. I mean, the treecats have all huddled around him, but they don't seem anxious. I saw some patches of burnt fur, but I think Jessica grabbed him before much worse could happen."

"That was really brave," Christine said, admiration in her voice. "I don't know if I could have done it. I mean, I didn't mind getting close to the fire because the suits kept out the worst of the heat and smoke. Opening up a suit when surrounded by fire..."

Jessica obviously overheard. Even before she fluttered open her eyes, she said in a very soft voice, "Brave or really dumb..."

She coughed a few times. Stephanie patted her hand, then moved it so Jessica could feel the oxygen mask.

"Don't stress your voice. If you need more air, take a pull on this."

"Okay. Can Valiant have some?"

"Valiant?" Stephanie realized Jessica must mean the treecat. "Sure. Take a drag and I'll see if he wants any."

Knowing that Lionheart would likely be with Stephanie when she went on fire duty, Richard Harrington had shown her how to adjust the flow for treecats. She did so now, glad that she hadn't been such a blackhole as to ignore good advice just because it came from her father. Dad had also included a variety of simple drugs—painkillers and stimulants mostly—that had been proven to work on treecats.

"Lionheart," Stephanie said holding out the mask. "You'd better show Valiant how to use this."

Lionheart took the device promptly. One of the females—an older one, Stephanie thought—hissed, but another treecat patted her and eased her back when she would have intervened.

His wife? Stephanie thought. *His mother? I can tell a kitten from an adult, but there's so much I don't know...*

The oxygen seemed to help Valiant. Lionheart then made a quick inspection of the other 'cat's bedraggled fur. It was burnt in places, but the skin was badly blistered only in one area—a long streak down the left shoulder and flank.

Stephanie took out some quick-heal and sprayed on a light application. In nature, burns healed best if kept clean and left to open air, but she wanted to do something for the creature's evident pain.

"Valiant got that," Jessica said softly, "when he pushed me into the stream. I froze for a minute too long, then I stumbled and did something to my ankle. He could have gotten away, but he stopped..."

Her voice choked with tears. "He's going to be all right, isn't he? I'll just die if anything happens to him, especially because of me...."

Stephanie's eyes widened. There was more here than just guilt or sympathy. She heard in Jessica's voice the same pain she had felt when Lionheart had attacked the hexapuma in an effort to save her.

She looked at Lionheart, wondering if he would confirm her guess.

"Bleek," he said, nodding. "Bleek!"

Me and Lionheart. Scott and Fisher. Now Jessica and Valiant....

Stephanie shook her head in wonder, then realized she hadn't answered Jessica's question.

"It's just a burn. I gave him something for the pain and his family has him all warm. Next thing you know, they'll be cleaning up his fur for him. You concentrate on getting well... Valiant's going to need you, too."

✧   ✧   ✧

Anders awoke to screams of panic.

He sat up, wondering who was sitting on his chest, then remembered it was the weight of the world—literally the world, all of Sphinx's 1.35 gravity. Switching on his counter-grav unit to the minimum setting alleviated the pressure, but did nothing to still the screaming.

It was Kesia.

"Oh God oh God oh God..." the linguist was saying without pausing for breath. Then she began babbling in some language Anders had never heard before but which, from the fluency with which she spoke it, must be her native tongue.

He glanced toward the forest, thinking that the fire must have reached the area. The picketwood grove, however, remained untouched. If anything, the smoke was lighter than before.

Kesia was pointing a few meters away from the islet in the bog on which they had made their new camp, pointing, apparently, at one of the patches of mud. An eddy of motion focused Anders' attention. He froze, for a moment believing that he was still asleep and that this was his worst nightmare yet. Then he had to accept what he was seeing was real.

The mud was slowly crawling toward them. This mud had teeth, teeth between which it whistled as it moved, an eerie sound, soft and gentle, completely at odds with the horror before them.

Other voices were joining Kesia's incoherent babbling. With a small corner of his mind, Anders realized he was not the only one who had fallen asleep. Exhausted from their recent labors and poor diet—probably also from breathing the smoky air—they had all drifted off. If Kesia had not awakened when she had . . .

Then Anders realized that Kesia's waking had not been a complete coincidence. A cream-and-gray treecat, certainly one of the two he had spotted earlier, was standing next to her. One of its upper paws—one of the "hand" set—rested on her shoulder as if it had just shaken her, while the other still pointed in the direction of the mud monster.

The latter was moving forward with more speed than Anders would have credited for something that lacked any apparent legs or even tentacles. Despite its lack of features—except for the teeth, those were all *too* evident—it must have had something that served as sound receptors, because Kesia's keening had caused it to pause, rippling in place.

. . . In thought? In anxiety? In contemplation of where to take its first bite?

One of the above. Some of the above. All of the above, Anders thought frantically. Certainly it showed no sign of retreating, so although Kesia's keening had disconcerted it, it wasn't about to be scared off.

And if the treecat had taken the risk to come out and warn them, then there was no way this thing wasn't dangerous.

Come out to warn them . . . Wonder filled Anders. As he got to his feet, he switched his counter-grav unit to compensate fully for the extra gravity. If they didn't get rid of this thing, well, they'd have more serious problems than functioning under an extra .35 gravity.

"A new species," Dr. Calida was saying. She sounded almost as much excited as scared. "It looks as it dwells mostly in this sort of terrain, so it might be amphibious."

"We've got that single tranq rifle," Virgil said tightly. "I don't fancy taking on that thing with a short knife, no matter what Stephanie Harrington did to that hexapuma. Who's a good shot?"

Virgil was looking directly at Dr. Whittaker as he spoke, but Anders' dad was shaking his head. "Since we were camping out," Dr. Whittaker said, "we were permitted to bring the tranq rifle, but I'm not a marksman. Our main defense was going to be a sonic perimeter. They've had a great deal of luck with those keeping off even hexapumas."

Dacey Emberly held out a hand. "Give the rifle here. I haven't shot anything for years, but Calli's father and I used to go hunting."

Everyone watched, tense and uncertain as the older woman took careful aim and fired. Clearly the powerful darts hit, but they didn't seem to have any effect.

"I think," Dr. Calida said, with detached scientific interest, "the darts embedded in the plants that grow on the thing. I wonder if it deliberately cultivates them as armor?"

"Either way," Dacey replied. "I'm not going to get through—and that was the last dart."

"This thing didn't seem to like Kesia's screaming," Anders mused. "I sure wish we had that sonic thingie."

Virgil dove toward one of the bags. "I think I saw..."

He raised an arm triumphantly. "Got it! I didn't bother to set it up when we were in the trees because we were pretty safe. It should still have juice..."

Anders had raced over to Virgil's side. The sonic perimeter guard consisted of a series of slender rods connected by an almost invisible wire.

"I have no idea how this works," Virgil said, thrusting a couple of the rods at Anders, "but I glanced at the instructions before deciding it wouldn't work well up in the trees. Set the posts in the ground, far enough apart that the wire is taut..."

Kesia had fallen silent, but she wasn't so far in shock that she couldn't help set out the rods. As they worked, Dacey looked at her daughter.

"Calli, remember that horrible campfire song you tormented us all with when you were eight?"

Dr. Calida started, then grinned. Without a pause she started singing, "Oh! In the cave there was a bear!"

The word "bear" was almost shouted, hitting one of those annoying minor-key notes that delight small children and make adults grit their teeth.

"While over the cave a puma howled!"

This was followed by sounds that might or might not have been a puma howling, but certainly made the mud creature ripple back.

The song went on, introducing more woodland creatures—owls, gautiers, screeching snakes, misty drakes—all of which made very annoying sounds. Anders noted that the treecat was shaking its head in evident distress. Nonetheless, it was counterpointing the raucous song with shrill wails of its own.

Assembling the sonic barrier required three rounds of the song. The first time they didn't have the rods in the right way. The second time the wire was stretched too tightly. At last, Virgil called out.

"Step back. I think we've got the rods in the right places this time. I'm going to throw the switch."

As the singers fell silent, the mud creature began to slide forward. For a horrible moment, Anders thought the sonic barrier wasn't working. He was opening his mouth to start again with the bear in the cave when he saw the treecat fold down its ears and wrinkle its nose in evident distaste.

The mud creature reacted far more violently. It reeled back, the ripples of its usual movement transforming into violent waves that revealed a sleek, rubbery hide beneath the coating of mud and ooze. It retreated at least fifteen meters, sinking down into a convenient pool covered with some tiny plants.

Anders didn't think it was gone, though, and no one else suggested that they try for shore.

"Did you see where the creature went?" Dr. Calida asked. "It retreated to where the air-van went down. I wish it had stayed where I could get some pictures."

Dr. Whittaker looked at her in shocked disapproval, but Kesia grinned.

"I'll draw you a picture, dear," Dacey said, reaching for her sketchbook.

"At least for now we're safe," Virgil said, wiping a muddy hand across his pants leg. He already had smeared streaks on his sweaty face. "It's not coming any closer."

"But our problem is the same as before," Anders replied glumly. Now that the emergency was over, he'd turned his counter-grav unit down again, and he felt doubly weary for having had the respite from the extra pull. "Power. We're safe until the battery runs out."

He looked over at the treecat who waited patiently, curled up against Langston Nez's side. There had been so much to do that no one had commented, but Anders saw his own awe and wonder at the treecat's presence reflected in everyone's eyes. Dr. Whittaker had even attempted to talk to it, but the only response his polite overtures had garnered was a definitely disapproving hiss.

Did I really see two treecats? If I did, where is the other? Could it possibly have gone for help? Anders swallowed a sigh, determined not to give in to the despair he could see on so many of his companions' faces. Instead, he kept his gaze fixed on the power-indicator light. *Even if it did, can help possibly arrive in time?*

❖   ❖   ❖

Climbs Quickly felt the awareness of Dirt Grubber's bond to Windswept spreading through the members of the Damp Ground Clan. Reactions varied, but he thought there was more approval than not. Like Death Fang's Bane, Windswept had demonstrated a strength of character that could not be dismissed.

He was thinking about the larger ramifications of this new event when he became aware of an eddy of alertness flowing through the clan. He was not precisely shut out. Rather, it took a moment for the "speaker" to remember to include him.

<My son, Left-Striped, is coming back from his scouting. He is very excited. Something about two-legs in our old home?>

This was followed by some non-verbalized grumbling along the lines of why couldn't young people learn to speak up?

Climbs Quickly extended his mind-voice, seeking that of Left-Striped, which he had come to know well during the days the twins had stayed with the Harrington family. He found it and sent an image of the Damp Ground Clan traveling packed into the back of the slowly moving air-truck.

<So that is what Mother was trying to say! Elders should learn to explain things more clearly! I see now why she depicted herself as moving, but I could sense no effort. Now that I have a clearer image, I will be there shortly.>

He fell silent, but they were aware of his faint mind-glow growing stronger. Now that he had a sense of the direction from which Left-Striped was coming, Climbs Quickly turned to Death Fang's Bane.

"Bleek!" he said, then pointed, making at the same time a motion similar to that of hands on the stick of the air car. He felt her flash of delight and amusement, then heard her making mouth noises to Shadowed Sunlight and the flier who drove the larger flying thing. The two vehicles turned almost as one.

<Useful,> commented Nose Biter grudgingly. <Can you always get her to obey so easily?>

<It has taken time,> Climbs Quickly admitted, <but once I felt certain that the mouth noises substitute for mind-voices, I knew we had to find a compromise. Their mind-glow is strong, perhaps as strong as that of memory singers, but largely they are mute. My throat cannot shape their noises. Even if it could, all but a very few seem capricious. Even names are difficult. The one who works the smaller vehicle and the vehicle itself are called by similar sounds. For a long time, I thought maybe they were the same.>

Nose Biter seemed interested and the discussion might have continued, but at that very moment Left-Striped came rocketing down from an overhanging branch, landing with studied skill first on the raised front part of the vehicle, then jumping down amid the members of his clan.

Climbs Quickly could hear Death Fang's Bane explaining the situation to her friend, whose cries of surprise when Left-Striped thumped down over his head had been loud enough to carry through the closed clear sides. However, he gave most of his attention to the excited and anxious Left-Striped.

<As requested, my twin and I went back to our prior denning place to see if the fire had reached it. We arrived to find that although the fire was not there, the grove was not as we had expected. We had expected to find ground-runners and other creatures taking shelter from the fire near where there was water—even if in this dry season there is not much. What we found was a cluster of two-legs.

<They were not behaving at all normally. Instead of moving about as they usually do, these were sitting out in the middle of the bog.>

Climbs Quickly wondered at the surge of horror that went through the members of the Damp Ground Clan, but he did not wish to interrupt. If it was important, Left-Striped would explain.

<We found evidence that for some days before they had been dwelling—I don't ask you to believe this, you can see it for yourself—in the rock trees. One of them was very weak. The others moved slowly as if burdened. Their scent was wrong, as if they had been eating bad foods. We guessed that when these two-legs smelled the smoke, they moved out of the trees, but, perhaps because of their injured one, they could not go far. Ignorant of the danger, they thought the bog would protect them best from fire.>

Again the shared sensation of horror.

<My brother stayed to watch over them, while I came back to inform you so you could decide which way the clan should go. I had not hoped to find two-legs so quickly, but I will admit, finding such would have been my next goal. These lost ones need help.>

<I agree,> said a rather fat and elderly female who Climbs Quickly now knew was Brilliant Images, the senior memory singer of the Damp Ground Clan. <We have been helped by these two-legs. We shall help these others. In that way, all debts will be even. We must move swiftly. I can just touch the edges of Right-Striped's mind-glow and I feel an urgency there.>

Climbs Quickly was grateful, but still confused. <You of the Damp Ground Clan react as if your former nesting place is a place of danger. How could that be?>

<Not the net-wood,> Left-Striped explained. <The bog. In it dwells a whistling sucker—a great mother. In this dry turning, she has not yet kitted, so there is just the one. We know to avoid her, but these two-legs have landed themselves directly within her favorite hunting grounds.>

14

STEPHANIE WAS AS STARTLED AS ANY OF THEM WHEN a treecat landed on the cab of the air truck, but when he bounced down and the collective green-eyed gaze of the treecats turned to him, she knew he was no stranger to the clan.

"I think he's giving a report," she said. "I can't tell what he's saying, but Lionheart is really intent. Funny... This 'cat looks sort of familiar. Karl, I'm going to send you a picture via my uni-link."

Karl's voice came back promptly. "I still have trouble telling them apart, but I think that's Left-Striped. His pattern is atypical."

Toby's voice followed. "Karl just showed me pictures he took, and I agree. It's the same 'cat, I'm sure of it."

"Interesting," Stephanie said. "Lionheart just turned to me. He's motioning that we should speed up. All of the other 'cats are hunkering down, so they're clearly waiting for it. Also, a fat and fluffy female is giving me the evil eye and pointing. I think she's helping with navigation."

"Any change in direction?" Chet asked. Stephanie could see Christine's face pressed to the rear window of the trunk cab, looking back in fascination at the passengers, all of whom were now facing front, bodies held low, evidently so that the side of the truck would cut any wind.

"Direction continues south," Stephanie reported, "but I think she's going to want us to cross the river to the south again."

"South," Christine said, "as in toward the fire?"

"The fire hasn't gotten this far west yet," Karl said. "We're still safe."

Stephanie was glad to hear this. She would have gone into the heart of the fire if that was what was needed, but could she have risked a clan of treecats and her human friends?

She said, "I'll keep an eye on the 'cats and let you know if they start to panic. Otherwise, let's go as fast as we can while staying beneath the tree line. This is not the time to get seen by anybody tracing the course of the southern fire."

"Seen with a truckload of treecats?" Chet laughed loudly. "I don't think so... Karl, take point. Remember, my truck needs more clearance than your runabout."

"Gottcha," Karl said. "Let's burn atoms."

✧   ✧   ✧

Anders was tinkering with some odds and ends from the cooking kit when the creature Dr. Calida had dubbed the Sphinxian swamp siren made its next move. Although the swamp siren had remained beneath its cloak of water weed and murky water, Anders felt certain that not only was it still there, but that it was studying them.

It might not be smart, not like a treecat is smart, but

it's a predator, and predators need to learn how to stalk or they won't get very many meals. This one is stalking us. I'm sure of it.

Turned out the swamp siren wasn't just stalking, it was doing some pretty good thinking, too. Somehow—maybe because the device was so strange—it had made the connection between those rods set in neat ranks around the hummock where its prospective dinner (including a tasty treecat) now huddled. When it moved, it slid down under the muddy water, working under and around the tussocks and hummocks, keeping its hearing receptors under the water so that the annoying high-pitched whine was muffled.

When the swamp siren lashed out, it brought one flipper into contact with the closest rod. Had it watched when they set the things up? Had it noticed the device didn't work unless the rods were anchored correctly? Or did it just slap at something that annoyed it the way a human swats at a fly? Anders would always wonder.

But he was also ready. He noticed when the swamp siren had started moving because the sodden area to which it had retreated looked flatter. The water weed moved sluggishly, not in the ripples that indicated the swamp siren in motion, but as if the muddy liquid had been stirred.

He frantically looked around just in time to see the weed-spotted flipper come out of the water and slap at the rod. Another flipper came up and another rod went down. If Anders had needed any evidence that the device was deactivated, he would have had it when the treecat's ears unfurled and it sat upright, hissing and snarling.

Anders brought his hand down on the bottom of the pot he had resting in his lap. He'd spent the short hiatus the sonic barrier had won them in rigging himself a drum kit, complete with cymbals made from any bit of jangly metal he could find. Now he beat on his drum with a spoon, while his free hand vigorously rattled a mismatched collection of camping gear.

The noise slowed the swamp siren. Kesia—her voice a bit hoarse—started in on the song about the bear. She was joined by the others, the eclectic collection of half-remembered words and tune making a god-awful racket. But either this time the swamp siren was ready or maybe it was just too hungry to care. Whatever the reason, it kept coming.

Their mini-island was surrounded by doubtfully solid bits of grass and water weed that (as Dr. Whittaker had discovered too late) created the illusion of solid ground. The still comatose form of Langston Nez was ample illustration that the mud could be as dangerous as the teeth-gnashing, whistling monstrosity boiling up at them, but at that moment, Anders had to fight an impulse to trust his luck and run.

He didn't. The hummock on which they'd made their camp didn't allow for a lot of moving about. Even so, a front and rear line of sorts had formed. In the front were Anders himself, Virgil, Kesia, and Dr. Calida. In the back, protectively huddling over Langston Nez, were Dacey and the treecat. Also in the back, protectively standing over the case holding his best artifacts, was Dr. Bradford Whittaker.

Everyone who could had grabbed something to use as a makeshift weapon. Everyone was shouting or singing or shrieking. The swamp siren alternated between hauling itself out of the water and shrinking back when someone hit a particularly discordant note.

Like most native Sphinxian creatures, the swamp siren appeared to be hexapedal. At least that was what Anders guessed when first one set of sea-turtle-like flippers, then another appeared—and the monster still seemed to be bracing itself against something that remained beneath the mud.

The swamp siren resembled a turtle in other ways as well, though instead of a shell, its body was a huge curving mass of rubbery flesh. Plants seemed to grow directly from its back, or maybe they were just stuck on. Instead of a turtle's long neck, the swamp siren had an elongated ovoid head, the entire front of which appeared to be teeth. If the creature had eyes, Anders couldn't figure out where they were, but along the top of the head was a fungoidal crown of flesh.

The swamp siren snapped at Virgil. Virgil danced back, stumbling into one of the bedrolls. This inspired him. He scooped it up and tossed the lot: doubled blankets, ground cloth, and pillow, over the swamp siren's head. The pillow flopped off and started sinking into the ooze, but the rest hung tight.

The swamp siren cast about, obviously confused.

"Its sensory apparatus," gasped Dr. Calida, "must be in the head. Perhaps those fleshy masses... Sonar, perhaps? Radar? A combination."

Anders really liked Dr. Calida and, even better, over the last couple of days, had come to respect her too. However, at this moment, he was seriously tired of fanatical scientists.

Virgil was more practical. The swamp siren was tossing its head wildly. Pretty soon it would either have gotten the bedroll off or those nasty teeth would have shredded it. Either way, he was readying another bedroll. Anders looked for rope.

Maybe we can tie the blinder on. Don't know if that will stop it, but at least it will slow it...

He grabbed a length of line, trying to remember how to make a slipknot. Dacey was out of reach or he could get her to do it.

Loop the rope, he thought. *Push an end through...*

Anders was partway into making his makeshift lasso when an air car burst through the trees. It was smoke-blackened, but he thought he recognized it. He had hardly registered this miraculous arrival when a second vehicle followed the first, swerved to go around it, and jerked to a halt.

I'm hallucinating, he thought. *That's Karl's car and that truck...It's full of treecats?*

The car was moving forward now, heading in their direction. Trusting Virgil and Kesia to deal with the swamp siren, Anders waved his hands over his head, then held both palms out, pushing back, trying to remember what Lionheart's gesture for "stop" had been. Whether or not Anders had remembered it right, Karl caught on. The car stopped and doors flew open.

Meanwhile, from the bed of the truck came a boiling mass of treecats. Stephanie Harrington was with them, running hard. She was dressed in a fire-suit, but the headpiece was down and her short, curly hair flew wild about her face. As she ran, she was ripping open the front of her suit, digging inside toward her shoulder, and emerging with a really lethal-looking handgun.

By this time, the swamp siren had succeeded in a combination of shredding and tossing that had effectively rid it of the encumbering bedroll. However, the sound of the arriving vehicles had distracted it. Lacking a turtle's long neck, it had to turn partially around to see what was going on behind it.

"Stiff motion," Dr. Calida was muttering, probably, Anders realized, into a recorder. "Could there be armoring under there? Note alteration of growths on head; from relatively tight knots, they've expanded, revealing multi-colored clusters."

Anders shouted toward the shore. "Don't come out here.

Dad thought it was a meadow and landed our 'van, but it's actually a bog. We're on a pretty solid spot, but..."

He didn't have the strength to explain that he worried that even taking the air car over the bog might disrupt their fragile island.

Stephanie called back. "Right! What *is* that thing?"

"All I know," Anders said, talking as fast as he could in case Dr. Calida decided to go all zoological, "is that it thinks we're edible and that it doesn't like loud noises. Oh... And it has lots of teeth."

"I see that." Stephanie had been holding the handgun— which looked far too big for her—as if she'd like to get a shot off. "I'd try to hit it, but, well..."

Virgil cut in quickly. "If you don't mind, I've heard you're a killer shot, but we're right on the other side of that thing... If you miss or it ducks..."

Stephanie nodded. "I know."

Anders saw her cast around for an angle from which she could get a shot without endangering anyone. The bog stretched out on all sides, effectively hemming them in. Stephanie would need to run a fair distance and even then might not find a clear line of fire.

While talking to Stephanie, Anders had noticed who was with her. Karl was there, of course, and with him Toby. The truck had been piloted by Chet, who now hurried up, hand in hand with Christine. Jessica was there, too, but she hadn't moved from the back of the truck. Neither had one of the treecats.

Meanwhile, the other treecats—Anders recognized Lionheart by virtue of his scars—were lining up along the edge of the bog. There were a lot of them. A whole clan, he guessed.

Behind him, Anders heard his father burrowing through the gear and realized to his embarrassment that Dr. Whittaker was searching for their best camera.

The center of the treecat line was a very fat and fluffy brown-and-white treecat. Despite the fact that she waddled when she moved, there was an enormous dignity to her that told anyone watching that she was a person of importance.

As far as Anders could see, the treecat leader made no gesture of direction, but at exactly the same moment all the adult treecats, as well as a few of the larger kittens, began to sing.

"Sing" might not have been the exactly right word for it. The sound was more like classic caterwauling. Anders didn't just hear it with his ears, he felt it in his bones. His eardrums ached and he stretched his jaw to take off the pressure. Behind him, still sitting protectively by Dr. Nez, the treecat who had first warned them of the swamp siren added a shrill piping note to the chorus.

For chorus it was, a chorus evidently created to home in on the auditory sensitivity of the swamp siren and hit it where it hurt.

It doesn't feel so good here, either, Anders thought watching the swamp siren contract, pull back, and dive back beneath the murky surface of the bog, *but I think it just might be the most beautiful music I've ever heard.*

From the satisfied reaction of "their" treecat, those gathered on the hummock had no doubt that the swamp siren was gone.

"I suppose," Dr. Calida said a touch wistfully, "that they gave it the mother of all migraines." She brightened. "Still, I did get some footage. What remarkable creatures!"

This last was said with a fond smile for the treecat who—just in case the humans hadn't gotten the point— was now motioning toward the shore.

Anders bent heavily to help raise Langston's stretcher, then he remembered.

"Stephanie! We're out of juice for our counter-grav units. Can we sync with your vehicle's broadcast power?"

"You bet!" came the welcome reply. "Go for it."

So it was with light hands, as well as light hearts, that Anders and Virgil carried Langston Nez back to the shore. Stephanie hurried over to help.

"What's the problem?" she asked.

Anders explained. "We think he got mud particles in his lungs, but by now he's also dehydrated and weak from lack of nourishment. We've gotten a little water into him, but he hasn't had anything to eat for five days."

Stephanie nodded. "Slide him up into the bed of the truck next to Jessica and Valiant. The kit Dad set up for us is pretty good. We can at least get Dr. Nez on fluids. And we'll go directly to Twin Forks and get him to a doctor."

Karl came up. "I called. Uncle Scott's at Twin Forks on stand-by in case there are any bad casualties from the fire. He said he'd drop everything when we got Dr. Nez there."

"Great..." Anders felt himself tearing up and looked away so that Karl and Stephanie wouldn't see. He saw Dr. Calida helping Dacey into the back of Karl's air car. Kesia was nearby, her very useful overnight bag dangling from one arm, her head tilted back so she could look up into the picketwood where the treecats—now that the emergency was over—sat, staring down at her with equal interest.

"Where's Dad?" Anders asked, even as he knew.

Dr. Whittaker remained alone out on the island in the middle of the bog, surrounded by his cases of artifacts. Now that the crisis was over, he seemed unaware that there were real living, breathing treecats within a few meters.

Seeing Anders turn his way Dad bellowed, "Well, aren't you going to help me with this? Certainly you can't complain anymore now that we have counter-grav."

Anders exchanged a glance with Virgil, then called, "We're on our way."

"We'll help," Chet said, his words clearly including all the rescuers.

"We will," Stephanie said and something in her brown eyes made Anders realize that she'd guessed at least part of what he'd gone through—and pitied him.

A FULL DAY AND A HALF HAD PASSED SINCE STEPHANIE and her friends had rescued both the treecats and the Whittaker party. They'd gotten Langston Nez to Scott MacDallan, then reported in. The focus on fighting the fires had kept almost everything from being resolved. In fact, about the only thing Stephanie was sure of was that she and Karl weren't being ousted from the SFS.

Now, an assortment of interested parties were gathering at the Harrington residence to catch up on the details and deal with a few unresolved points.

"Langston Nez is dehydrated and suffering from malnutrition," Scott MacDallan said as he, Fisher, Irina, and Karl joined those already in the Harringtons' large living room. "However, we were able to siphon out the garbage in his lungs. The level of immunization before his arrival kept pneumonia from setting in. If he wishes, he should be able to do deskwork in about a week. I'd say he could be cleared for light field work within two."

Stephanie sighed in relief. Somehow a lot of the shine of their rescue of Dr. Whittaker and his associates would have diminished if Dr. Nez hadn't made it—and, if there had been a fatality, it would have been nearly impossible for Dr. Whittaker to retain his role as Crown consultant.

She looked over at Dr. Hobbard, who had brought out Dr. Emberly, Dacey Emberly, and, best of all, Anders. The other members of the expedition had also been invited, but Kesia and Virgil were both making up time with their spouses, and Dr. Whittaker...

"Dr. Hobbard," Stephanie said, "what's going to happen with Dr. Whittaker? Do you know?"

Dr. Hobbard looked thoughtful. "Right before coming out here, I had a quick meeting with Chief Ranger Shelton. We're all in a tough position."

She looked apologetically at the Emberlys and Anders. "May I speak frankly?"

"Do," Anders said before the two adults could. "You can't possibly say anything worse about my dad than I'm already thinking."

Anders had been widely praised by almost every member of the expedition for how he had kept a clear head when almost everyone else was flustered. Kesia Guyen had gone as far as to say that without him and Dr. Nez, they likely wouldn't have made it.

For someone who was being lauded as a hero, Anders didn't look very happy. In fact, he looked so miserable that Stephanie had to fight back an impulse to go over and wrap her arms around him.

She fought back a blush. Anders might get the wrong idea—or, worse, the right one. And what would she do if he pushed her away?

Lionheart, however, had no such qualms. He leapt lightly up next to the young man and patted him reassuringly on the arm. Stephanie knew Lionheart had turned on his best soothing rumble. Anders visibly relaxed.

At this latest display of treecat/human interaction, Dr. Hobbard looked as if she wanted to stop and take notes, but she continued speaking with only the slightest pause.

"Our first impulse was to ask Dr. Whittaker to leave. However, he and his team arrived with enough fanfare that we couldn't do that without publicizing a reason. If the truth came out, both the reputations of the Forestry Service and of Landing University would suffer. We could try and hold back the full story, but enough people were involved that it's likely the truth would leak out."

"I believe," Dr. Emberly said, "you could count on the members of the expedition to keep quiet. I know that Kesia has spoken to John and he's agreed to drop the lawsuit he was contemplating. Peony Rose and Virgil have too much resting on their association with Dr. Whittaker to want to make trouble. Mother and I . . . Well, we came through intact, and I've been credited with the discovery of a new species. It's already beginning to seem like a wonderful adventure."

She smiled with satisfaction. The informal name "Sphinxian swamp siren" was already in use among the few informed parties. Remembering how good she had felt when her term "treecat" had been accepted, Stephanie understood the smile.

"It's good to know the newsies won't get much from you," Dr. Hobbard said. "As to Dr. Whittaker . . . His behavior was not the best. However, he didn't do anything that harmed any Sphinxian native. There was some discussion of asking him to leave, of putting Dr. Nez in charge, but Dr. Nez lacks Dr. Whittaker's academic reputation. So a compromise has been suggested. Dr. Whittaker will be permitted to remain, but only if he and possibly the members of his expedition agree to carry tracking beacons with them whenever they leave their residence."

"I think I could agree to that," Dr. Emberly said, glancing at her mother.

Dacey nodded. "As long as I'm not tracked when I'm at home, I'm fine. Actually, after what we've been through, I'd be happy to know I could be found."

Anders nodded agreement. "I don't think I ever realized just how big a planet could be until after we went down and I started thinking about how hard it would be for even an intensive search to find us."

Dr. Hobbard nodded. "That's good. Hopefully, the rest of your associates will feel the same way. Meanwhile, when we have time, we're going to come up with a variation on events that will be close enough to reality to work. Stephanie, just how many of your friends know how Dr. Whittaker's group ended up in the wrong place?"

"Just me and Karl," Stephanie said. "Anders told us later."

"Good. Right now the planned cover story is something like this. Dr. Whittaker and his group were heading out for their assigned locations but decided to divert to take some pictures of the site for comparison. They landed in the bog and the rest is history."

"That should work," Dr. Emberly agreed. "It's close enough to the truth. The only thing it leaves out is that Dr. Whittaker intended to do a bit more than take a few pictures. If you leak out the fact that he was enough of a rube to land on a bog, that we didn't even have the right uni-link programs, well, we'll come across as laughable, but not willfully arrogant."

"Which Dad was," Anders said. He turned to face Dr. Hobbard. "I mean, how do you deal with that?"

"We deal with it," Dr. Hobbard said, "by adding a

few members to your team. The Forestry Service is still stretched thin with fire watch, but I think a couple of probationary rangers would be happy to help with the first couple of shifts."

Stephanie felt herself flushing with excitement. Spend days with Anders? Watch anthropologists and how they studied cultures. Do a lot of camping?

"I'd love it!" she said.

"Me, too," Karl agreed. "I'll need to talk with my folks, though."

Stephanie glanced at her parents. "Uh, me too."

But, judging from their expressions, Dr. Hobbard had already spoken with the Harringtons and they were open to the idea.

"Calida, I want to ask you about that swamp siren," Dr. Hobbard said. "Why do you think the treecats would choose to live near something so horrible? It's evident they knew it was there."

"Well," Dr. Emberly said, "I'd guess they didn't have much choice, not if they wanted to take advantage of the bog. There's plenty of advantage to such a location: rich soil that grows a wide variety of edible plants, fishing, good hunting. So, I figure they simply avoided the deeper areas where the swamp siren lived."

"Still," Marjorie Harrington said, "it does seem dangerous. I'm guessing that many people would argue this is a point against the treecats being sentient."

"Not as much as you'd think," Dr. Emberly said. "The treecats obviously knew how to drive the swamp siren off. Remember, humans have chosen much more dangerous environments in which to settle. For example, on Old Terra there were enormous carnivorous fish called sharks. Tours would spread offal on the water to attract the sharks, then send divers down in light metal cages to take pictures."

"I see your point," Marjorie agreed. "Even here in enlightened modern times we have people who insist on going hunting with bows—just for the thrill."

Stephanie had to add, "Think about the risks the colonists here take with fire. Even with the SFS constantly issuing warnings, still, too many fires are caused by human carelessness."

"What is the situation with the fire?" asked Scott MacDallan.

Karl was opening his mouth to answer when a knock at the door interrupted him. Jessica and her mom came in, accompanied by a much-recovered Valiant. The bond between treecat and human had been another element that had diverted criticism from Stephanie and her friends when their choice to go in and help the treecats had come to the attention of the Forestry Service. It was evident that the treecats, at least, wholly approved.

Moreover, Dr. Emberly and Dr. Whittaker's holo-images of the treecats coming to the rescue of the stranded humans, of how they had confronted the swamp siren, had shown that treecats as a community—not merely those who had been dismissed as isolated eccentrics, like Fisher and Lionheart—were willing to assist humans. This news was already having a marked effect on human opinions about treecats. Diehards might not be willing to admit that treecats were "people" any more than tales that dolphins had saved drowning sailors had automatically stopped fisheries from damaging practices, but the general attitude was much more positive.

After greetings were exchanged, Jessica and Naomi Pherris shared a news bulletin they'd heard on their way over.

"Both fires are officially contained," Jessica announced. "There are still pockets, but short of something really unexpected, the threat is over. Not a single town or holding was lost. Property damage was reported as 'minimal.'"

When the cheering died down, Stephanie said somberly, "But even so there was a lot of damage done, a lot of animals lost their homes."

She found herself remembering what they'd seen after they'd dropped off Dr. Nez at Scott's emergency clinic. They'd gone over to where Richard Harrington was treating animals brought in from the fire zone so that he could look at Valiant's injuries. Jessica had insisted that hers—Stephanie had wrapped her swollen ankle—could wait.

Whereas over in the human areas Scott had been able to immediately turn his attention to Dr. Nez, the situation at the veterinary clinic had been different. Animals injured by smoke and flames, sometimes by acting foolishly in panic, waited in carriers, boxes, and crates. Larger animals were outside in trailers. Valiant's minor burns were ruled noncritical, although Dad had promised to take another look when he had time.

Over to one side of the clinic, waiting patiently, had sat Trudy Franchitti, carriers large and small clustered around her feet. A very limp near-otter lay across her lap. She was holding an oxygen mask to its face. At first, Stephanie had been inclined, as always, to despise Trudy for keeping so many animals captive. Then she had caught a scrap of what Trudy's father, who was standing glowering down at his daughter, was saying.

"... and you deliberately defied me. What if you'd been hurt?"

Trudy had stuck out her chin defiantly and Stephanie had seen that her skin was smudged with smoke. There were even a few small burns.

Trudy didn't shout, but her words still carried. "I wasn't hurt. I couldn't leave them there to be burned alive or smothered. Anyhow, it's over. Maybe I'll just get rid of them, but only after the vet tells me it's okay for them to go wild."

"Well," Mr. Franchitti said, turning on his heel and striding from the room, "you can take his bill out of your allowance."

So maybe even Trudy wasn't all bad. Maybe.

While they waited for Dad to be able to look at Valiant, Stephanie and her friends had done what they could to help out. None of them had vet training, but able hands to carry water and ointments were readily accepted. Stephanie guessed that somewhere in the course of this, Dad—and Mom, who was also helping—had figured that they weren't too mad at her for taking risks.

Stephanie thought about that later that night when the party broke up. She was walking with Anders, trailing the group heading out to Dr. Hobbard's car.

"You could stay here," Stephanie suggested. "Karl and Jessica are. I could fly you back tomorrow."

Anders shook his head sadly. "Dad's doing better now that the stress is off, but I'm afraid to leave him for too long. You don't know how...He got really scary out there. I'm still trying to figure out how to write Mom the truth. She needs to know all of it, not just his version, not just the official version."

Stephanie nodded, thought about risks, then she reached up—Anders was really very tall—and kissed him. It was only on the cheek, but it was a kiss, a real one. The first she'd ever given to someone other than family.

Anders looked surprised for a minute, then smiled. The shadow that had haunted his features since the rescue lifted.

"Thanks, Steph." He squeezed her hand. "You know, when we were out there, after the car went down, I had this impulse to just curl up, let the adults take charge, since they'd messed everything up by not being willing to challenge Dad. Then I remembered you, how you took risks for Lionheart and all, not bothering to worry about whose fault it was, just because it was right. That reminded me that one person really can make a difference."

Stephanie felt embarrassed, but really happy, too. "I'm glad. From what everyone says, you were the one who got them going, who pretty much saved the day."

"Ah, they're exaggerating. If Langston hadn't gotten the gear..." Anders trailed off and squeezed her hand again. Stephanie had been acutely aware that he hadn't let go. "I'm looking forward to seeing more of you..."

Anders paused and she waited for the inevitable, "And Karl," but instead he grinned again, "A whole lot more."

He pulled her close for a moment into a sort of half-hug. Then, with a return of his usual energy, he ran for Dr. Hobbard's van.

As she walked back to the house, Stephanie glanced at her counter-grav unit. She discovered that—as was pretty usual when at home—she wasn't wearing it. How odd. For some reason she felt as if she were walking on air.

✧　　✧　　✧

Climbs Quickly sat up near the top of his favorite crown oak. The two-legs had long gone home or to sleep, but he had invited visitors of his own. They had been long coming, for they did not have vehicles that ate distance, but now they were here.

Right-Striped and Left-Striped arrived with Brilliant Images, the memory singer of the Damp Ground Clan. Slightly after, Twig Weaver and Stone Biter joined them, escorting Sings Truly. Ever since the day when she had led the Bright Water Clan to rescue Climbs Quickly and Death Fang's Bane, Sings Truly had continued to challenge the convention that females, especially the highly-valued memory singers, remained where their clans could keep them safe.

As was evident from Brilliant Images' presence at this meeting, Sings Truly's influence was spreading.

The People had already shared images of what had happened over the last several days. Investigation on the part of several clans who lived near the big fires had confirmed that these fires were natural in origin, the result of lightning strikes on crown oaks.

<*Everyone agrees,*> Brilliant Images said, <*that the two-legs worked hard to stop the fires, even before the winds shifted and the flames threatened where they have their dwellings. This—and also how Death Fang's Bane and her young band came to our aid—show that two-legs are not as uniformly dangerous as the fate of the Moonlight Dancing Clan or those preyed upon by Speaks Falsely would have us believe.*>

<*Yes,*> Stone Biter said. He was a clan elder of Bright Water, not as conservative as, say, Broken Tooth, who still occasionally lamented the day Climbs Quickly had first been spotted by Death Fang's Bane, but still not certain whether this young two-leg and a few others were exceptions to a generally depraved species. <*But the People have dealt with wildfires before. You yourself admit that the two-legs' arrival in their flying things caused panic that delayed your retreat.*>

Brilliant Images retorted tartly. <*We still might have been too late. Certainly elders and kittens—even plump matriarchs like myself—might not have been able to run fast enough to escape the fire after that near-pine crashed down over the stream. I am glad Climbs Quickly heard our confusion and brought help—even strange help.*>

Discussion followed as to where the Damp Ground Clan might relocate until their favored area near the bog had an opportunity to recover. The net-wood grove they had chosen was burned beyond use for a year or so, but other well-watered areas not currently in use were suggested.

The debate continued for a long while, weighing this point, contrasting it with that. Climbs Quickly participated, but he was careful not to over-state his thoughts. His opinion—bonded as he was to a two-leg—was considered by many to be radical and suspect. Even so, although the People were not quick to change their minds on important matters, they were also not so foolish as to refuse to see a flood when their feet were already wet.

Or a fire, Climbs Quickly thought to himself with amusement, *once their fur has been singed.*

Still, he thought that the others had not yet realized what the presence of two-legs meant to the People.

Even today, as they have discarded a few areas as unsuitable because they are too near to settlements of the two-legs, they do not seem to have realized that our world has become a bit smaller. Now we need share it not only with each other, but with these strangers as well.

Then Climbs Quickly looked up through the leaves to the stars, thinking of things he had seen, of how these two-legs had apparently come from beyond the sky.

Or maybe the world has not gotten smaller. Maybe it is simply that my *world has grown much, much larger.*